MW00816922

# CROOKED ISLAND

Also by Victoria McKernan
*Osprey Reef*
*Point Deception*

# CROOKED ISLAND

Victoria McKernan

Carroll & Graf Publishers, Inc.
New York

First Carroll & Graf edition 1994

Carroll & Graf Publishers, Inc.
260 Fifth Avenue
New York, NY 10001

Library of Congress Cataloging-in-Publication Data

Manufactured in the United States of America

To Scott, always and any way, and for keeping the red phone plugged in.

Special thanks to Lori Annaheim, a steadfast friend and (not a nerd) computer genius who managed to salvage this manuscript (several times) from my sometimes cannibalistic old machine.

Also thanks to the librarians and aids at the Arlington County Public Library main branch for research help and general graciousness, and to the architects who designed a building that made long research joyous.

*"I understand there are six people in Dartmore [prison for the criminally insane] who say that they are the real Prince Charles. I often wonder if perhaps one of them **is** the real Prince Charles and I am the insane one."*

—Prince Charles

# Prologue

*August 1714*

The sun rose red beneath a low slab sky. The heavy air pressed the water flat. The sails flapped in the feeble breeze, but the captain knew, by the way the hairs sharpened on the back of his neck, that a squall was on the way.

"All hands," he directed the mate.

"All hands, aye, sir," the mate called the order. Below deck, the crew roused quickly, tumbling out of their hammocks and scrambling to the hatches. Most were experienced sailors, who had also felt the pressure of the approaching storm and had been awakened by the stillness of their ship.

"Port watch for'ard. Furl topsails!" The breeze was freshening, the air smelled metallic. Small whitecaps skittered around the ship as the crew scrambled aloft to secure the sails. The cook and the ship's boy hastened to secure things below deck. They had been lucky so far. Eight days out of Jamaica with good winds and gentle seas. The change was inevitable. A few more hours would have been welcome. They were almost at the end of the Caicos Passage, and another twenty miles or so would put the ship in open seas.

Captain Avery had some crude charts of the area, but he did not know these waters well. He had chosen this more obscure passage to avoid the heavy traffic along the coast of Hispaniola, where English, French, and Spanish warships hunted one another and pirates lay always ready.

"Capt'n, sir, the topsail is fouled."

Avery looked up with irritation to see a rigging line had snapped. The loose end snaked around the spar, preventing the sail from being dropped.

"Brooker lad, go aloft. And keep a sharp watch!" he directed.

Brooker was a strong, nimble deckhand who climbed like a monkey and had the eyes of a hawk. Few men, even the bravest, most seasoned sailors, would climb the mast in the face of a squall, but Brooker actually loved it. He scrambled up and perched on the spar, lashing himself to the mast with a line about his waist. From this vantage point, he had guided the *Christiania* safely through many a reef.

"Haul up now! Lively there!" the boatswain called. The clouds boiled in the west. The helmsman braced as the first gusts hit. "Starboard haul! On the main now!" Avery felt the cold clear thrill of it. He had nearly twenty years at sea. Voyages to the Far East, to Madagascar and China. He had seen his share of storms, and while he was not fool enough to lose respect for the elements, he was not easily daunted. The *Christiania* was a good ship, well outfitted, with the best crew money could buy. He had been paid handsomely for this passage.

"Mr. Hawkins," he summoned the first mate. "Please see that the lady and child are made secure."

"Aye, sir."

The edge of the squall was galloping toward them now with a gray curtain of rain. The wind howled in the rigging.

Below deck, huddled in the stifling safety of the purser's cabin, a young woman tried to comfort her screaming toddler. If they lived, she vowed, she would have the ship turned back to Jamaica. England be damned. She wept with fear and with sorrow and loneliness. Years of talk and planning, finally the right time, finally a ship that would take them, then just as it had all come together, Edward had fallen ill with fever. Yes, he was finally going home, but his berth was a coffin, his destination the grave.

On deck, there was a measured calm, even as the waves grew and the wind shrieked. The storm hit with a crash, a low explosion like a cannon shot that left ears aching. Cold rain hammered the men. They could not see from helm to bow.

"Down helm! Down helm!" Avery commanded. The masts creaked from the strain, and the helmsman threw his full weight against the wheel. The ship lumbered up the rising waves, and crashed into the troughs beyond. Men struggled to hold their places. And Brooker, unable to descend now, clung to his perch with all his might. The sea churned and the wind roared. For half an hour they sailed through the tempest, then just as quickly as it had arisen, the fury eased. The rain moved off, and the low clouds thundered on past. Men peeled off wet clothing, Avery sent the cook below to start the breakfast. The sailors cheered their luck and hurried to restore full sail. Then the cry came out.

"Ship ahoy, sir! Black flag on the starboard beam!" Brooker shouted from above, pointing to the horizon. The men rushed to the side. The pirate ship had appeared out of nowhere, out of the dawn, bearing a black flag and skimming the waves with a frightening speed.

Avery called for the glass and, bracing against the pitch of the ship, stared through the brass scope at the approaching vessel. It was a schooner like his own, though smaller and much lighter, outfitted not for an ocean crossing but for just such a mission, a lightning dash out of the rising sun, with full sail set for attack.

"Stations, men. Steadfast now!" Avery ordered. "We will stay our course." The first mate looked at the captain in surprise. "It is the devil and sword," Avery explained in a quiet voice. "Flag of Bartholomew Cross. No friend of mine, but no enemy, either. He may not interfere once we are known to him . . ." he stopped short. The woman had appeared on deck, her face white, terror in her blue eyes.

"Lady Catherine, you must stay below."

"What is it? What is happening?"

"Hawkins, take her to my cabin and stay with them." But she had heard the cry, and seen the fast approaching ship.

"It's a pirate ship, sir?"

"They're not after you or the baby," Avery explained tersely. "They don't even know he's here. They are common thieves after treasure. We are prepared for that. Go now." Hawkins took Catherine's arm and steered her to the hatch.

The pirate ship was closing. It would be only minutes now. Avery knew the plan well: a dashing approach, cannon fire, chainshot through the rigging, the pirates swarming aboard the crippled ship. How many times he himself had been at that command! His only hope was that Cross would respect their shared profession. How absurd it would be for the famous Buccaneer Henry Avery, legend on all seven seas, who had seized the greatest treasure

ships of all time, to die at the hand of a third-rater like Bartholomew Cross.

Avery's instinct, and his pride, bid him stand and fight, but he
would raise the white flag, spare his ship from bombardment, give
over what they must. There would be payment enough when they
reached England. *If it all works out as they say,* he thought, *I
would certainly be in excellent standing with the royal court.*

If they had not had to furl sail for the squall, they might have
had a chance to outrace her, but now there was no other option
but appeasement. The flag of surrender was raised, and Bartholomew Cross did not fire.

"I sail under protection of the governor!" Avery shouted as the
ships neared. "And by orders of the English queen. There will be
reward for our safe passage."

"Avery!" The pirate Cross recognized him now. "What new
trick is this?"

"No trick, my friend." The whole crew was watching. Many
had sailed as pirates themselves. Tension was high, the watch
neglected. Young Brooker, who should have been watching the
water for reefs, was watching the pirate ship instead. The low
morning sun made it difficult to see submerged coral from the
deck.

With a sickening scream, the *Christiania,* this fine fast ship,
crashed against the reef with a violent crack and the screech of
splintering timber. Men went flying. Avery was hurled against the
wheel, and two sailors on the port bow were tossed into the water.
Far above, the mast whipped violently and Brooker was flung
screaming from his perch, the safety line snapping his back. Men
clutched at any hold as the ship lurched sharply to one side.

Below deck, Hawkins crashed against the sail locker. Dazed
and bleeding, he did not at first believe what he saw. The timbers
had split open like green sticks, and the ocean was rushing in.

"Lady Catherine! Lady Catherine!" He pulled himself up and
sloshed through the rising water to the aft cabin where she and
the child had been hidden. He yanked open the door and saw
her, huddled against the wall, clutching the baby, her face white
with terror.

"Quick, m'lady." He grabbed at her and pulled her out. The

water was up to their knees already, and they struggled forward to reach the ladder. Suddenly Catherine pulled away.

"Edward!" she screamed. Her husband's coffin was sliding toward the hole in the hull.

"There's no time!" Hawkins dragged her on. "Leave him. The sea is as good a grave as any." He caught hold of the ladder and pushed her in front of him. "Quick now, m'lady." Her skirts were wet and cumbersome. "Give me the child!" She turned to hand him her son, but the boat lurched again and she fell, knocking them both into the rising water. Hawkins clutched for a handhold. He opened his eyes, but all he could see was dark green. He felt for the woman, his arms swinging wildly. Desperately, he pulled his head above the rising waters and caught a breath.

There! She had caught hold of the mast, and struggled to hold her child's face out of the water. Hawkins tried to find footing, but the ship was tilted so drastically he could not. Kegs and other debris bobbed around them. He managed to grab the ladder again.

"Take my hand!" he shouted. Her eyes were wide with fear. "My hand!" He leaned as far as he could; if she would only reach out! Hawkins felt the ladder shake beneath his hand. The whole *ship* was shaking with a low, terrible shudder. It was as if time had slowed down. Catherine was sinking, her long hair swirling around her. Slowly, her arms uncurled, and she pushed the baby toward him. Slowly, his own arms moved to catch the child.

He saw the little white gown, the chubby little arms and legs disappearing beneath the green water, the soft black curls on the round little head sinking, the huge eyes open in astonishment, looking straight at him. Hawkins let go of the ladder and plunged after the boy. He touched his gown, lost it again. Desperately, Hawkins felt for the baby in the dark water. His hand hit a piece of wood . . . then nothing! Cloth . . . then gone! His lungs burned. He had to get out. Just a few more seconds. Cloth again . . . then flesh! Soft baby flesh, a small soft limb, a tiny baby foot. He pulled the child to him and struggled to the surface.

"Hawkins! Hawkins! Here, man!"

Avery was lying on the deck, reaching down into the hatch. The water in the hold was barely two feet from the top. Hawkins kicked toward the ladder, finally curling his fingers around a rung. He felt hands clutching at him, grabbing his clothes, his arm, his

hair, pulling him up. His foot found the wooden step, but everything was at such an angle now, the ship almost on its side.
Hawkins and the baby were pulled to the deck just as the water
began to pour up through the hatch.

On the pirate ship, the men were leaping to adjust the sails,
trying to keep their own ship off the reef. The morning air was
filled with screams. The sun had come out by now, and it seemed
a cruel mockery. Men clung to barrels and splashed frantically
toward the pirate ship, their only hope of rescue. Avery took the
baby from Hawkins and half dragging the staggering mate, they
made their way up the steeply tilted deck to the last high point
of the sinking ship.

"A bag of gold!" Avery shouted toward Bartholomew Cross's
pirate crew. "A bag of gold to the man who saves this child!"

# ONE

*December 1991*

Annabel Lee was a peculiar child. Quiet, pensive, entirely too
serious for a little girl, she had huge solemn brown eyes that gazed
at the cook with a disconcerting steadiness.

"That's disgusting! What do you want to play with fish guts
for?" The man grimaced up at the girl, who sat quietly on the
deck dangling her skinny legs over the side. He was on the dive
platform, cleaning a handsome grouper that her uncle had just
speared.

"I just want to see what it looks like. If you want, I'll gut it
myself. I'm old enough to use a knife. My father lets me."

The cook stared at the scrawny child, wondering if he should
take her seriously. The captain was always insisting that his crew
do everything possible to accommodate the passengers, but never
before had a child asked to play with fish guts. Well, what the

hell. Her dad had brought his whole dive club down here for three years now. Keep 'em happy, the skipper insisted.

"Tell you what. Get you that bucket there and I'll dump 'em inside. Then when I'm done, I'll let you down here to play." He sure didn't want her getting blood and guts all over the deck. Scrubbing up was his job, too. Annalee considered the offer. Grown-ups could be so annoying with all their conditions. "Okay, but can I see inside before you take them out?"

"Inside the fish, you mean?"

"Yes. Please." She added politely, "To see where everything goes."

The cook wiped his brow on his forearm. Sooner done, sooner he could catch an afternoon nap. "Get you a life jacket then, and come on down." The girl sprang up, grabbed the life vest, and climbed down the ladder to the wooden platform, carrying her little bag of tools. She squatted eagerly by his side. Loose hairs whipped around her face. Her father was not so good at braiding, and the tropical breeze quickly made tatters of his pigtail. She was wearing her usual outfit, an old T-shirt and faded shorts, both a few sizes too big. Her mother had packed a whole week's worth of coordinated shorts and pretty tops, but Annalee preferred her brother's raggy old clothes.

Huge dark eyes and this ragamuffin style had resulted in the family nickname Lay Miz, so closely did she resemble the waif on the poster for the musical *Les Misérables*. Her brothers, of course, came up with many variations of the name, all of which were a variation of "misery," and all of which little Annalee ignored. She watched happily as the man sliced open the shiny belly of the fish.

"There, you see." He held it open for her. "'At's the liver ... heart ..." He pointed the knife blade at the only two organs he knew. "Rest is just guts ..." Annalee didn't say anything, for she was trying to fix in her mind the exact picture of where everything went.

April McGuire sometimes accused her husband of creating their child's peculiar personality by naming her after a character from an Edgar Allen Poe poem. But Jack McGuire, who had actually been somewhat alarmed to be presented with a baby girl, at the age of forty-three and after so many boys, could not have been happier to have the little thing turn out the way she did.

"She's the charm of my old age," he joked.

Annalee's main peculiarity had to do with animals. The family house in Madison, Wisconsin, offered a nearby woods and lake, so from the time she could catch her first tadpole, she was stocking jars and pens with her catches.

A devotion to animals was not so unusual in a little girl, but this particular little girl's interest extended to realms her mother found a little odd, if not disturbing. While the child adored her creatures and took the most tender care with them, if one should happen to die, Annalee was just as interested. While proper little girls were having tea parties with stuffed bears, Annalee was autopsying her pets.

It was not as if she was eager for their deaths. She would bring home wounded birds and nurse them tenderly, but if one should die despite her care, Annalee had no compunctions about cutting it open to see what was inside, or feeding it to the black snake that lived under the garage. When Tornado, her beloved dog, was hit by a car, the seven-year-old had wept hysterically for days, but the next summer, she had felt no compunction about trying to dig up the bones.

"She's just curious." Jack had stuck up for her when April wanted to take their daughter to "see someone." As an archaeologist, he found his daughter's interests quite normal, and even refreshing, but April just didn't have the heart, or stomach, for her daughter's odd fascination with the viscera of life.

"Had enough?" the cook asked, beginning to feel uneasy about the little girl's intense interest in the dead fish. She nodded, and he dumped the guts out into a bucket. She sat on the bottom step and waited quietly as he cut the fillets off.

"No, wait!" she squealed as he was about to toss the skeleton over the edge. "You want that, too?"

"Yes." He shook his head, slid the fillets into a bowl, and climbed up on deck. "It's all yours. Knock yourself out."

Annalee sat down happily and began to examine the fish skeleton. Her father appeared at the railing for a minute, to be sure she was safe. The little girl looked up at him with her most contented angelic smile. Jack felt good to see her so happy. It was the first

time he had brought her on the annual dive trip, and it had taken
a lot of convincing for his wife to let her go. None of his sons
had really developed his passion for the sport, and the youngest,
at nineteen, was spending this Christmas vacation on South Padre
Island with his college buddies. His ten-year-old daughter, however, had turned out to be an ideal companion.

Right now, Annalee was happy down to her toes. She loved
being out on the water, living in a boat, and she was nearly delirious at all the wonderful new things to explore underwater. She
went snorkeling every chance she had, and twice now, when they
were near shallow water, Uncle Peter had let her sit on the bottom
and breathe on his scuba tank. He was a scuba instructor, and
promised that next year, when she was a little bigger, he would
really teach her, and take her on a real dive.

"Scream loud if you fall in, Miz, I'll be up here reading."

"Okay, Daddy," she said as she turned back to her fish.

It was Jack McGuire who insisted they let the girl "bloom as
she may," while his wife tried to get her interested in more
"healthy" activities. Jack brought her to the campus with him on
weekends where she soon made friends with graduate students in
the biology lab. She loved assembling skeletons, and Jack had
taken to carrying around heavy-duty trash bags and a hooked stick
in the car, in case they came along a road kill. Father and daughter
constructed a cage of wire mesh which they kept hidden in the
woods and into which they would put the carcasses for a "swift,
natural cleaning."

The skeletons were then soaked in bleach, dried in the sun, and
packed in a box labeled *Museum of Natural History—model skeletons.* That was a well-thought-out ruse they employed to convince
her mother that the skeletons were really some sort of mail-order
educational toys. Annalee had so far put together the skeletons of
a raccoon, a fox, a rabbit, a seagull (the wings kept breaking off!)
and her all-time prize, a beaver with six-inch-long curved red teeth
that could be pulled down out of their sockets. Her bedroom
looked like a museum; no little schoolfriends ever came to play
with Barbies there!

On her tenth birthday, Jack had finally agreed she was old
enough to handle a scalpel. It was this scalpel that Annalee now
used to dissect the grouper. She lifted out the heart and laid it on

the piece of cardboard. Next she picked up the stomach. It felt like a regular stomach, but there was something hard inside. Maybe the grouper had swallowed a fish right before it was speared! Eagerly, she sliced through the stomach wall.

The object tumbled out and almost fell between the slats. She grabbed at it, catching it just in time. Though it was black and encrusted, Annalee immediately saw that it was some kind of necklace. There was a chain, frozen into a crumbled knot by the centuries, and a charm, a half circle, with a jagged edge.

Why would a fish swallow such a thing? While most of the medallion was dark and crusty, part of it sparkled. Perhaps it had only recently been turned up by a current, or something. The shiny bit might have attracted the grouper's attention. Annalee turned the medallion over and examined it closely. There were scratches on the back. No—actually the marks were tiny words carved into the metal! And now she saw that the jagged edge was actually a shape, a cross maybe. Her mother had a charm with a heart cut in the middle. Maybe it was something like that.

She clutched the necklace in one hand and climbed up to the deck, where her father was snoring, a book open on his chest.

"Here, Daddy" Annalee shook him excitedly. "I found some archaeology for you!"

Jack McGuire's first instinct had been that of an archaeologist: identify the piece, define the site, examine the historical records, and consult with colleagues. Fortunately for him, his less academically minded brother was also along on the trip. As soon as they saw that the medallion from the grouper's stomach, was indeed a very old piece and not some bangle that had fallen recently from a passing cruise ship, Peter had insisted on secrecy.

"Don't you get it—we might be looking at real treasure here!"

"Here where?" Jack pointed out sensibly. "The fish could have picked it up anywhere."

"But groupers are territorial! That reef where I speared him was only what—a quarter-mile long? The necklace had to have come from somewhere along there. Do you have any idea how many undiscovered shipwrecks there are in these waters?"

"Come on, Pete, everybody and his brother have been scouring the Caribbean for treasure for years."

"Yeah, but look where we are. We're *nowhere.*" Peter waved his hand toward the vast expanse of water. These few tiny cays and reefs, some fourteen miles off the coast of Mayaguana near the Caicos Passage, were not a regular destination for the dive operators of either the Bahamas or the Turks and Caicos. The operator for their annual trip had wanted to scout out new dive sites and offered them a bargain rate to help him explore.

"I doubt that many ships ever sailed through here," Peter said. "It wouldn't be a very direct route anywhere. Most of the treasure hunters focus on areas of heavy shipping traffic." Jack smiled at his brother's enthusiasm. Peter had always been the wild one, the speculator. While Jack plodded along with his old bones and artifacts, securely settled in his academic career, his younger brother had plunged into the stock market and made a small but respectable fortune in the Chicago commodities market.

"I'd love to find a shipwreck, Pete, but I just don't see how we go about it."

"Oh, come on, man—you're a damn professor, let's hit the books."

Between Annalee's excitement, Jack's scholarship, and Peter's visions of gold doubloons, they began their research. Photos of the medallion were sent to the Smithsonian in Washington, D.C., where a curator placed it in the late seventeenth century.

*Closer examination of the engraving will probably show that the piece was inscribed before it was cut. It was probably a circle with a cross cut from the center, which then broke at the weak points. The weathering of time makes it impossible to tell from these photos, but electron micrography may help there. The necklace is consistent with British workmanship of the period and so I have forwarded the photos on to a specialist in London.* Careful cleaning had uncovered part of an inscription on the back, fragments really. There were at least three lines, but all they could make out were bits of the ends: "my heart . . . thee . . . my home." *Possibly a lover's charm, a token for a soldier going off to battle, or a sailor.*

Through the rest of that cold Wisconsin winter, and long into the spring, the brothers wrote to dozens of small museums, and archives, consulted historians, shipwreck enthusiasts, and cataloged accounts of every reported and rumored shipwreck within a hundred miles of the site where the grouper had been caught.

By the time the prairies began to thaw, the McGuires' living room was piled high with books and papers, and April had bought a new file cabinet just to handle the "grouper" correspondence. There was a great stack from the British Museum, another from the shipwreck museum in Florida, and some impossible documents in Spanish that seemed to have something to do with a fleet of warships that went down in 1694. They studied current patterns, underwater charts, and ancient navigational techniques. Three ships eventually began to emerge as possibilities.

The first big break came almost a year after the fateful dive trip, when one of Jack McGuire's archaeology journals did a feature story on an excavation in Port Royal, Jamaica.

"There was a huge earthquake there in 1692—buried most of the city," Jack explained. "They've been digging for a few years now, and recently uncovered a courthouse, or county office. Hundreds of records and papers, shipping manifests, tariff books . . . it's a gold mine."

Jack called the author of the article, and got his list of contacts, British and Jamaican archaeologists who had worked on the dig for years. The phone bill that month was three hundred and eighty-seven dollars and forty-one cents and April McGuire's already waning enthusiasm for the project plummeted dramatically.

The stacks of boxes and papers now crept out of Jack's study and overflowed one of the boy's old bedrooms. By summer of 'ninety three the focus of their search had narrowed.

"The *Christiania*," Peter insisted. "She sailed from Jamaica in 1714, and reportedly went down nine days later in the Caicos Passage."

"That's perfect, Daddy!" Annalee commented enthusiastically.

"But it doesn't make sense," Jack pointed out. "That wasn't the normal route for the time. Not even close."

"Well, it makes sense in light of the rest, doesn't it?" Peter countered. Nothing they had learned about the *Christiania* made sense. There were no passengers aboard except for an unidentified woman and a baby, and almost no cargo. Only a coffin, said to contain the remains of the woman's husband for burial in England.

"And the woman died, but the baby was rescued." Annalee looked at the photocopy from an old Port Royal ledger.

"So she was a rich widow! There's a treasure with our names on it down there, Mizzy!" Peter said gleefully. "I can hear it calling."

"If she was so rich, why was she wearing a *bronze* charm?" Jack asked.

"It didn't have to be hers, could have belonged to one of the sailors."

On and on they went, digging, probing, speculating, through the summer. Shortly before Thanksgiving, a letter arrived from London, a report from an assistant curator of antique jewelry at the Victoria and Albert Museum, a Miss Margaret Haversford, confirming the medallion as belonging to the late seventeenth century. *The quality of the workmanship is interesting,* her report noted. *Both styling and engraving are exceptional, of a quality available only to the upper class, yet worked as it is, in a base metal . . .*

"She thinks it might be similar to papal rings," Jack explained.

"What's that, Dad?" Annalee propped her skinny elbows around the photos and her braid swung down over one shoulder as she scrutinized the photos. "What's a papal ring?"

"The rings given to emissaries of the pope to identify them as messengers. They traveled on horseback, and the rings were large enough to fit over a leather riding glove, and to be seen from a distance. Bandits, or highwaymen, would see the ring and know, before firing off an arrow, that the rider was only carrying messages, not valuables. The rings themselves were made of base metals, so there was no value in stealing them."

"I don't get the connection." Peter frowned.

"Miss Haversford suggests the charm might belong in some sort of colonial situation. Jamaica in the seventeenth century was a pretty well-developed English colony, but still a rough place. A woman didn't want to bring her best jewelry to the Colonies, where it might be lost or stolen, but she still wanted pretty things—and, of course, the display of wealth. Fine craftsmanship from base metals made clear that she had the means to have better things but chose not to under the circumstances."

Peter looked again at the photo of the medallion. He had been disappointed to discover it was made of bronze, and not gold, but this information was starting to make the whole situation sound more interesting.

"It's looking better for the *Christiania*."

Jack nodded. "There were quite a few European women in the New World by then; wives and daughters of sugar planters, shipping company officials, government appointees. Stands to reason they would have jewelry."

"Are you going there to dig, Dad?"

"To Port Royal? No, hon."

"We don't have time to look under old rocks," Peter said, tugging her braid playfully. "We've got a sunken ship to find."

"Are we really? Are we going? This Christmas, Dad? Are we?"

"We are not going anywhere." Jack glared at Peter for getting the child all excited. Peter, who believed in an uncle's sacred duty to insure a bit of anarchy in young lives, just winked at her.

# *TWO*

*December 1993*

Chicago stared into the lustrous brown eyes and held her breath, hoping the turtle would come closer. What a stunning fellow he was. He circled slowly, his brown eyes appraising her carefully. Then, with a sudden flip of a fin, he was gone.

She watched him swim away into the blue, until he was just a shadow over the reef. She heard a distinctive "Thwuunk" and turned to look for Alex. He was snorkeling nearby, trying to spear some fresh fish for dinner. Here in the Bahamas you could only fish with a "Hawaiian sling," a simple three-pronged shaft, propelled by a rubber sling. Less powerful than a regular spear gun, it required stealth to get close enough, and a certain "fish sense" for aim, something Alex hadn't quite developed yet.

He looked at her and shrugged, then pointed to a rocky mound across a small patch of sand, a promising spot. She waved and watched him swim away, his body outlined against the sky. She felt a little stab of sadness. Alex was getting restless. Somewhere in the back of her mind she had known it for a while, but as she watched his body fade into the blue, it suddenly became real.

It had been six months since they left Miami, and Chicago was actually amazed that they had come so far, not only not killing each other, but actually growing closer. Life on a boat was difficult, even though the *Tassia Far* was a spacious one. She had grown up on boats, and was used to the life, but Alex had never really been to sea, not like this anyway.

At first the trip had been perfect for him, a time to escape, to heal, to finally sort himself out. For a while, he seemed to have a new sense of calm. She knew he loved the diving, loved the adventure of sailing, but she also knew that in the past couple of months, there had been a subtle change. He seemed restless and distracted. He was beginning to chafe.

She turned over and floated in midwater, looking up to the distant blue, watching fat clouds, bent by the weight of water, drift across the sky. Her bubbles shimmied upward. She could feel the sun warm through the water. The reef here was like a garden, with waving soft corals and anemones and little fish like flocks of butterflies.

She watched Alex floating on the surface. When he spied a potential quarry in the rocks below, he took a few deep breaths, then piked and dove. The sunlight rippled across his body and glinted for a second on the spear. She would miss him.

Chicago turned back over, her scuba tank shifting a little with the motion, and slowly drifted back down to the top of the reef. With an easy kick of her fin, she glided around a great stand of elkhorn coral, then hung motionless, slightly upside down, to look under its orange branches for whatever might be hiding there.

She watched an arrow crab walking with its elegantly goofy little toe-step. The crab was a common species, and looked like a daddy-long-legs spider, with delicate little limbs and two tiny claws. As she watched the little crab, out of the corner of her eye she saw a dark shadow. It might have been just a large cloud shadow, but her instinct prickled and she turned, only to find herself looking eye to eye with a large, fat bull shark.

They startled each other, and both jerked away, the shark

maneuvering far more gracefully. Chicago dropped down among the staghorn branches and watched from the relative safety of the coral cage, her heart beating fast. The shark circled once, then seemed to dismiss her, resuming his cruise. Chicago relaxed. There was no threat posturing, no tension in the fins, no arc in the back that signaled a challenge. They had simply surprised each other. He looked for all the world like an old man out for a stroll in the garden.

She knew, however, that calm as the shark was right now, it probably would not be a good idea if Alex should happen to spear a fish. She looked around and saw him about thirty yards away, hunting the back side of the reef. She let herself drift up out of the coral, then with slow easy kicks, the better not to interest the shark, she began to swim toward him. She was halfway there when Alex tucked his body, pulled the spear into position, and dove to the bottom. Chicago followed his direction and saw a perfect quarry: a nice-size grouper sitting placidly in a basket sponge like he was ready to be checked out at the supermarket.

*Not now, Alex,* she thought. Alex pulled back on the rubber sling and took careful aim. *You've missed a hundred times, babe,* she thought as she swam faster, *let's make it a hundred and . . .* Thwuunk! A perfect shot, straight through the gills!

The grouper thrashed mightily. Alex pulled it in, grabbed hold of the spear, and, with his lungs bursting for air, kicked for the surface, the struggling fish flopping against his legs. Chicago's heart began to pound. She could almost feel a pressure wave as the shark thundered past her, excited by the wounded fish. Horrified, she watched as it shot up toward Alex's dangling bare legs.

The shark was excited, but also cautious. He circled slowly, his back arched, his narrow head weaving back and forth. He dodged close, ducked away, made a closer pass and arched out again. Along the sides of his head, just below the mouth, tiny sacs, ampullae of Lorenzini, capable of sensing one one-millionth of a volt of electricity, were picking up a veritable lightning storm. The grouper was still twitching, its muscles churning out an electrical Morse code that registered on the shark's primitive brain like a dinner bell.

Let it go! Chicago thought angrily as she swam in as fast as she could. What the hell was Alex thinking? Certainly he had seen the shark by now. Let the damn fish go!

Alex kept his eyes on the grouper as he tried to disentangle himself. Once on the surface, in those few seconds before the shark appeared, he had threaded a keeper line through its gills. The still-thrashing fish had got the cord knotted with the string of Alex's swim trunks and wrapped around his leg.

The shark circled closer. Alex felt the swirl of its tail. He spun around and got most of his leg free when the shark suddenly darted in and bumped the dangling grouper with its nose. Bumping was not good. Bumping was the shark equivalent of tucking in your napkin. Why hadn't he worn his dive knife? Desperately, he gave up trying to untangle the cord. He yanked the fish in, and tried to shove the toggle tip back through the fish's gills.

Suddenly he felt a bump against his hip, then something clamping hard. The shark had him! He swung around in horror as he felt the pressure raking down the sides of his legs. Was this what it felt like then, to be caught in the jaws of death? But there wasn't any sensation of pain. Absurdly, he thought that maybe it was an old shark who didn't have any teeth. This didn't feel like jaws, it felt more like . . . hands.

Those hands gave a powerful tug, and yanked his shorts off. Alex stared with surprise at Chicago, while out of the corner of his eye he saw the shark seize the grouper and dash away, Alex's yellow swim trunks, still tangled with the fish leader, zipping after him like a flag. Chicago was glaring at him through her mask, holding out her extra regulator and urgently signaling to go down. Alex understood. They would be safer underwater, hiding in the coral if need be, until the shark went on along its way. He quickly took the octopus, slipped the mouthpiece in, and took a breath of the compressed air. Together, they swam down to the bottom.

The shark returned, looked them over, but did not approach. The grouper had been an opportunistic little meal; these large ungainly creatures with their bubble blowing and odd electricity were not registering in any of his major food groups. Finally, he disappeared into the distance. Chicago and Alex looked at each other and burst out laughing, bubbles boiling, and water flooding their masks.

# THREE

Mark Whitstone adored the queen. The Queen Mother more properly. To most of the world it was Elizabeth II who now reigned, but to Whitstone, the Queen Mother was and always would be the Queen. Her picture hung on the wall in his modest apartment, in a carved and gilded frame he had bought for six pounds at an antique store in 1953. At the time, this was more than a day's pay, but he could do no less honor to the queen who had treated him kindly.

In 1944, while war was blistering through Europe and buzz bombs were hammering London, King George VI and Queen Elizabeth often visited the wounded neighborhoods to show their support. Whitstone was six years old, small for his age and frail, with a twisted foot and a bad lisp. His older brother, and longtime protector, had gone off to war, leaving the child at the mercy of schoolyard bullies. His father, a librarian, was dying of cancer, and his mother had taken a job in a boot factory. Women of their class, modestly middle class, did not usually work, but she was saved, just barely, from social embarrassment since it was patriotic to support the war effort.

The child's life was bleak. Wartime and sickness had colored every day of his young life, and his memories until that day held no color. The streets were gray with cinders, the buildings black with soot, even the sheets flapping on the lines were dingy, for there wasn't enough soap. The whole world seemed ugly and gritty and mean, but on that fateful morning, color had bloomed for him.

A bomb had landed three streets away, and the king and queen were coming to visit. A huge crowd turned out, but somehow the young boy managed to work his way to the front as the royals arrived. There were guards on motorcycles, then police cars, then

24

finally, the shiny black car with the queen. It was early summer and she wore a blue dress. In his memories, it was pale blue silk, with a sweeping skirt and jewels round the neckline, but as a matter of fact, it would have been dark blue at best, serge or linen, and closely cut, as was the thrifty wartime fashion.

But there she was, the beautiful queen in blue, like the statue of Mary in the Catholic church, where he sometimes slipped away to hide from his tormenters while being chased home from school. The crowd cheered and surged forward, and the little boy was pushed down, scraping hands and knees on the paving stones. As others, unaware of his fall began to press around him, he crawled out into the street and struggled to his feet. He was bloody and dirty and horribly ashamed.

Then she looked at him. She smiled at him. The queen's gentle eyes fell on his, and it was not a smile of scorn or pity, but the sweet smile of a good mother who understood the pain of little boys. She smiled right at him, and the sky opened up and he was bathed with a warm golden light. When the queen moved her gloved hand ever so slightly, one of the guards was at her side. She spoke a word, and suddenly the man was walking toward him, a white handkerchief in hand.

As it was fixed in his memory, it was the queen's handkerchief wiping the blood from his hands and knees that day, though in reality the attendant had used his own handkerchief, and used it roughly, annoyed to be chosen for such an inglorious task. But in the stories Whitstone told over the years in any new pub where they had not heard it a hundred times already, it was the queen's own handkerchief, with embroidered initials: pure silk, white as snow, smelling like lilies and bordered in fancy lace.

Mark Whitstone loved the queen as one loves a saint, with a distilled purity and honest devotion. It was his sacred duty to protect her.

"Well, I wasn't sure just who to go to, gov. So I was glad when you said you would see me. I have heard of you." Whitstone smiled earnestly. Adrian Spencer worked at being patient with the man. As head of palace security, he knew the type, lonely old fellows whose hobby was royalty, who phoned up the palace guard to report on plots and suspicious characters, fantastic concoctions of paranoia and evil. They dreamed of being knighted, but would usually settle for an autographed photo. Spencer had encountered them many times.

"I checked you out myself a little I did." Whitstone made a sly, confiding gesture that came across as comical. "You been wi' the family for twenty-three years. Knew the prince at school, too. This whole matter you see, it's very delicate. It mustn't go out of this room. Or, well, I suppose you might have to check with some experts, some *other* experts," he stressed, clearly proud of his own scholarship.

"Yes, well, you may be assured, Mr. Whitstone, that your confidence is safe with me. Are these the papers you spoke of?" Spencer nodded at the packet clutched on the man's lap.

"Oh, no! Oh, my goodness, no. I would never carry around three-hundred-year-old originals. No, these are copies."

"Of course." Spencer smiled. It was a thin unconvincing smile that wavered at the corners, as if being tickled by the light fringe of mustache above it. This mustache was gray, as was the man's hair, though his lip was faring better than his scalp in terms of volume. His eyebrows boasted the most luxurious hairs, however, white bristles that crept in swirls toward the sides of his forehead, as if trying to escape the stern brow. He was fifty-three and trim, on the slender side even, though this was an accidental benefit of genetics rather than any devotion to fitness. It was a great source of irritation to him that as he aged, he had come to look dreadfully like a butler, and on occasion, had been mistaken for one by unknowing visitors to the palace.

"Mr. Whitstone, why don't you just explain to me exactly what you have uncovered that concerns you so."

The little man leaned forward, glanced side to side, and, satisfied that no one else had mysteriously appeared in the man's office, spoke in a hushed voice.

"I'm an archivist at the British Museum, you see. I take care of all the documents that come in. Treat them, store them properly—it's a very technical process, a lot to it."

"I have a general familiarity with the subject, Mr. Whitstone. Why don't you explain your concern about these particular documents."

"Yes, sir, very good." Whitstone, never much at ease outside the seclusion of his archives, was even more uncomfortable to be talking to such a high government official. He took a deep breath and wished he hadn't forgone his usual morning nip of sherry before this meeting. "Well, it's like this. Over the past two years now, we've been receiving a lot of material from a dig. An excavation, I mean, a British archaeology project in Jamaica. The whole city was buried in an earthquake three hundred years ago, when, as you know, it was a British colony. It's been very exciting! Last year they found a courthouse. Some sections of it were remarkably well protected, yielding all sorts of documents—legal papers, shipping manifests, letters, ledgers, oh, birth certificates, marriage records . . ."

"And there has been some American interest in them, you said?"

"Yes, sir. That one sheet there," the man pointed a wavering finger at the top sheet, "is a list of all the documents I've sent them copies of over the past year. I mean, I didn't know, I didn't realize at the time, what it was all pointing to. It was only because, well, I'm a bit of a history buff, specialize a bit in, well, we call it apocryphal history. I guess you would call them rumors, odd bits of history, quite a lot of it really, most fascinating . . ." Whitstone knew he was digressing, he was trying so hard, but how to explain?

"Well, one bit of a rumor has always been around . . . oh, not in regular circles, no credit to it at all, no evidence—well, until now, that is."

"And what is this evidence that you refer to, Mr. Whitstone?"

"Well, it's come together as I looked over all the Port Royal documents. But I didn't see any pattern, as I've said. Not until now. Pulling up all those copies for the Americans . . . Oh, dear."

"My good sir," Spencer decided to use his kindly butler looks to put the man at ease and perhaps get to the point, "I'm quite sure you have done nothing wrong. What is it exactly that you are worried about exposing? What could these papers possibly show?"

"What could they show? Well, I'm afraid, Mr. Spencer, they could show . . . Well, oh my goodness, sir—there could be a pretender to the throne!"

# FOUR

"You didn't bring even one towel?" Alex asked forlornly.

"You know I never bring a towel; it just gets wet in the dinghy. What—you think you're going to catch pneumonia now or something?" Chicago patted his bare bottom as she squeezed past him. "We'll go slow, keep down the draft." She was trying hard not to mock him, but standing buck naked in a bobbing rubber dinghy made him such an easy target. Mostly, though, laughter kept the real fear at bay. Things had looked nasty there for a minute.

Now that the actual danger had passed, the shark attack slipped into an abstract, almost surreal, kind of fear. It was as if the event had been slipped into a museum case, where they could look in from a distance. It was a strange and somehow beautiful fear, so typical of the sea. Fear was not even the right word, but there just wasn't a word to fit.

The image of Alex's legs dangling at the surface stuck in her mind. One minute his body had been beautiful and strong, the next, there were those suddenly ridiculous limbs. One moment glory, the next, bait. Such was life in the sea. Alex slipped up beside her and put his arm around her, the touch of his flesh somehow shocking. He brushed a strand of wet hair off her forehead. Her pale blue eyes revealed little emotion to those who did not know her, but Alex had learned their shades by now. They sat there a few minutes, in their own silent resolutions, bobbing gently as the sun warmed their dry-earth bones.

"Hey, thanks for the rescue. I owe you one."

"Yeah, well, I didn't want the poor shark to get a bellyache." She turned and crouched over the motor, pulled the cord once, and twisted the throttle as the outboard roared to life. Alex slipped to the bow and began to pull up the little anchor. "Careful with

28

the chain, honey,'' she admonished him cheerfully. ''Don't get anything caught.''

He turned and scowled. Chicago watched as he pulled, the tanned shoulders working in easy rhythm. He looked like a real sailor now, sinewy and a bit ragged, but balanced, tuned in some imperceptible way to the sea. His hair, shaggy as it was at the moment, trailed into wet black curls at the nape of his neck. Alex had a smooth, leonine muscularity, but the skin was marred with scars. Most were faint, incurred long ago in a life he spoke little about. Some she knew about, a few she didn't. One, an almost matched set—the entry and exit wounds of a bullet just beneath his ribs—she knew too well. They were less than a year old and still faintly purple. He pulled up the final bit of chain, then turned around, holding the anchor in front of him like a fig leaf.

''Anchors aweigh, Cap'n.''

''I'll say.'' She laughed. ''Now you can ride masthead for a change—and I'll drive. I kind of like this view.''

''Like hell.'' The dinghy was too small for much of a tussle, and it didn't take long for Alex to reverse their positions. He took the throttle and Chicago stood in the bow, holding on to a loop of rope, her legs spread for balance like a trick rider on a circus horse. Alex wasn't sure if she had ever even sat on a real horse, but was quite certain that if one did try to buck her off, it would have a hard time of it.

Chicago was not one to surrender easily, to man or beast. She was a tall woman, at five nine only three inches shorter than Alex, and strong. She had inherited Viking bones from her Norwegian father, but her mother's Caribbean heritage had softened the broad shoulders and given a graceful curve to those sturdy legs. Alex missed her long dark hair, which she had unceremoniously lopped off to shoulder length the first week of the voyage. Not that it didn't look good this way, with a slight waviness that hadn't shown before. He knew such long hair was impractical with all the diving, but for some odd reason, he now felt she needed it. It was weird, he decided, but the hair had always seemed . . . Well, a protection.

He twisted the throttle down as far as it could go. The same patch of elkhorn coral that provided such a lovely underwater garden also posed a dangerous obstacle for the little boat. They had to thread their way through it slowly, with Chicago looking for passages in the maze, pointing out the way as Alex steered. Once inside the reef, they zipped along, the palm trees blurring past.

They slowed as they approached the *Tassia Far*. Chicago always liked the sight of her boat from the water. The hull had nice lines and perfect balance. Forty-two feet long, she was a little beamy, but still fast and responsive. Originally a ketch, Chicago had removed the mizzen mast and converted to cutter rigging. The old mizzen mast had cracked in a storm anyway, and since she would be living on the boat, Chicago had opted for more room on the aft deck.

Her father had built it almost thirty years ago, working on it for a few months at a time between his commercial voyages. Chicago remembered walking with her mother, Tassia, to bring him lunch each day, excited to see what else he had done. She loved the smell of the wood, and all the different stories he would tell.

"This is where the horses will live," he said, leading her through the skeletal ribs. "And this will be the crocodile pen, where you will sleep," he teased.

"With the crocodiles?"

"Of course with the crocodiles, so they won't get lonely."

He drew pictures of fantastic boats for their amusement, boats like Indian palaces, or Turkish harems . . . deckhouses eight stories high, with a hundred colorful flags streaming behind and a crew of monkeys to work the sails. "We will just sit back and enjoy, and the monkeys will do all the hard work," he explained. "Only we'll have to stop often to pick up bananas. In the galley there will be one tap just for Coca-Cola, how about that?"

In 1962, Coke was still a rare treat in Tobago. Chicago was five, and the boat was almost finished when her mother grew ill. They had been saving money, intending to live on the boat, just the three of them, and sail around the world, but suddenly the dream was shattered. Before her father could even finish painting the name on the stern, her mother died. And so the intended *Tassia Fair* became *Tassia Far*.

"Great—the whole neighborhood's out to greet us!" Alex noted sourly. There were only three other boats in the anchorage, but it looked like everyone was buzzing around. Mel and Joan of the *Fine Romance* looked like they were getting ready to sail, and Lee Bob of *Defiance* was in his dinghy, tied up to the stern of *Carolina* talking with a couple they hadn't met yet. "Go around the other side," Chicago suggested. "I'll climb up and get you some shorts."

They were rinsing off the scuba gear and hanging it to dry when Lee Bob puttered over.

"Hey—you know a radio call came through for you this afternoon. Caught it on the noon report."

"A call for us? You sure?"

"Don't know any other boats with a name even close. Reception was clear, too. Here you go." He handed up a slip of paper. "Just the name and phone number, no message. Except call ASAP."

"Thanks, Lee." Alex looked at the name, Chicago saw his expression change. "Philip Greenway," he said with a nonchalance that wasn't convincing.

"I'm headed in to make a phone call myself. The station here is only open from four to six. You want a ride in?"

"Yeah, sure. Let me get my wallet."

Chicago watched them go, puttering toward the dock in Lee Bob's dinghy. The sun was dropping and the bay was so clear and shallow that each man was a long, split shadow, one floating on top the water like oil, the other steeply bent and scraping across the sandy bottom. Chicago shivered. Philip Greenway. The message unnerved her. Although they had not planned to vanish off the face of the earth, they had been enjoying a certain blissful anonymity down here. Suddenly, here was an intrusion, the real world scratching at the door. Fast behind the calm, she could feel the wind changing.

She went below to change and shower. The interior of the boat was well designed and practical, but there were unconventional touches, totems and artifacts from her father's many voyages, African masks, Indonesian fabrics, a Japanese sword, a table made from the foot of an elephant.

There were all the necessary practical aspects for a life at sea, berths built along the sides, a fold-down tabletop, and rails on the shelves, but there was also a real couch, a heavy antique brocade claw-foot sofa that her father had dragged home from some voyage. It was a ridiculous thing to have on a boat, but Chicago couldn't part with it. She had bolted the feet in place, however, and made sturdy covers to protect the upholstery.

She stripped off her wet swimsuit and got in the shower, rinsed off, then switched off the water while she soaped her hair. Greenway was a banker in Maryland, whose murdered daughter had drawn Alex and Chicago into a series of catastrophes. What did he want with them now?

She had learned early in life never to count on too long a stretch of joy. Her mother had died when she was only five, she had lost her husband after two short years of marriage. Last year she had seen a good friend murdered. Alex had already left her once. She did not expect destiny to be smooth. Six sweet months had been a generous run of fate.

# *FIVE*

Except for a fringe of palms around the shore, Rum Cay was a shadeless island, with an interior of salt flats, scrub brush, and hard-baked ground. Thin, dusty dogs peered suspiciously from dry front yards as Alex and Lee walked down the road to the telephone office. The few houses along this road were small, built of cement block with gleaming linoleum floors visible through open doors. Tough little chickens scratched in the dirt or ruffled down for a dust bath in a patch of shade. Like many of the smaller islands, Rum Cay was fading, blistering away layer by layer until one day there might be no village here at all, the houses open and abandoned.

The island had once thrived, as it was named, by distilling and shipping rum, but the industry was long dead, and the few remaining inhabitants were mostly elderly, supported by their families working in the tourist business elsewhere. A dive resort had been built here, but folded shortly after opening, victim to poor investing, speculation, thievery ... No one ever knew for sure, since it was common enough in the islands. Today the buildings stood empty. The few visiting boats supported two small bars, but otherwise there was not much going on. The telephone office was a small wooden shack about a ten-minute walk from the dock, standing alone in a bit of clearing.

Alex sat on a rock and waited for Lee to make his calls. The afternoon heat hugged the land, and big, slow nuggets of insects droned from bush to bush. He felt a strange, dry desolation, as if a great hunger had seized him. The torpor of the island, this sad, faded place reflected too acutely his own spirit. He was miserable. Yet he had no right to be; and the very admission gave him a pang of guilt. This was a great life. How could he be miserable with the woman he loved, with this chance at life and love, after so many years?

It was the shark started all this. Gave him that feeling again. His hand, where he had smacked the beast, still tingled. He closed his eyes and remembered the sight of it, cold eyes and silver fins charging him. The power of his own body responding to the challenge. Even now he shivered. God, was this some sort of addiction? He had broken with all that. All the danger and the tension, the hunts and conquests. That life was over. But the thrill wasn't over. Every taste hooked him again, and the shark was another taste.

He had no idea what Greenway wanted, but he was sure it would be something. He stood up and walked back out to the road. Lee, still on the phone, saw him and held up an apologetic hand. Alex gestured no hurry. There was no hurry. There was never much of a hurry out here, except for catching the occasional tide or avoiding a storm front. He craved action, motion, challenge, quest, but there were so few real quests anymore, and he would not tilt at windmills.

A fierce squawking interrupted his thoughts. Alex turned toward the noise and saw a swirl of dust, and feathers flying in the brush. In a tumble of color, two cocks screeched out of the scrub, hackles raised, tail feathers fanned, fighting. They broke away, then tore

at each other again. The phone operator ran out of her booth
screaming and waving a kerchief at the birds, a futile gesture, for
they were blinded by instinct and the smell of blood. She kicked
at them, and Alex, afraid she would try to break it up further and
suffer for it, grabbed her arm. It was a normal scrap, he thought;
these were barnyard cocks, not bred for fighting, but there was
the chance one could be torn open, and a good breeding rooster
was probably valuable on this poor island.

Lee looked out of the booth to see what the commotion was all
about, and saw Alex, in one sure, quick movement, snatch up one
of the cocks. When the other flew up at the bird in his hand, Alex
jumped easily out of the way, launching himself into a sort of
handless cartwheel.

'What the hell was that—some kind of chicken kung fu?'' Lee
exclaimed as he hung up the phone.

Alex smiled. ''Must be the old farmboy busting out.''

''I never seen any farmboy move like that,'' Lee said quietly,
scrutinizing him. He had seen Alex a few times, practicing an odd
sort of martial art on the beach, but the movements were always
studied and slow. He had grabbed up those chickens like something in a Ninja movie.

The phone operator hurried to take her rooster, and was about
to storm off down the road in furious search of the owner of the
other bird that shouldn't have been let loose at all, because it was
a vicious bird, always causing trouble . . . When Lee reminded her
that Alex still needed to make a phone call.

When Alex returned he found Chicago reclining against the
cushions in the cockpit, drinking a beer, watching the first golden
tones of sunset wash across Rum Cay with Lassie curled up in
her lap.

''Well?''

''Well—damn, you look great.'' She was freshly showered, her
wet black hair combed straight back. She wore a sarong wrapped
native-style just over her breasts, with, Alex knew from experience, nothing on underneath. He bent over her and kissed her,
drinking in the clean soapy smell, the heat of her body. He sat
down next to her and gently lifted the boa constrictor out of the
way.

"Go away now, Lassie, there's a good snake." The boa uncurled itself with a languid indignation, and slowly slithered toward a patch of sun. Alex ran his hand up Chicago's tawny leg, and kissed her again just above the patterned cloth. One thing he had learned early on with this woman was that a good day of diving made her incredibly lusty. Chicago roused to his touch, and Alex felt himself growing hard.

"How did Greenway track us down?" Her curiosity was, however, controlling her desire for the moment.

"Called the marina in Miami, and they made the radio call with the message," Alex mumbled into the top of her sarong.

Chicago pulled his head out. "And what does he want?"

"Wants us to find a sunken treasure."

Chicago rolled her eyes. "Any one in particular?"

"A ship called the *Christiania* went down in seventeen something in the Caicos Passage." He grinned. "Since we were already in the neighborhood, he wondered if we wanted to go treasure hunting."

She looked at him closely, suspiciously. He looked excited. It was a dangerous look for him.

"Alex, if a boat went down a week ago, broadcasting its precise location at the time, we would still have difficulty locating it. He's talking about an ancient shipwreck. He needs someone with sonar, metal detectors, recovery gear, storage tanks, all kinds of stuff. Not to mention permits and ... well, all kinds of stuff. There are professionals for this."

"Actually he's got one. Got them all lined up, a professional treasure-hunting operation, but he needs some divers, and wants someone there he can trust."

"He's expecting big treasure?"

"Not exactly. The whole project came from an associate of his in Wisconsin, a guy named Peter McGuire who's been researching the wreck for two years now with his brother, an archaeologist. They think they have enough now to take a look, and Greenway helped them arrange financing. They've got the money together to hire a boat for three weeks, but they're on a tight budget and they need some divers. He's offered us six hundred bucks plus expenses."

"Six hundred bucks is not a lot for three weeks of professional diving, my dear."

"I guess he heard I had a cheap scuba babe."

Chicago would have smacked him except he might move his hands to defend himself and she kind of liked what they were doing down where they were.

"Okay, the money is very tight. It's probably going to be a historical find if anything. Archaeology doesn't exactly rake it in. But it's also six hundred more than we have in savings right now," Alex reminded her. "And we're diving all the time anyway, might as well be looking for treasure."

Chicago did not seem enthusiastic. "I've only done salvage work, Alex, treasure hunting or archaeology is a whole different specialty."

"Well, this captain they've hired, Ross Shepard, evidently knows the business well enough . . . what's the matter?" he asked, noticing her eyes had widened in surprise.

"Ross Shepard?"

"Yeah. You know him?"

"Yeah—he and my father go way back. I haven't seen him in, wow, probably twenty years. But yeah . . ." She was smiling, and Alex was glad. "They both shipped out of Norfolk for a while when I was a kid, used to get together if they were in port at the same time, sailed together a couple of times. God . . ." Chicago smiled with the memory. "His wife, Martha, gave me my . . . well, you know, girl talk, when I was twelve or thirteen."

"Is that right?" Alex murmured as he unfastened her sarong. "What did she tell you?"

"About, you know, boys. Sex . . ." She sighed with pleasure as he began to kiss a trail down her body.

"Hmmmm—and did you pay attention?" Chicago nodded and stroked the back of his neck, shifting to accommodate his caresses.

"To the good parts," she said, laughing. Alex stood and pulled her up to him in one fluid motion, then walked her backward toward the companionway.

"So where are we going?"

"Not far." Alex kissed the side of her neck, behind her ear. Her hair was warm and wet and heavy. "Mayaguana," he whispered in her ear as his hands took firmer control of her body.

# SIX

At a party in a loft in Soho on a Saturday night in early December, Margaret Haversford finally remembered where she had seen the inscription before. It had been one of those nagging things in the back of her mind for some months now, ever since she had examined the photos of the medallion sent her by the Smithsonian.

The party was wild, full of London's arty set, all dressed in black and spandex, with hair of many colors, tattoos, pierced noses, lips, and nipples. Margaret was slumming. Just a week ago, she had spent a perfectly respectable weekend with her perfectly respectable family in Chelsea, in a Laura Ashley dress and clear nail polish.

Now she wore a pair of shredded blue-jean shorts over bicycle shorts, a transparent blouse, and a streak of fluorescent pink in her blond hair. This, of course, would wash out in the morning, before she returned to work at the museum. Margaret was from the very upper class of British society, old money, a few titles, heavy silver, finished in all the best schools and now employed, as were most of her friends, in a respectable position. A career to Margaret's class was what a lady did between earning a degree in fine arts and marrying a man from a good family. Right now, at age twenty-four, she had the former, and a promise of the latter, and was just trying for a little fun in between.

She did not take them seriously, these frantically hip young punks and mods, for they seemed to her, in their own way, just as pretentious and conforming as the smart set in Chelsea. But it was different, and it was fun. Margaret liked the music—loud and relentless. In the museum offices, they usually listened to chamber groups.

The loft had been transformed into a sort of free-form art gallery

37

for the night, and performance artists occasionally writhed on the floor, smeared themselves with canned pie filling, or recited passages from *Mein Kampf* in pig latin. Several "rooms" had been built in the open space from doors and sheets, and in these, one could see grainy avant-garde movies, write a few lines for the poetry tree, or join a computer conversation network. In one of the rooms, a tall man, frightfully thin, with tiny orange glasses and a braided goatee that hung to his waist, was doing some sort of projection art concept. Margaret hung out by the entrance watching as he placed torn pieces of newspaper headlines on an overhead projector, combining and recombining them into various anarchist slogans.

It had nothing to do with ancient jewelry, or with the medallion, but the fragments of words sparked the memory. Last spring, while cataloging part of the seventeenth century collection, she had come across a curious piece. It was a half-circle with half a cross cut out of the center, just like the one the Americans had found. It could, of course, be a common style from the period; the seventeenth century was not her primary interest after all, but still there was something uncanny about it.

As if the words were being projected on the screen in front of her now, she remembered there were fragments of sentiment engraved on the back. Could there be a connection? If she remembered right, the museum piece was the opposite of the McGuires', with the smooth side on the left, and the cross cut from the right.

That Monday, when Margaret got to work, she found the catalog with the picture of the charm, pulled up the computer file, and stared in amazement. This piece was the same size, same style, and, as best she could tell from the photos, a good chance to be the missing half! And there was an inscription. Arched across the top, *King of . . .* and across the bottom, *King of . . .* She pulled out the photos of the McGuires' piece. . . . *my heart, . . . my home. King of my heart, king of my home.* But there was a middle line missing. There must have been a third piece! The charm was a triptych. All she had of the middle line was *God pro . . .*

Most intriguing, however, was the catalog description. *Late seventeenth century,* the label read. *Said to belong to Queen Mary of Modena.* Margaret had to dig up an old history book to find out who she was. Of course, Mary Beatrice, second wife of King

James II. They had fled the country, driven into exile, some said, in 1688, when William and Mary took the throne. James the second and Mary Beatrice were the last of the Stuart dynasty in England.

Mr. Pratt, the chief curator, was intrigued with her speculations, but could offer little else in the way of information. He suggested she pop over to the British Museum and talk to a certain Mr. Whitstone.

"A bit eccentric, but he knows his royalty. Perhaps he could be of some assistance."

# *SEVEN*

"Adrian, come in," Crawford Hayes greeted Spencer at the library door and waved him into the elegant room. They were meeting at Corwyn House, a small but well-appointed old row house that had come into possession of the government in the fifties and had been used since then for a variety of discreet purposes. Upstairs, it was rumored, various spies had plotted daring adventures, and Soviet moles had been discovered putting microphones in the draperies. In reality, however, although the building did belong to the MI5, the activities here were far more mundane. The downstairs parlor bore an air of shabby gentility with overstuffed furniture and frayed but immaculately white antimacassars.

"Buffed up the old place a bit, have they?" Spencer remarked as his eyes adjusted to the dimmer light. He had only been here once, some five years ago, on a matter of minor interest, and could not suppress a little thrill to have been summoned back today.

"Have they?" Hayes replied without so much as a glance around. As Director General of the British Secret Service, he used the place so often it had become almost a second home. Hayes was fifty-seven, a compact man of average height who, once handsome, had not aged particularly well. His face had the fortune of good bones, but the skin had gone spotty and slack, paling to a disturbing translucency that showed wormlike blue veins around his temples where the hair was thinning. He moved with an economy of motion that as a younger man had marked him as an athlete but now just seemed a trifle fussy. He led Spencer down the hall to a small library.

"Adrian Spencer, Colin Teneby." Hayes introduced the other man who rose most of the way from a wing chair and accepted Spencer's outstretched hand. "I've assigned Mr. Teneby to special charge of this case." Hayes sat behind the desk and opened the file folder, pulled out the copies of Whitstone's documents.

"This case?" Spencer was surprised to see the file. "I'm afraid I don't understand. I mean, I wasn't aware this had become a case." Although he thought them fairly ridiculous, Spencer had passed Whitstone's information along to Hayes. Files were kept on all threats to the Royal Family, and while this hardly seemed to fit that definition, Spencer was a by-the-book man.

"I mean, you're not taking this seriously are you? As a threat to the crown?"

"It's my business to take things seriously," Hayes answered quietly.

"Well . . . certainly," Spencer replied, chastised.

"Of course it is absurd, hence the name." Hayes had named the case after the Gilbert and Sullivan operetta, *Pirates of Penzance*. "But I think you'll see our concern." Hayes drummed one heavy finger on the thick file. "First of all, how many people know about these documents?" Spencer, still taken aback, tried to switch grooves. He had assumed the meeting today was about routine damage control, efforts to keep the ridiculous story out of the press where it might cause embarrassment to the Royal Family.

"Well, bits of them—maybe a dozen. I mean, several people have seen some of the various papers. Members of the excavation team certainly, and a few assistants at the museum, but no one put much of it together until it got back here to Whitstone. Even then I don't think it went anywhere until the American inquiries came in and the little fellow got worried. He went through a few ranks before he got to me, but did it all discreetly. You and I are still the only ones with the whole picture."

Spencer shrugged, a gesture meant to be reassuring that struck Hayes as unseemingly blithe.

"Mr. Teneby has read through the documents as well," Hayes added. "But I'd like you to give him your thoughts."

"Certainly." Spencer nodded. "Well," he began, "from time to time, someone, usually one of our cherished English eccentrics, has brought up rumors and speculation about the royal lineage. Pretenders to the throne," he explained. "Some chimney sweep discovers evidence that his great-great-grandfather was really Prince Whomever, switched at birth, and just found the papers to prove it. This information seems to fall into that case. Our primary concern, as I'm sure Mr. Hayes has told you, is to keep another wild round of monarch bashing out of the tabloids. I'm sure you can appreciate that after, as Her Majesty so perfectly put it, this *annus horribilis,* we would want to avoid a new mess. My goodness, after all that business with those girls." He spoke the word "girls" in a disapproving whisper.

"I'd be happy if all we were looking at was a little royal scandal here," Hayes said grimly.

Spencer's fluffy eyebrows raised. The man made him nervous. Technically, he was Hayes's equal in rank, though government service levels did not compare well. Spencer, under the auspices of Scotland Yard, directed a largely routine and long-established security corps within Buckingham Palace. Hayes's men crossed borders and plunged daggers into the hearts of terrorists. Or so Spencer imagined.

He stared at Hayes. "How can you even consider . . . there is something? A real threat?"

"We must consider it a possibility, Mr. Spencer." Teneby sat silently, observing the two men. At forty-five, he had been an agent for twenty years, and always found the power struggles between his superiors amusing. The small slights and glancing jabs, the polite barb, silly, ineffectual little struggles. Teneby, like most agents, had not exactly spent much of his career in James Bond exploits, but he had from time to time seen real action. The petty jealousies between these two men were trivial but entertaining.

As if reading his thoughts, Spencer glanced at the agent, uncomfortable with his silence. Colin Teneby actually was a large man, but he somehow gave the impression of averageness. Average height, average coloring, average face. His was a visage for a purse-snatcher or con man, unidentifiable, common. Upon closer examination, however, one would pick out features that were all a little too much of something or the other. His brow was slightly heavy, his jaw a trifle long, and under his chin, the tip of which was a bit square, if he tilted just so, one could make out a small but jagged scar. But these details took scrutiny, and a familiarity that Teneby was not wont to grant casually.

"What exactly are you worried about, Mr. Hayes?" Spencer persisted.

"It is a tremendously flimsy chance here, but if the Port Royal documents are genuine, and a certain other evidence is located, then there could be an argument against the House of Windsor as the rightful monarchy."

"Oh, please, Mr. Hayes. Begging your pardon, but have you checked this out with someone? I mean—there are rules of succession."

Hayes nodded. "Everything got a bit messy back then. Some feel there was basically a coup. King James was booted out and William of Orange brought in."

"It was still three hundred years ago!"

"Spencer, working so closely with the Royal Family, you might not absorb the full extent of popular feeling these days."

"Oh, come now." Spencer was so rattled he got up and paced the narrow room. "I'm fully aware of the fringe movements, that fool MP and his bill, but no one is going to throw out the monarchy. Why the queen, God keep her, is paying taxes now! We're English. It just isn't done."

Teneby wondered if Spencer realized how many times that sentiment had been uttered in the ever-shortening shadow of the Union Jack. It was inconceivable at various times that England would ever be driven from her colonies and diminished as a world power. Teneby wondered if Spencer realized that these days, the sun actually *did* go down on the British Empire.

"We are in complete agreement, Adrian." Hayes leaned forward and clasped his liver-spotted hands. "The chances are preposterous, and if it were any other situation, I'm sure we would just let it go, but things are a bit stickier."

"How so?"

"What we are worried about here, is stirring up the fringe groups, giving the radicals, the antimonarchists, a rallying point against the queen. Mr. Teneby will explain." Hayes gestured toward his agent, who now handed Spencer a thin file.

"If you trace the lineage from the Port Royal registries," Teneby explained, "the true heir to the throne of England is Cory Fitzroy MacClannon."

Spencer looked puzzled for a minute as he tried to place the name. "Cory MacClannon—the Scottish oil man?

"He owns substantial shares of refinery and shipping companies," Teneby explained. "And several factories."

"And he makes a fine whiskey," Hayes added. "Still young, I think he only opened five or six years ago, but it's coming up nicely. If you wanted to put together a royal family from scratch right now," Hayes went on, "the MacClannons would be it. Outside of being Scots, that is. We aren't talking about 'King Ralph' here, Spencer. They're titled. Genealogy full of heroes. Cory's father is a decorated war pilot, good Anglicans from cradle to grave. And popular. The family money was largely lost by the time Cory came along, so he's, how do the Americans say, 'pulled himself up by his bootstraps'? He's a self-made man, and he plows his self-made millions right back into Scottish industry. He's pulled many a bloke off the dole."

"MacClannon's wife is a major force in the charities," Teneby added. "She's lovely, gracious, and of a good English family. Three sons—one is a judge, the other runs one of the companies— and two lovely daughters—one a solicitor, both intelligent, and . . . ah, well behaved. There is also a brood of happy grandchildren."

"Oh, I see. Yes. I do see." Spencer frowned. "We've got the royal brood scrabbling and fooling around and toe-sucking all over . . . but come now, gentlemen. We English are not about to boot out our queen over this. It just isn't done. And why does it matter so that your 'king' would be MacClannon anyway."

"He's an active member of the Scottish National Party," Teneby informed him gravely. "A big force for cessation." The men were quiet for a long minute. Teneby looked through the file again. The ancient documents were hard to read, written with few rules of grammar and using creative spelling and small thin script. They had been transcribed, however, and what a story they had to tell.

"Gentlemen, I suppose you've convinced me that there is reason to keep a tight watch on this matter, and of course I remain at your service, but honestly, aside from the possible scandal and gossip, I just don't think we have to worry." Teneby glanced toward the window.

"Is there?"

"There could be. Aboard the wreck of the *Christiania*."

"The McGuires have hired a boat," Teneby explained. "To look for it."

# *EIGHT*

"Isn't it romantic?" Margaret Haversford twirled her spoon in the china cup, enjoying, despite herself, the pleasure of the fine porcelain and antique sterling. In the London flat she shared with two other girls, they drank out of mismatched cups from the Oxfam thrift shop. The middle class did lack a certain appreciation of the finer things.

"Margaret Mary, one doesn't speculate on such things," her mother reproved in a tone of mock disapproval. "A love child, indeed. How would a queen go about having an affair back then in the first place, and in the second, I thought you said she was a devout Catholic."

"She was, Mummy, that's what got them run out in the end, after all, but an affair would have been easy enough." She sipped her tea and grinned. "Those old castles have pretty thick walls."

"Oh, please!"

"Mary Beatrice was only fifteen years old when she married King James. She hadn't even met him! I can easily imagine that somewhere down the line, she could have fallen in love with, say, a groom, or a knight or somebody. She bore the child in secret, and sent it away, but before she did, she had the necklace made as a token.''

''It's preposterous.'' Mrs. Haversford put her cup down on the silver tray and rang the little bell for the maid. ''Come on now, I told Dame Atchins we would be there by four. If you want a chance at the real story, she might be able to help you get started.''

As Margaret and her mother rode down the country lanes to Dame Atchins's estate, Margaret pulled the photos of the two medallions from the envelope and stared at them. What was the real story behind the charms?

## *November 1673*

*Mary Beatrice stood at the ship's rail, shivering as a slow fog swirled over the water. "There, m'lady," the captain pointed. She strained to see, hoping, with childish hope, that she would see no land, no horrible England, but there it was, a shadow on the horizon. Her small hands clutched the ship railing and her heart gave strange little flutters; nerves, she supposed, and the motion of the ship. She had not eaten in two days, though she pretended well at the court dinner last night. Perhaps it was the wine, full of bubbles. It had made her feel dizzy and, for a little while, almost happy.*

*Why was the channel so narrow, this passage so brief? Why couldn't the sea just go on forever? She imagined sailing to the far-off colonies, sailing beneath blue skies and full, glowing moons. There she would find warm sun, strange beautiful birds, and flowers big as platters. She would see whales and savages. She would disguise herself as a man and steal away and live on an island where no one could ever send her away.*

*But it could not be. Visible through the mist were the stark white cliffs of Dover. Would she ever be happy again? She closed her eyes tightly as the chill fog settled on her face. She wept for the warm sun of Italy. Would she ever feel it again? Once the boat reached that ghostly shore, her life would be forever changed. No more playing with her friends, or romping with her father's hunting dogs. No quiet, sweet days in the convent, singing or sewing with the nuns. No more angulus in the courtyard, with the noon sun shafting through the dust, sparkling off the backs of her hands.*

*As they sailed nearer the shore, the white cliffs were clouded again, not with fog this time, but with her tears. Waiting for her on those shining white cliffs was her husband, a man she had never met, James II, Duke of York, brother of the English king. They had been married already, by proxy while she was still in Modena, and as soon as she landed, there would be an official ceremony.*

*"Is he handsome?" she had asked her uncle while the negotiations for the marriage were going on.*

*"You will be treated well," he had replied.*

*Mary Beatrice, sheltered, privileged, resigned to an arranged marriage since she was a little girl, had never even felt the first bloom of love for a man. What now did fate have for her?*

# NINE

"No, James wasn't king yet when he married Mary Beatrice," Dame Atchins explained in her high, breathless voice. Not until 1685 when his brother Charles died. James's first wife had died, and left no male heirs, just two daughters, Mary and Anne. King Louis XIV of France arranged a marriage between James and Mary Beatrice of Modena, Italy. This was a very turbulent time in the history of England, remember."

Margaret squelched her exasperation and nodded. "I do remember, right after the Restoration, of course." *Please, you old windbag,* she begged silently, *get on with it.*

"In 1660, after Cromwell died, and the monarchy was restored . . ."

The parlor was incredibly overheated, and Margaret struggled to stay awake. Dame Atchins, a member of the Kensington Ladies' Historical Society, had a large collection of antique jewelry, and was regarded as an authority on the subject. Margaret was merely hoping for some background on the two medallions . . .

"Now, this whole time there was also the beginning of a lot of Catholic–Protestant conflict in England. Charles II was a proper Anglican, but his brother James II was a devout Catholic, and so was Mary Beatrice. When Charles II died, and James was crowned, suddenly there was a Catholic king of England. The Protestants, to put it mildly, were upset. But Mary Beatrice had still not produced a male heir. Her first four children died. So it looked like James's eldest daughter Mary, by his first wife, would be next in line for the throne, which was fine with the English, since she was a Protestant. Now she was married to William of Orange, also a Protestant, but he was Dutch . . ."

Margaret's face was starting to tire with the strain of the artificial smile. She was beginning to regret her zeal in investigating the medallions. She did not want the history of England, she wanted to know—to whom had the queen given the other pieces of the triptych? She stared out the window over the bleak winter landscape and let her imagination loose to play once again.

"So as long as King James and Mary Beatrice produced no son, the Protestants were happy. . . ." The quavering old voice faded to a drone. "But then in . . ."


## October 1687

*It was autumn, and the leaves were red and gold in the woods. The sun was setting with a gloss of crimson over the hills. Mary Beatrice sat by the castle window, watching the hunters returning with a stag, gutted and slung between poles, its antlers dragging patterns in the dirt. She could smell the blood, heavy and wet in the clear air. But of course she could not really. She was too far away, it was just her imagination. Still, the smell made her sick.*

*"Your Majesty?" Her lady in waiting rapped lightly, then slipped into the chamber. "Shall you dress for supper? The king is already in the library with the guests." Queen Mary nodded*

*and left the window. The smell was still there, sharp, thick blood, the stench of flesh and death and meat.*

*"Will you take some comfrey, m'lady?" The maid poured her a steaming cup. Mary sipped the grassy brew. It had been flavored with honey, the way she liked it, but right now, the sweet taste sent a wave of nausea through her.*

*"Katey gathered it this afternoon, just by the Whistlebridge gate." The servant chatted on as she helped the queen on with the petticoats and corset, all the time looking for signs of what might be ailing her. She had been nervous lately, drawn and tired. The servants had been whispering. "Hold now." Mary gripped the bedpost and Katey pulled the lacing tight. "There will be a frost tonight . . ." she chattered on. "Too tight, m'lady?"*

*"No." Mary Beatrice steadied herself and smiled. She selected an emerald necklace that had been a gift from the Duke of Exeter. Mary Beatrice steeled herself for her royal duties and went downstairs.*

*They were giving a small dinner for the Duke of Exeter, the Earl of—oh, god* where? *Was it Cornwall? Lords and gentlemen and bishops, up for a shooting party and politics. Queen Mary smiled as she walked into the room and took her place beside her husband. King James had become a dreary old man, but after fifteen years of marriage, Mary Beatrice had grown used to him. There might once have been something handsome about his dark looks, but now he was sour and rigid and ugly, with a thin, pinched mouth that always seemed locked in a sneer. But he had treated her kindly, and there had never been expectations of love.*

*They had never been close, but since he ascended to the throne two years ago, the strains of royal life had increased. Two years on the throne, now fifty-five years old, and there was still no heir. Four times she had given birth. Four times tiny coffins had been lowered into the ground.*

*The musicians played, wine was poured, the candlelight sparkled on the silver. Mary tried to smile and listen, but the voices kept fading to a drone. Figs appeared in front of her, one of her favorite dishes, stewed in brandy with lemons, but she ate only a bite of them. Then came roasted quail, filet of salmon, but each time the servant's hands descended over her shoulder with another course, she felt more desperate.*

*Finally the main course was brought in. A suckling pig, roasted whole, its skin crackled and brown, its snout puckered with the cooking, shriveled little ears moving slightly as the carver took his knife. The smell of the pork was overwhelming, a dark smell of fat and blood. It was simply too much. Queen Mary fainted dead away. The gossip of the servants had been right, and on November 14 there was an official announcement. Queen Mary Beatrice was once again pregnant.*

"Even before she had the baby," Dame Atchins spoke in a gossipy tone now, and Margaret realized she had been day-dreaming, "there were rumors circulating. There had to be a boy, and it was said there would be a switch if it were not. Law required that there be witnesses to a royal birth, and the room was packed with people, but still there was controversy.

"The Protestants did not believe the Catholic witnesses. They claimed that a healthy baby boy had been smuggled into the queen's chamber in a warming pan to take the place of a stillborn, or a girl. Now this was absurd. A warming pan had been brought into the room, but more than two hours before the delivery. That anyone could stuff a live infant in a shallow metal pan, and have him lie quietly . . . well, it was absurd and the rumor was pretty well put to rest, except among the most radical supporters of William of Orange . . ."

# TEN

". . . So for a few months, everyone just basically hung back and waited to see if the infant would live . . ."

At about the same time, across the Atlantic, Jack McGuire and his daughter Annalee were telling much the same story that Margaret Haversford was hearing, though in much more comfortable circumstances and with a variety of colorful commentary. Margaret

had faxed them the information on the other medallion, and Jack
and Annalee had made an immediate trip through the blizzard to
the university library, where they checked out every book there
was on King James and the Stuarts.

The three McGuire sons were home for Christmas, and they
were all gathered around the kitchen table playing a game of Risk
and drinking beer.

"Mary Beatrice had been ill throughout her pregnancy," Jack
went on. "The birth had been difficult, and the baby was
sickly—"

"Oh, tell what they fed him," Annalee interrupted with the
unique gleam of a child about to relate something particularly
disgusting.

"You tell them. You're the color commentator here."

"Okay. Well, we don't know why, but they didn't just nurse
him like a regular baby. Because he was a prince, all the palace
doctors got all into it, and of course they knew nothing, so first
they made a mush of flour and oatmeal with currents. They're like
raisins, little raisins, and canary wine. Only we don't know what
that is. The book didn't say; but it's probably wine made out of
canaries; 'cause now it gets really gross."

She swiped her hair off her face and went on breathlessly. Warren was wondering if he had shared a little too much of his beer
with her.

"This stuff made him sick . . . of course. So then, they gave
him this medicine that had ground up *deer* antlers in it, and dried
*snakes* and raw silk, and . . ." she gave a dramatic pause, "the
*skull* of a person that was hanged. Honest. A real human skull."

"Dad!" the brothers groaned in unison.

"I thought you said she would grow out of this," Warren said.

Jack shrugged in hopeless acceptance of his daughter's maca-
bre tendencies.

"That's what the book said."

"And it could burn a hole in a piece of cloth!"

"It was, after all, the seventeenth century," Jack reminded
them. "People believed in magic potions. They believed the king
could cure them with his touch. Anyway, it does appear that the
baby had been terribly sick at court, due primarily to the interfer-

ence of the king's doctors. Whether or not this was an actual attempt to poison the heir is another matter. Finally, however, the queen put her foot down, found a wet nurse, and had the baby fed simple mother's milk. Soon Prince James Francis Edward grew quite robust.''

"So the Protestants got worried and drummed them out of the country, and brought in William and Mary to rule," John finished. "And it is now time to defend Irkusk from the marauding invaders." He laughed and handed his father the dice.

"Well, yes. Basically," Jack said with a twinge of hurt feelings at their lack of historical zeal.

"So how do we get from there to your treasure boat at the bottom of the sea?" Trevor asked, puzzled.

"Well, that comes a little later . . .''

# *ELEVEN*

Ross Shepard had been treasure hunting in the Bahamas and Florida Keys for twenty years. He had been successful enough to keep himself in business, and occasionally make the newspapers (features, not headlines) but never successful enough to retire in proverbial splendor. A big operation such as he now had aboard the *Golden Goose,* with metal detectors, side-scan sonar, mailbox blasting, and a good team of divers cost thousands of dollars a day.

The McGuire brothers, primarily through Peter's contacts in the investment business, had assembled enough money to hire him only for a three-week initial search. Shepard wasn't exactly thrilled with this, but there wasn't a lot else going on at the moment. He was waiting for salvage permits from the Dominican Republic which might not come through for another couple of months, so he figured he might as well keep busy. Mayaguana wasn't that far, and the wreck of the *Christiania* sounded interesting. He steadfastly refused to have divers hired by the client, however, until he found out one would be Chicago Nordejoong.

"Chicago? Little Chicago?" His wife Martha was thrilled.

"Little? Never been nothing little about that girl," he reminded her. " 'Specially her temper."

"Oh, you don't know. She must have been, gosh, thirteen or fourteen the last time we saw her. Nineteen seventy . . . one of two?"

"Naw—couldn't be that long. Remember we ran into Nordy in Venezuela that time . . ."

"That was years later. She was in boarding school then."

"Can't be twenty years."

"Shep—we're old! Everything there ever was is twenty years ago by now!" She laughed. Shep just growled. Although they were both in their sixties, they lived a fairly ageless life out here on the water, free from society's oppressive reminders of youthful glory and the bleakness of old age. Except for occasional creakiness, and a bit of a breast cancer scare for Marty in '89, they were healthy and active. Shep was a little stooped, and one knee, shot up in the Korean war, had stiffened with age and did not bend much. The only thing he was bitter about was the ear trouble that kept him from diving. It took so long to equalize now, that a half hour into the dive, he was still making his descent.

Curly hair ringed a bald and bumpy skull, but he had a handsome face, an aristocratic face. His grandchildren joked that he should be hosting a PBS show. He didn't know about that, but he did know that Martha was still beautiful. It was not just the fondness of old married people for each other, she was honestly an attractive woman, with dark brown eyes and a calmness of disposition that gave her a sort of glow.

It had been tough for her around forty-five, he vaguely remembered, when she began to show a little wrinkle and sag, and a couple of stubborn extra inches settled in around that previously tiny waist, but Shep had not even noticed these changes until she burst into tears one evening when she found she could no longer zip a dress that had fit perfectly twenty-three years and three children ago.

Her hair, though gray now, was still shiny, and her hands were as pretty as ever. Women at sea usually had bad hands—hell, everyone at sea had bad hands, dry and calloused and rough—but somehow Martha had always taken care of hers, even though she had hauled nearly as many lines over the years as he had. They were small and soft, her hands, with nails like little petals. And her smile—God, he would come into the wheel house sometimes, even now after all these years, and she would smile, just that regular smile, the same ordinary daily smile she gave to shop clerks, and he would just feel struck with some kind of glory.

"I was so sorry we couldn't make it to her wedding. Or the funeral. What a tragedy. I don't think they were married two years even." Martha scanned the horizon once again. She had been keeping an eye out for the *Tassisa Far* since morning. "But she's sailing with a young man now. Maybe . . . Oh, look. That must be her now!"

Ross took the binoculars. "No. That's not . . . well . . . yeah, sure is—look at the curve of the bow. She must have taken down the mizzen, but I'd recognize that hull shape anywhere. Never seen a man bend wood like old Nordy."

Ross and Erik Nordejoong had crewed together for years on merchant ships, starting in the late fifties. As they climbed in the ranks, and eventually came into command of their own vessels, however, their lives intersected less often, and the friendship slowly dwindled. The long lapse had built up gradually, due to nothing more than time and tides, sailing schedules, family obligations, and hemispheres. For a while in the late seventies when they had both shipped out of Norfolk, Erik and the twelve-year-old Chicago frequently spent shore time with the Shepards, but it was true, they hadn't seen Erik for eight or ten years, and Chicago for nearly twenty.

Martha waved as they approached and watched eagerly as they anchored and puttered over in the dinghy.

"Oh, my goodness—look at you!" Martha threw her arms around Chicago, then pushed her back for a good look. "You see!" she said in a mock scolding tone, glancing at Chicago's chest. "I told you they would grow!"

Shep, though he was equally happy to see her, was characteristically gruff. He was of the old school, where the emotional folderol of life was a wife's job, and best kept that way. He kissed her on the cheek and shook hands with Alex, sizing him up and down with an abrasive glare that made Chicago laugh. "He's able-bodied, Shep," she said supportively, patting Alex on the shoulder, letting her hand linger, a gesture Martha picked up immediately. She looked at the two of them and felt the wistful satisfaction of an old lady looking at young lovers.

"This is Stanislaw Czychech, my partner," Shep explained as Stan came out of the wheelhouse. He was a big man, in his mid-fifties, sinewy and lean, with a strong upper body and neck muscles like hawsers. Stan had been a professional diver, working oil rigs and bridge construction, before joining Shepard's operations some ten years ago. He had rough reddish hair in need of a trim, and a couple days' growth on his chin.

"I've got a local guy coming out this afternoon, name of Wodie. Young kid, but supposedly a good deckhand and diver. He's bringing his launch, so we'll be able to keep the *Goose* out here, run in for whatever we need. Probably a slacker. Hard to find good workers these days, but it's good business to hire a local or two. Well, let me show you around the *Goose* . . ."

"Just the short tour, Shep—don't go dragging Chicago all through the engine room. I've got lunch ready." Martha remembered how Chicago, even as a girl, had liked to mess around with machinery.

"Stan oversees all the diving, Martha handles navigation and supplies, I run the boat."

"Is this your old dive boat?" Chicago asked. "Dad said you bought one in Puerto Rico."

"That she is, but mostly just the hull and the aft cabins are left from the original. We put in a new engine and electronics, rebuilt the wheelhouse five years ago. Pushed it forward here," he waved to where the cabin had originally stood, "to give us more room on the aft deck for equipment. Put in the winch, the compressor there."

"Wow." Chicago was impressed. The dive area was well organized, with racks built in near the compressor so that tanks could be filled where they were positioned.

"She originally could sleep twelve, plus six crew, but we tore a couple cabins out below to put in storage tanks and work areas."

"For all the treasure," Stan explained with a good-humored irony.

As Shep went over the boat, he never checked to see if they were following him, or spoke of anything but essentials. He reminded Alex of one of his uncles, a short and snarly man who did not tolerate fools gladly. His loyalties were hard won, but highly valued.

The wheelhouse was enclosed only on three sides, though the back could be shut off with slatted boards and a heavy-duty canopy. The radio and electronics were clustered in the forward section. There was a captain's chair, a small chart shelf, and a narrow berth, where three could sit, or one could sleep.

Below deck, everything likewise was spare and utilitarian, but comfortable. The salon was spacious, with a long table, padded benches, and fold-down bunks. The galley was smaller than one would expect, also compressed from the charter days in order to make more space. Just forward of the main salon, there was a well-designed work area with the chart table, another radio, and various drawers and boxes of equipment. Shelves and cubbyholes ringed this space, crammed with history books and papers, research on the various shipwrecks Shep had hunted for.

Shep and Marty shared one aft cabin, Stan had the other, leaving two smaller cabins for divers and crew. Alex and Chicago would be staying on the *Tassia Far,* but as Alex watched Martha laying out platters of sandwiches, bowls of potato and green bean salads, and a still-warm pound cake, he silently prayed they would be eating their meals over here.

Chicago's cooking had not improved with experience. Alex had discovered that it was not simple ineptness, or a streak of rebellion. When it came to cooking, she had a mental blank spot, a sort of culinary dyslexia. A pot or pan was always a new object to her, and while she could rip through complicated formulas for celestial navigation, it was all she could do to remember that spaghetti only needed to boil for seven minutes.

Alex's experience was not much better, though he did try. His training, and a good deal more personal experience than he would have liked, had given him the knowledge to live off the land in any jungle or desert. Dining on the occasional grub or root was not unknown to him, but during the periods of normal life in civilization, he relied on sandwiches, pizza, and the microwave. With no corner store or deli accessible out here, their meals aboard

the *Tassia Far,* outside of grilled fresh fish, were spartan, repeti-
tive, and usually canned.

They sat around the table and ploughed into the food with the
sort of appetite only sea air can give.

"Can you tell us more about the ship we'll be looking for?"
Chicago asked. "We really don't know anything."

"It's a schooner called the *Christiania,*" Martha explained. "A
couple of years ago, the McGuires found an old medallion in this
area, evidently quite an unusual one. Their research led them to a
ship that reportedly went down in seventeen something. The ship
was reportedly carrying a coffin with, well, they think it could be
the body of the real king of England. James, was it?" Martha
looked at Shep, who just shrugged.

"I never could keep any of 'em straight, I ain't about to start
now."

"Wait, I'll get the letter." She disappeared below, and returned
a little while later with some of the papers Jack McGuire had sent.

". . . Switched at birth," Stan was explaining, rolling his eyes
at the obvious absurdity of it, "and sent away to Jamaica."

"It was King James—the second. In 1688. The queen had just
borne a son, and there was some political upheaval, and they were
fleeing the country."


*November 1688*


*Huge waves crashed against the rocks, and ships in the Ports-
mouth Harbor were tossed at anchor. Mary Beatrice sat quietly
by the fire, her eyes burning as if with fever. It had been four
months since the birth, but the stress, plus this trip into exile, had
taken further toll on her. The king had sent her here three weeks
ago with the child, to be ready if necessary to flee to France. She
was thin and her eyes were sunken in her pale face. Her skin was
taut and her hair, once lustrous and thick, felt coarse. But she
minded none of this as she gazed at the sleeping child in the
cradle. Edward was a sweet, fat baby, vigorous and happy, thriving at last.*

*"Your Majesty, it is madness, pure and simple." Abbe Rizzini*

paced the small chamber, nervous and alert to every sound, like
a mouse in the master's kitchen.

"It has been madness for a while now, Zizi." The queen
smiled sadly.

"But this is . . . this is so drastic! The king has many supporters,
he commands powerful allegiance. Two months from now it might
all be over, and then what will you do? How will you explain?"

"I am taking command of the only thing I can, in the only way
that I can. I have no power over the forces that conspire against
the king. In my heart, if you would know, I should almost like
for it all to end tomorrow, for James to abdicate, and to hell
with England."

"Your Majesty—"

"No. Let them war each other for another hundred years. I'm
tired." Her eyes filled with tears, and she reached for the sleeping
baby, drawing him fiercely onto her lap as if pulling him from
drowning. "Look at him, Zizi. He will grow up. This one will live.
I know it! I don't care if he ever becomes king, I just want him
to live!"

Abbe Rizzini was a trusted friend of her brother, the Duke of
Modena. It was he, and King Louis of France, who had convinced
James to let her and the baby flee to Portsmouth, and he who had
guarded their hiding here. She trusted him completely, but she did
not hope to make him understand.

"This is the only way." She laughed. "And it's sweet, is it not,
that the idea was theirs?" She brushed her hand over the baby's
dark hair and kissed his sleeping face. "The notion came right
from their very wicked hearts. All of them, claiming the baby was
a changeling. You must do this, Zizi." Huge tears rolled down
her tortured face. "Soon, before I lose my courage."

They both jumped at the sound of approaching hoofbeats. There
was a sharp rap on the door. Queen Mary clutched the baby. The
door to the bedroom opened, and Genevieve, the baby's wet nurse
and the queen's confidante, came out in alarm. Rizzini motioned
for them to be silent, as Mary took the child into the other room.
Rizzini drew his dagger, and waited for the visitor to relay the
password. When he was convinced all was safe, he unbarred the
door. There stood a young man spattered with mud, his short

*woolen cloak soaked and dripping, steam rising from the back of his horse.*

*"M'lord, I bring word from Lord Dover." The man swayed on his feet from exhaustion, and his chest heaved beneath his jerkin. "William of Orange has landed this afternoon at Brixham. He marches to London."*

*When the messenger had gone, Rizzini sank into the chair. So it had started. William intended to take the throne from King James, and Rizzini knew there was every likelihood he would succeed. What now? James's support was weak, but were the English really ready to see him deposed? Perhaps it would just be a lesson of sorts. Perhaps a few months, or years, of exile, then a triumphant return. If so, then the infant prince must be protected. Perhaps the queen's scheme was not so absurd. How much had she really planned?*

*The bedroom door opened and Queen Mary emerged. Standing beside her in traveling boots and cloak was Genevieve. Both women had been weeping. Genevieve held the baby.*

*"It will be tonight then," the queen whispered. Rizzini stood and quietly assembled his own boots and clothing.*

*"M'lady, I am at your service."*

*"There is a sailors' inn at the dock," Mary told him in a carefully controlled voice. "Ask for Joden. You may trust him. He is an emissary of the king of France and has been standing by, awaiting command. Once you have turned my maid and the child over to him, you are to go to the abbey." Mary's voice began to quiver. Genevieve reached for her hand, but the queen pulled away as if pained by the touch. "Ask for Sister Agnes Carmel. She knows nothing but that a foundling is to be adopted."*

*"She will wonder at my arriving at this late hour."*

*"Tell her your carriage was delayed by the rain. The parents have been taken to the boat already, and must sail in the morning. She is old and the orphanage is crowded; they will be glad to be rid of one baby. His name is Michael. Be sure of this. Genny has been careful to chose one of near resemblance."*

*"M'lady, I will do your bidding. Only I implore you one more time." Mary Beatrice shook her head. A strange composure had crept over her face and her eyes looked distant.*

*"At least consider the ruse. Won't someone discern the truth back at the palace?"*

*"We've been gone nearly a month. Babies change quickly. The king does not know him beyond a bundle in the royal crib, and a burden on his throne. Here are the papers."* She handed him a thick packet wrapped in oiled leather and sealed with wax. *"They are to go by courier to Modena, to my brother the duke, to be secreted until I should someday want them."*

*"Is your maid to pass as the baby's mother then?"* Mary nodded. *"I know her as an honest woman, a good Christian and a trusted friend. Moreover, she has the wits necessary to help make this ruse successful. She will not betray us."* Rizzini gave Genevieve a slight respectful bow of acknowledgment.

*"Very good, Your Majesty, but might I suggest, the child is dressed rather well."*

*"Oh, goodness yes, mum!"* Genevieve's eyes grew wide as she fingered the fine linen dress and soft blankets.

Mary looked alarmed, the first thought of all that could go wrong with the plan really hitting her. She had thought it out so carefully, but of course she had overlooked this one obvious thing.

*"What, what is there? Oh, dear god . . ."* Mary's careful control was about to crack. Gennevieve put the baby on the bed and helped her mistress to a chair.

*"The little vest and suit, m'lady! The one Katy's daughter knitted. Bless her heart, the child spun the yarn herself, and the stitches are so loose, it really is quite shabby."*

*"Yes . . . yes. And it will keep him warm. It was so dear of her to make it for him."*

*"And we can wrap him in this blanket here!"* Genny pulled a worn blanket from the chair. Quickly she changed the baby, pulling off his lacy frock and slipping the clumsy sweater over the prince's chubby arms.

*"What about this, m'lady?"* Genevieve fingered the small chain that hung from the child's neck, and held the cross in the palm of her hand.

*"I had them made a fortnight ago,"* Mary explained. *"It isn't gold, so no one should value it."* Mary's hands trembled as she fingered the little cross. The chain had been fashioned with no clasp, and made just slightly smaller than the baby's head. Fastened around his neck by the jeweler, it could not be removed without breaking. Hidden beneath her clothing, Mary Beatrice

*wore a similar chain, bearing a half-circle charm with a half-cross cut from the jagged side. She reached into a small velvet bag and drew out a third chain with a similar token.*

*"Keep this with you always. See, the piece was engraved straight across, then cut into these three pieces. No one can make a false one." Genevieve examined the charm in her hand, then bent over the baby and placed it next to his cross. The pieces fit perfectly together, the cross enclosed by the two half circles, the inscription lining up perfectly. "King of my heart, King of my home, God protect and return thee."*

*"It must stay—how else am I to ... how else will I know him?" Mary Beatrice began to sob.*

They were all silent as Martha finished telling them the queen's sad story.

"But I thought you said the *Christiania* went down in seventeen fourteen," Alex finally said. "That's twenty-six years later. What happened in the meantime?"

Martha shrugged. "They don't really know. We can only guess."

# TWELVE

"Okay, Crawly—tell me you're joking." Teneby paced slowly, then stared out the window of the Director General's office. It was the sort of dark, sleety afternoon that could make London appear especially bleak. The Christmas decorations still hanging in the shop across the street looked feeble. "These Americans pull up a coffin, Cory MacClannon is king of England and he cuts Scotland free? Just like that?"

"Essentially. Yes."

"There's no way the Scots are going along with cessation even if their local hero is crowned king of the universe. The SNP has never polled more than thirty percent, and even when they've done well at the polls, there were always other issues on the ticket. No one honestly believes that if there was a vote exclusively on separation, the Scots would vote it through. It's preposterous. For all their storm and fury, it's still a romantic notion. They've been talking about a split since the bloody place joined up. And what's that now, three hundred some years?"

"Things are different now."

"So they've got all the oil, okay, what else?"

"They've got the Maastriht Treaty, currency balance, a new European Common Market that could let them trade just as easily with Brussels as with London. And yes, the oil money is important. There's billions of dollars a year flowing out of the North Sea so far, and Cory MacClannon controls a lot of it."

"But break entirely? Why?"

"Because they're Celts, damn it! Because they're bloody Highlanders who can hold a grudge for three hundred years and never liked us much to begin with."

"They might storm and bluster and write a few more ballads, Crawley, but pick up and leave?"

"Have you looked at a map of the world lately? Balkinization is the fad. Small ethnic countries carving themselves off."

"Off at the knees likely."

"It's a bit of a vogue one might say, but psychologically significant."

"Psychologically significant? You mean the Scots are inspired by some rotten peasant revolt in Azerbaijan or wherever?"

"Never overlook national psyches. You don't really think we lost the Colonies over tea, do you?"

Teneby gave a half-nod, a tip of one shoulder, a reluctant acquiescence.

"They're pissed off about the poll tax, about our meddling in their local affairs, school boards, local health boards."

"So why don't you just send a few lads to blow up Whitehall?" Teneby asked with good-natured sarcasm. "Kill off all the politicians who've been messing them around."

"It's more than that, Tenny. The recession has hit Scotland hard. British Steel pulled ten thousand jobs out of there in the past few years. MacClannon is right now collecting investors to reopen the Ravenscraig plant. You don't think those ten thousand young men will follow him to hell and back for work?''

''Well, Capt'n, I'm still not convinced, but I'm on the case if that's what you want.''

''Good chap, Tenny. Of course the whole thing is ridiculous. But let's just stay on top from the beginning and spare ourselves the mess. First of all, I'd like you to pay a visit both to Mr. Whitstone's apartment and his office. Spencer says he's given him everything he knows, and is slavishly loyal to the queen, but I want to know for myself. Is he holding anything back? Or falsifying all this to inflate his own role.''

''You think he's a crackpot?''

''I don't know. I don't think so.'' Hayes leaned back and the old leather chair creaked. He noticed lately that his body didn't seem to take up as much space in the chair as it used to. Could he be shrinking with old age? ''I've checked everything out through other channels, and the whole thing looks awfully tight.''

''His story is true? The baby switch . . . all that?''

''I'm afraid there is some good evidence. That girl from the Victoria and Albert Museum—what was her name . . .''

''Margaret Haversford?''

''She's muddled things up a bit.''

''What do you want to do about that?''

''Do? Oh, nothing right now. She's convinced it's some sort of lover's token, that the queen had a bastard and sent it away.''

''There's an idea,'' Teneby pointed out. ''A three-hundred-year-old royal scandal.''

''I'll keep it in mind. Meanwhile, let's have a good look through Whitstone's papers.''

''Shouldn't take long.'' Teneby got up.

''Good, because then you're going to the Bahamas.''

Teneby brightened at this. ''Am I now?''

''Don't get too excited. Mayaguana is not one of the leading resort destinations. In fact, there's precious little there at all: one town, a couple of hotels. Sand and water. But I want you to keep an eye on this salvage boat, the what is it . . .'' He shuffled a few notes aside. ''The *Golden Goose*. Just be there in case they find anything. We'll need a reason for you to be there at all, probably development speculation or something. Put your mind to it. You'll go with another agent, probably Collins or Griffith.''

"What about Harry Willis?''

"I've already got him on mission next week.'' Teneby of course didn't ask where. "Well Christ, Crawley, don't we have a sweet young agent around somewhere can pose as my girlfriend? I thought we were supposed to be recruiting a few spy girls, equal opportunity and all that.''

"We have, and they're all in nice safe offices where they belong and where they're going to stay.''

"Well, pardon my bluntness, sir, but I won't have Collins. The man's an idiot and I haven't trusted him since the Falklands.''

"Very well, you'll have Griffith.''


# *THIRTEEN*


"Well?'' Annalee burst into the kitchen as she had done every day since the search began, her cheeks red, her eyes bright with expectation. Once again, April McGuire quelled the girl's expectation with a sad shrug.

"Sorry, hon. No treasure today.''

"Oh.'' She looked crestfallen, and April's annoyance with Jack went up a notch. Two weeks of this. It seemed like the longest Christmas break in the history of the world. Every day, the girl running home expecting to hear about a discovery in Mayaguana. It was worse now that the boys were gone again. April was getting skilled at smoothing out the daily disappointment, though inside she was seething over the folly of the whole affair. Somehow her husband had managed to take a simple lucky discovery and inflate it into world-breaking proportions. One old necklace, and now he was trying to change the history of the world. Well, let him, but why did he have to set their daughter up for such disappointment?

"Where have you been?"

"Skating." The girl dropped her knapsack and headed straight for the cupboard.

"On the lake?"

"Uh huh." She pulled out the jar of peanut butter, and dipped out a spoonful while she rummaged for the crackers and jelly. She had been in a growth spurt lately, seemed to have shot up two inches, and eating like the boys used to.

"I'm joining the hockey team."

"No, you're not," April responded calmly. "Use a plate." Annalee spread two crackers with peanut butter and jelly and mashed them together to make a crumbly sandwich, and was eating it over the sink.

"Why not?"

"You'll get your teeth knocked out."

"Warren and Trevor and John all played. Did Daddy call? Maybe they called his office."

"Annabel, your father told you not to get your hopes up."

"My hopes are not up." She brushed the crumbs off her sweater. April felt lost. She had never known what to make of this child, and didn't feel ready for her budding adolescence and all this ridiculous shipwreck business on top of that. She had been fairly proud of the way the boys had turned out, but the vicissitudes of their puberty now seemed simple compared to dealing with Annabel Lee.

"Why don't we go over to the arena and sign you up for figure skating?" April suggested hopefully.

"Mom, I don't want to twirl around! I want to play hockey!" Annalee picked up her knapsack and headed to her room.

Annabel Lee's frustration with her mother over "girl things" would probably never end, but her frustration with the lack of news from Mayaguana was about to.

An hour later, and hundreds of miles away, aboard the *Golden Goose,* the metal detector suddenly began to beep.

"Something big, Capt'n!" Stan cried out excitedly. "Reverse sweep!" They had been dragging the magnetometer in a grid pattern, up and down and up and down for two weeks.

Shepard watched the blips on the screen as they doubled back, and the metal detector once again signaled wildly.

"Neutral, Marty!" he called out to his wife at the helm. Marty throttled down and shifted, then hurried to his side to look at the screen. Alex caught them exchanging excited smiles, like kids on a new adventure. "Drop the hook, let's check it out," Shep ordered. Wodie, the Bahamian deckhand, scrambled forward to unchain the anchor, while Alex reeled in the fishing lines. While trolling for treasure had proved futile so far, they had at least been lucky with the fish. Chicago checked the GPS and wrote the co-ordinates in the log. There was a guarded excitement aboard the *Golden Goose.*

They had picked up strong signals twice so far. On the first dive they had discovered a collection of oil drums, and on the second a couple of steel girders that had probably fallen off a supply boat.

"I got a good feeling, Shep." Stan grinned as he began to assemble his scuba tank.

Shep just shrugged and leaned over to look down into the clear water. "We're in sixty feet."

They were far enough out that it was more likely that a ship could have gone undiscovered this long, and very close to one of the likely sites, a small reef that might once have been a shallow scrap of cay.

"Well, what are you waiting for?" he growled. "Check it out." Because of the ruptured eardrum, Shepard himself no longer dove, and the irritation of having to stay on deck showed. Alex and Chicago quickly suited up, the boredom suddenly broken. This was like Christmas morning, going downstairs to see what might be under the tree. Marty pulled on her wet suit, old and faded and almost worn through in places, she insisted it still had many good dives left in it. Most of her equipment looked as if it had come out of a museum, though she had finally bought a new mask when her old one began to leak.

When they were all ready, Stan briefly went over the dive plan. They had a few different search patterns they could use, based on the sort of bottom configuration they found, and he went over the signals for each one.

"Okay, Shep, turn out your pockets," he directed as they assembled on the dive platform. Shepard dug into his shorts and came up with a handful of change. With a minimum of ceremony but a definite reverence, he flung the coins out over the site. It was a treasure hunter's superstition, a gift to placate the spirits of the dead who guarded the wreck.

With the easy rhythm of two people well used to each other, Shep held his wife's tank and weight belt while she jumped in the water, then handed them down to her to put on. This assistance was her only concession to advancing age.

"All set?" Stan checked his watch then looked at his dive computer, making sure both were working. They slipped beneath the calm surface, and, hopes high, began the descent. The water was clear, visibility a hundred feet or more.

Stan's instinct started humming as soon as he got in. The water was clear. Stan Czychech was a quiet and superstitious man, with a collection of charms that he had accumulated over the years, and which he swore led him to treasure. There was a graveyard feel to this place.

He drifted down slowly, feeling the slight current, turning to survey the surroundings. They were not looking for sparkle and shine, but for tiny clues. Whatever was down here would be covered with layers and layers of sand and muck and sea grass, hidden beneath boulders dislodged in undersea earthquakes, scattered by currents, or simply too battered by time to be recognized by the untrained eye.

They were looking for a certain shape that didn't quite belong to the natural reef formation, a pattern of growth that might reveal the ribs of an ancient hull. Saltwater was a remarkable preservative. Wooden timbers had survived for hundreds of years in the right conditions. He and Shep had pulled up shoes, clothing, even a wooden crock still full of butter.

He dropped another twenty feet and began to survey the bottom. How would a ship settle here? Would it tumble and shift for a few years until finally reaching a rest, or simply settle where first it landed? Those boulders, could they have cracked the ribs, split the hull, and scattered its contents in the deeper water? What was growing here? The types of corals and sponges might give some clue.

He did not register all this information consciously, did no calculations or measurements. It was an intuitive process. And it worked. There was a long arch of coral, a little too regular. As

Stan swam over to check it out, he heard excited rapping. He turned and saw Alex signaling to him, pointing to the metal detector. Stan, Chicago, and Marty all swam over, and watched with satisfaction as the light kept blinking.

The divers began to search. Moving slowly, with perfect buoyancy so as not to stir up the bottom, they floated around boulders and peered under chunks of coral. Beneath a large mound of brain coral, covered with great blue basket sponges, Chicago finally saw something. One shape slightly out of place. It was covered with growth. Fuzzy little Christmas tree worms perched all over it, and a fat anemone nestled between some branches of fire coral, but Chicago, raised on boats her entire life, could clearly see the shape of an anchor.

# FOURTEEN

Prince Gloom they called him, or variations thereof—His Dismalness, or The Royal Sour; names whispered about the back corridors of the palace. The queen's servants generally had great devotion to the royal family and would not stand for anyone on the outside making a slighting remark, but for servants to mock their masters is natural and so there were names. At least "The Prince of Tails" had faded by now, as there had been no more embarrassing tapes.

The prince sat by the fire, his thinning hair in disarray, his cheeks flushed, his trousers still flecked with mud, straight from the paddock where he had spent the afternoon working with a new polo pony. The prince was most comfortable here, amidst the splendid disarray of his study, decorated to his own desires, and not to the demands of history or palace fashion. Highgrove in Gloucestershire had always been his special retreat, and for the past few years, as everything else soured around him, he took greater solace in its halls, especially after the intensity of Christmas with the family.

Right now he had a rare two days between public engagements, and was enjoying the solitude, listening halfheartedly as Adrian Spencer briefed him on security arrangements for the next day's trip to a biscuit factory in Manchester. There had been a recent escalation in IRA activities, and Spencer planned a change of route and a decoy motorcade—the usual dodge. Damn factory tours. There were issues of substance he could be concerning himself with, the prince's trust school leaver initiative for one. Or an essay to finish, a philosophical paper on how ancient architectural styles reflected man's changing relationship with the natural world.

But tomorrow he would be strolling down some assembly line watching a machine trowel out vanilla creme fillings.

"Is that satisfactory, Your Majesty?" Spencer's inflection alerted the prince to the end of the briefing and he nodded.

"Very good, Spencer. I rest securely in your capable hands."

"Is there anything else you wish to know then?"

"Yes, actually there is. Do sit down, Spencer." The prince waved toward the facing chair. Spencer, who had known the prince since his college days, had a good sense of the man's moods, and knew he was worrying over something. It had been a hellish year. The breakup of his marriage was bad enough, but to be cast so uniformly as the villain was unconscionable. Of course there had been problems but . . .

"I'd like to know about the Penzance affair," the prince said casually. Spencer blinked twice, but otherwise displayed no evidence of his surprise.

"Excuse me, sir?"

"I believe that's what you are calling it. Clever name."

"It is of minor interest, Your Majesty." Spencer recovered quickly. "A bit of an inquiry we have going on, based on some rather wild suppositions of an elderly documents man at the British Museum. Certainly of no consequence. We check such things out as a matter of course."

"Yes, I expect you would." The prince enjoyed seeing the fellow's surprise. For many years he had taken occasional pleasure in browsing through the palace security files. Raised from infancy in the rarefied world of royalty, the prince was fascinated by the peculiar obsessions of some of his subjects. He examined letters by psychics claiming they had messages for the queen, notes by inventors seeking funding for fantastical schemes. The prince found the files, from the eccentric to the psychotic, fascinating. It was ironic, really, that he read them with the same guilty indulgence that a million tabloid readers enjoyed—at his own expense—every day in the *Sun* and the *Mirror*.

Since the gossip of his affair had been broadcast all over the world, obviously from leaks within the palace, he had begun to take an even greater interest in the security files, cultivating his own sources to keep him aware of all goings-on.

Now and then, alone and brooding, it struck him that this was the first manifestation of an old man's paranoia, a sort of prickly impotence. It was a bitter satisfaction to know exactly what your enemies were up to.

"I believe it involves a historical matter. An allegation, I understand, that there may be a question of succession. A possible claim to the throne."

"Entirely frivolous, Your Majesty. Some vague old papers dug up in Jamaica."

"Yet there is an American team mounting an expedition to search for a shipwreck?"

"Hardly an expedition, sir." Spencer felt the side of his face growing hot from the fire and shifted in the chair. "A couple of brothers, one an archaeologist. They've hired a boat and a couple of divers for a little exploration."

How had this come to the knowledge of the prince? Spencer feared he was being tested in some way, but could not figure exactly how. Spencer adhered to the long palace tradition that it was best not to involve the family too closely in the details of their security. The sheer number of threats, most of them groundless exercises of the imbalanced, would distract and possibly frighten anyone without the balanced perspective of his office.

Could Crawford Hayes himself have gone to the prince? Was there a connection he did not know about? This thought angered him. The Royal Family was his responsibility.

"So what would you say the chances are of these Americans actually finding something down there?" the prince asked, obviously relishing the story.

"No way to know." Spencer tried to make his tone nonchalant. "Some of these fellows search for years before they find anything."

"But they did find a medallion at one location?"

"Yes, sir."

"A natural starting place, one would think. That's where they're going? Those MI5 chaps?" Spencer's heart gave a lurch. So the prince knew this, too. What did that mean? Was he being investigated? Was his own position in danger?

"Yes, sir. An island called Mayaguana. I'm a bit surprised the higher ups gave the go-ahead. It does seem a wild-goose chase. It's hard to imagine records from the period were so well kept, so detailed, to stir up all this."

"Shipping was the foundation of the Colonies, Spencer, the backbone of commerce. And you know with what fondness our noble countrymen have always held writs and deeds and such." The prince smiled, and leaned back, assuming a less royal posture to help ease the man's tension. Enough of the toying. Spencer was a good and loyal servant and didn't deserve to worry.

"I'm quite pleased with your handling of this case, Mr. Spencer. Well done. Now tell me, how quiet is this thing? Honestly?"

"Thank you for your kind words, Your Majesty. It was of course never my intention to withhold any information from you or from the queen. I'm sure you know that in matters such as this, well . . ."

"Yes, yes. I'm sure I know." The prince waited for the answer to his question.

"How quiet? Well, sir. We are taking extraordinary precautions. I take some relief in the fact that nothing has hit the tabloids yet. These documents turned up a couple of years ago, and really don't mean a lot unless you connect them with other events: allegations, old stories, that sort of thing. Even if someone on the excavation team, or at the museum, did read the documents and did understand them and had heard of these obscure old rumors, well, it's still a dead end. Nothing starts to fall into place until you piece together a whole variety of other circumstances from the next twenty years."

"Which is what these Americans, these McGuire chaps, appear to have done."

"Well yes, Your Majesty, so it appears."

The prince smiled, a beaming, contented smile that puzzled Spencer. He could not see what in the conversation would have pleased him so. There was a bright flush of excitement on his cheek, and a gleam in his eye, as if something deeply satisfying had been revealed to him just now.

"Very good, Mr. Spencer." The prince rose, and Spencer immediately stood. "I should like to be kept informed on this matter."

"Yes, Your Majesty."

# FIFTEEN

Colin Teneby was a little disappointed that Whitstone's apartment was so easy to break into. Things had been so dull lately, not much to challenge a spy anymore. The only real action these days was in Yugoslavia, and he had little background in Eastern Europe. He picked the lock with ease, and slipped quietly inside.

The efficiency was small, spare, and as he had expected from a man who sorts and files papers for a living, meticulously neat. As far as creature comforts, there was a single bed with an old frame but a good mattress, a dresser, one old comfortable chair, a small wooden table and two chairs, and a twelve-inch black-and-white TV. The rest of the space was crammed with a desk and computer, bookshelves, and file cabinets. Teneby was even happier. Whitstone was not the sort of eccentric who keeps everything in heaps of moldy old boxes and ledgers.

He stood for a few minutes in the center of the room, simply observing. The wear on the carpet showed a triangular path, from bed to desk to chair. The sink, though old, had no water stains; Whitstone of course would not allow a dripping tap to disturb his scholarship.

The only curious thing was on the wall above the dresser. It looked like a shrine of sorts. A handkerchief, a man's handkerchief, faintly stained, hung in an ornate frame, surrounded by photos of the Queen Mother. There was a bulging album atop the dresser, and it, too, was devoted to the queen, a scrapbook of her life, focusing particularly on wartime news photos, clipped from magazines. Spencer had mentioned the chap had a devotion to the Queen Mum. Well, it looked harmless enough, no alterations to the photos, no unmailed letters of adoration, not even candles.

After memorizing the exact layout, so as to leave nothing in disarray, Teneby flipped on the computer, opened the first file cabinet, and began a methodical search. Whitstone was as logical as he was orderly, and everything having to do with the Penzance case, the Port Royal documents as well as Whitstone's own thoughts and cross-references were all together. For two hours, Teneby checked the files to be sure that Whitstone had given them complete and accurate information.

Document for document, everything checked out. It was all so neat, so perfect. The Penzance case was looking like another dull assignment.

"Good timing, Teneby," Hayes greeted him when he returned. "I was just talking with Dunagh here about your little trip. You do know each other?"

"A bit." Steven Dunagh rose and extended his hand. The two men nodded, automatically sizing each other up. Teneby had had only minor interaction with him, but it had been positive enough. Dunagh was in his late thirties and had been with the service for six years, after time in the military. He spoke with a trace of a northlands accent, and an occasional hint of the work that had gone into erasing it. He was not tall, but he had a strongly built torso atop legs that seemed slightly bowed, broad, restless hands and ruddy features. He was dressed in a rough wool jacket and corduroy trousers and held his cap in hand, his bearing meek, his step hesitant as if unaccustomed to walking on thick carpet. He was a tradesman or lory driver perhaps, down to London on business, awkward in the presence of gentlemen. A ruse, Spencer noted immediately, but a good one.

"We've pulled him off an undercover, a minor trade union investigation." That explained the clothes.

"What happened to Griffith?"

"Didn't you hear? Had a rotten accident last night. Drunk driver jumped a lane or two on the motorway, ran him into a bridge strut. He'll be all right, but has to be in hospital for a few days at least. I knew you nixed Collins, so Cranbourne recommended Dunagh here. He's got the right credentials." Hayes handed Teneby Dunagh's personnel file. "So why don't you look through this, have a talk, and see if we can't get you both off to the Caribbean tomorrow or so. Oh, by the way, did everything check out with Whitstone?"

"Just fine, Chief. All on the level." Teneby looked quickly through Dunagh's file. One item caught his attention. "You're a munitions expert?" He looked at Hayes with suspicion. "Sub aqua?"

"We want to keep all our options open, Teneby."

"We're being sent as watchers."

"And that's all you'll be doing, I'm certain." Hayes smiled.

# SIXTEEN

Chicago picked up the spoon. It was an ordinary piece, heavy and plain, with a bent handle and a deep bowl.

"It's so strange to think about someone three hundred years ago, sitting around the table on the *Christiania,* eating with this. All this stuff—does it seem spooky to you?"

"It used to." Martha laughed. "It still does when it's something personal. We pulled up a pair of boots once from a sunken freighter. You could see how the man walked, the sides of his heel worn down, one side more than the other. And he had lost the toes on his left foot. All but the big toe. There was cloth stuffed inside; you could see the indentation of a big toe." She smiled. "Now, that gave me chills."

In the week since they found the wreck, they had uncovered spoons and plates, pieces of the ship's stove, iron rings and a small cache of weapons, ancient pistols so encrusted with coral that they would have been missed by the casual eye. The smaller articles were kept on board in tanks of seawater, those items too big for such storage were kept in special containers on the bottom until they could be assured of proper handling.

There was always a tug of war between archaeology and profit in a shipwreck, but since Jack McGuire had pushed hard for the historical evidence, and secured part of the funding through an archaeological grant, they were taking special care with the *Christiania*. Artifacts that had lasted three hundred years under the sea could be destroyed in a matter of weeks in the open air.

Martha finished cataloging the new finds and looked out toward the low gray sky. Every sailor in the Caribbean had been monitoring the brewing in the South. It had begun three days ago as a vague swirl of clouds, five hundred miles southeast of the Bahamas, moving slowly and giving hope that it would dissipate. But then the swirl began to tighten. Hurricanes in January were rare, but not unheard of. This afternoon, the weather service upgraded it to a tropical storm.

The women heard Alex and Stan surface from their dive and went to the stern to take their gear.

"Find the chest of gold yet?" Martha teased as she took Stan's weight belt. So far, the *Christiania* was turning out to be a very stingy wreck.

"Damn it, we did!" the man growled as he peeled off his tank. Chicago and Martha realized he wasn't joking.

"Well, we found a chest anyway," Alex explained. Chicago lifted his tank and Alex pulled himself up onto the platform. "But we don't know what's in it. Looks like a plain seaman's chest, though. I doubt we'll find any ruby tiaras."

"You couldn't bring it up?"

"It's pretty broken up. Might be leather," Stan explained. "Hard to tell, but we need to box it before we lift it. And it's heavy. We didn't have enough bottom time left."

Chicago looked at her watch, then reached over to her own gear to check her dive computer. She and Martha had been up from their last dive only an hour, and neither had much bottom time right now, either. They were far from any decompression chamber out here, and diving so much that they had to be extra cautious about nitrogen absorption. A proper salvage of the chest might take an hour, and it looked like no one on the *Golden Goose* could dive that long right now without risking the bends.

Stan peeled off his wet suit and shook his shaggy head like a dog. "First thing tomorrow we're down for that baby," he said. "I'll be one sorry puppy if we lose our first chest of gold to a hurricane. What's it doing anyway? Any news?"

"Shep is in the deckhouse glued to the radar," Martha told him.

"Where's Wodie? I don't see the skiff."

"It's Saturday, remember? We sent him in to meet the weekly plane. To send the videotapes to Madison."

"He should be back by now," Stan objected. "Probably tomcatting around." Alex laughed at the quaint expression. "Well, what do you expect a guy to do on his rare shore leave!"

# SEVENTEEN

"Sheet, mon, yes, it a ship down dere, but notin' to find, I tell you. Dey dive all day bring up some piece of old broken-up dish, no treasure dis wreck, believe me."

Wodie took a long pull on his Heineken. The sky was cloudy over Abraham's Bay. He was in a hurry. Shepard wanted him back on the *Goose* by sundown, and Wodie was hoping to spend at least an hour of this shore trip in the sweet strong arms of Mary Blue. She, like many of the local women, worked in Nassau during the tourist season, but had come home to tend her sick mother. After months of hotel bed-making, she was ripe for some good bed-*un*making. Wodie was aching at the thought of her.

"You know dey been looking a week now and find nottin'." He shrugged and shifted on the wooden chair, the roll of bills a comforting bulge in his pocket. "Some guns, little silver, but not so much."

"Look, Wodie, as I have explained before, it is not a treasure I'm interested in," Teneby went on in a cool voice. "If a chest full of gold is found down there I'd be very happy for you all, but entirely uninterested." Wodie shifted uneasily.

"Yeah, dat what you say, but it don' make no sense to me. Everybody interest in gold."

Teneby laughed. The young man was not as dumb as he thought. He signaled for another beer.

"Have they told you much about the wreck—about what they're looking for?"

Wodie shrugged. "They find some lady necklace." Even if he had been inclined to trust white men and foreigners, he would not easily trust these two. Colin Teneby looked like the bad guy in every movie Wodie had ever seen, the quiet bad guy, the one you really had to worry about. The other one, the one called Dunagh, was harder to read. He was square and solid, could have held up a corner of the courthouse.

"You seem nervous, Wodie," Teneby said in his soft voice.

"I got to be back da boat. Cap'n worried the storm com'n."

Teneby looked out over the sea where the sky was low and gray.

"They're saying it might turn into a hurricane. What is Captain Shepard planning to do?"

"Don't know. The *Goose* she a good boat, got a good engine, he talk'n stay it through."

"And the other boat, the couple with the sailboat?"

"Dey worrying. Man, I got no more to tell you. I got to go, you see?"

"Sure, Wodie, of course, just a couple more things. You said the McGuires are flying in to join the expedition."

"Ya, dey come in Thursday." Wodie had told them all this already.

"And you'll be bringing the launch in to pick them up here?"

"Das right"

"Okay." Teneby gently slid a hundred-dollar bill across the table. The first offering had also been a hundred, but in twenties it just didn't have the same effect as one crisp note.

"Have they said anything about a coffin?" Teneby asked quietly. Wodie's eyes narrowed.

"That's all we're interested in, Wodie. No gold, no jewelry, no treasure. A coffin."

"What you want wif a coffin, man?"

"How long has your family been here, Wodie?" Dunagh, quiet until now, began to play his hand.

"I don't know. Long way back. Me mother side anyway. We come from de Indians, de Caribs."

"Hundreds of years then?" Dunagh looked impressed. "They were here before Columbus." Wodie sat up a little straighter, his narrow chest held a little higher.

"Das right."

"And you respect your heritage, don't you? It's a noble heritage. Your ancestors were important people—chiefs, healers, hunters." Wodie went on listening. "How would you feel if someone dug up one of your ancestors and desecrated him? Cut up his body and put his bones in a museum. Have you seen this?" Dunagh handed the young man a copy of *National Geographic* with a picture of the "Iceman" on the cover. The ancient corpse had been uncovered in a glacier in the Alps, where a freak accident of nature had dried and mummified him.

"Look inside," Dunagh insisted. "Look at all those pictures. There are two countries fighting over who gets to keep the poor fellow, who gets to cut out bits of his skin and saw open his bones and then put him in a museum for thousands of people to gawk at." Dunagh's voice had taken on a slight tremble of rage. Teneby was surprised and impressed. He had no idea the man was this smooth.

"Well, here's the thing. That coffin down there holds the body of one of my own ancestors. He sailed to the New World three hundred years ago. He married an Indian woman and they had children, six children." Dunagh checked himself before he got too involved in his own fantasy. "That man started my family, and now we are a very rich family, and I do not want my ancestor dragged from his grave." He leaned forward with the weight of his emotion. "D ye understand, lad?"

Wodie nodded, still transfixed by the gruesome pictures.

"There ye go. Of course you do."

"But what you want me to do if dey find it?"

"Just let us know. Call us on the radio. We'll give you a wee bit of code, something that sounds like a regular call and won't tip anyone off, but we'll know it means you found the coffin."

"Then what?" he asked suspiciously.

"Then you get another of these little bills." Wodie's eyes brightened.

"But what you going to do about it? Steal it?" Teneby looked expectantly at Dunagh. Yeah, mate, what are we going to do about it?

"No, no, of course not. We'll file an injunction with the Bahamian government to stop the salvage."

Wodie flipped through the pages on the iceman. "Read this bit here." Dunagh was playing his trump card. "Read about how they pulled him from the ice so roughly they ripped off his . . ." Wodie's face took on a look of horror as he read the paragraph, and he reflexively crossed his legs.

"You'll do it then?" Dunagh smiled. "You'll let us know?"

Wodie closed the magazine and tried to look tough. He was only twenty-three, and it was hard. He shrugged, with a noncommittal sort of nod, and got up.

"Be listening to de radio."

# EIGHTEEN

*1692*

*"My dear Bea,*

*It is frightfully hot here, and I fear I may never grow accustomed to it, though my husband says I will. The heat does not seem to bother the children, however. Little Edward runs and plays outside all the time. He loves to splash in the water, and he is so strong! He looks out for Clarissa like a proper big brother, though he is eager for her to walk so she can play with*

*him, and so takes her out of the cradle and tries to stand her up. I
wan: to scold him, but he looks at me with those beautiful dark eyes
and I cannot. He is quite the charmer, and a very bright child.*

*"The little suit you sent was most elegant, but I'm afraid he is
so big I had to squeeze him all over to get him in it, and within
a fortnight he was out of it! But he knows you are thinking of
him. I do not let him forget. Of course, he cannot yet understand
really. Richard loves him like his own son, and we will all be sad
to see him go, but if you say it is time, then I will put him to the
safety of the Lord and send him to you."*

Mark Whitstone put the letter down, his eyes strained by the
faint print and tiny writing. He pulled off the cotton gloves,
slowly, so she would not see that his hands were shaking.

"Tell me again, Miss Haversford, how you came into possession of this letter?" Her cheeks were flushed from the walk over,
and from excitement. Her hair was windblown, and Whitstone was
startled. He was, he had to admit, highly unused to pretty young
scholars bursting into his tiny office.

"One of mummy's club ladies, you know, Lady Huxley-
Atchins, is quite a renowned collector. Always off to Sotheby's,
china figurines mostly." Her voice dropped to that certain tone
the wealthy employ when disparaging one another for bad taste.
"Those ruffly shepherdesses and dancing ladies, you know the
sort; but she also collects jewelry. I asked her about the charm.
She thought it wasn't a lover's charm at all, but maybe a sort of
... token. Women sometimes gave such things to men going off
to war, a locket or charm in two pieces that each would wear to
symbolize their union. She wasn't sure this was the case in the
seventeenth century, but still, we thought it might be something
like that."

"Yes," Whitstone agreed cautiously.

"But now—it might not be that at all! You see, Lady Atchins
is also a member of the Kensington Ladies Historical Association.
I don't think she's seriously interested, but they do a nice lunch-
eon, and often have private tours of the great houses. Anyway,
she took me along today, to see if any of the ladies might know
more about this sort of piece, and the most marvelous thing! Mrs.
Bartlett, Lady Huxley-Atchins' friend, collects vintage letters and

postcards, you see. Victorian era mostly, a lot of valentines, but she did remember that another lady friend, a librarian in . . .'' Margaret's voice faded as Whitstone tried to think what to do. Could the letter be real?

Of course there was no proof who the sender and receiver of this particular letter was, but using Bea for Queen Mary Beatrice, Edward for Prince James Francis Edward, made sense. He knew from marriage records found in Port Royal that a woman named Genevieve married a young English shipping clerk in 1690, and that she had already at the time a young child called Edward whom she said was her nephew. This fellow, Richard Brixby, eventually purchased his own ship, then another, and another, and apparently made quite a name for himself, shipping rum and molasses to England and bringing back slaves from Africa. It would have been relatively easy for there to be correspondence. And it did seem to fit.

''. . . so there was the letter, and I asked if I could bring it to you,'' Margaret concluded. ''She was most reluctant, but in the end agreed.''

''And what . . .'' he tried to keep his tone casual, ''what connection do you find between this letter and the charm?''

''Well, the charm reportedly belonged to Queen Mary Beatrice. This letter, Mrs. Bartlett has always believed, though has not been able to verify, was sent to the queen. I think . . .'' and here Margaret paused, her excitement momentarily subdued by her gentle upbringing and sense of propriety, as if suddenly she remembered that she was not talking with her girlfriends in the pub after work, but with an elderly gentleman scholar in his dusty archival office.

''Perhaps, Mr. Whitstone, the queen, being so much younger than King James, perhaps she had, well, taken up with a younger man. Perhaps even . . .'' she sat with finishing school grace, and dropped her gaze demurely. ''Perhaps there was a child. She would have gone away to hide the pregnancy, maybe then entrusted the baby to a nurse. I really don't know, but I would love to investigate! Do you think you could help me?''

''Help you?'' He was momentarily relieved by the fact that she was so far off the track. But it wouldn't take much more for her to discover the truth. It had taken him years to realize what he was looking at in all these bits and pieces, yet here was this young woman, barely out of university, remembering one odd bit of jewelry she cataloged months ago, then this . . .

*"My dear Bea, it is frightfully hot here . . ."*
"May I keep this a little while?" he asked softly. "I would like to do some tests—age the paper, test the ink, and so on."
"Oh, dear. I told Mrs. Bartlett I would have it back to her today. She was terribly reluctant to let it out at all, you know."
"Well, she might have some confidence in my position," Whitstone pointed out with a twinge of indignity. "I do, after all, handle a great deal of archival material. Quite carefully, I might add."
"Oh, of course! Of course I'm sure she would let you. But she wanted it back for this weekend, you see. A tour group from America is visiting her collection. A history group, you know. She's so awfully excited."
Whitstone felt desperate, but he tried to smile. What should he do? Mr. Spencer would know. He should call someone. He placed the letter carefully in a clear plastic folder and got up to escort Margaret to the door.
"Perhaps after the weekend then? You will let me know?"
"Of course, Mr. Whitstone, of course."
Once she was gone, Whitstone sat a long time, just thinking. He pictured the queen weeping as she read the letter, alone in her room, reading by candlelight in her lonely exile. Lying on her bed, peacefully asleep, was the foundling baby she was raising as her own, while her true child lived only in the carefully worded pages sent from Jamaica.
What had happened that the true son was never returned? This letter spoke of such a return, but it had not happened. Written in 1692, it would have been soon after the Battle of Boyne in Ireland, where King James had been soundly defeated while trying to retake his throne. It was also the year Mary Beatrice gave birth to a daughter. Maybe this mitigated her grief, and she began to accept that her real son was lost to her forever. Or the earthquake. Of course. Perhaps the Jacobites had gone to Jamaica, but the earthquake disrupted their plans.
Whatever the answer, the letter had to be treated carefully. The last thing this case needed was a bunch of old society birds stumbling on to the damaging truth. He knew how women were. On

the outside all smiles and friendliness, but inside, vicious and gossiping. They would all turn out to a tea with the Queen Mum, and brag about it, too, but if they had a chance to take her down a peg, why they would be at her like hyenas. Elizabeth, dear pure Queen Mother. He had to keep them away from her. He should call Mr. Spencer. He would know what to do about this girl.

# *NINETEEN*

Martha came into the cabin, her thick gray hair still damp from the shower. Shep was once more glued to the radar terminal, watching the storm.

"Wodie's back," she told him. "He looks happy."

"All this time, he'd better be smiling." Shep stared dismally at the radar.

"Stan says it's looking good," she said, always the positive one. "It might pass far off."

"If it stays on course it will. We'll get banged around a little, though."

"Well, I've made a big pot of stew. At least we won't go down hungry." Shepard smiled and patted her hip with a casual affection while he continued to stare at the screen. For days they had debated their options. Mayaguana didn't really offer an anchorage with enough protection. They considered running down to Providenciales but that was a long trip, again for dubious shelter. He was reluctant to leave the site unguarded for that long.

Though there hadn't been much treasure to speak of so far, he was sure rumors were spreading. They were isolated out here. There was probably talk going on this minute in some bar up in San Salvador or Great Exuma, about bars of gold and chests full of jewels.

"Wind's picking up," Stan announced as he swung into the cabin. "Smells good, Marty. Can't say I'd even mind a hurricane with a belly full of stew." He squeezed into the galley and lifted the lid, sighing with exaggerated pleasure.

"Oh, go on and have some," Martha said. "And it's not a hurricane, it's still a tropical storm. Don't talk us up any bad luck here."

Stan spooned up some of the stew and stood over the sink devouring it.

"We'll be fine. We rode out worse than this before, eh, Shep? Damn, that typhoon came through in Truk . . . When was that? Seventy-nine? There was a mother."

"Eighty-two."

"Yeah, well, you get this old, they all start to run together." He rinsed his bowl and set it in the dish rack. Though Martha did most of the cooking, cleaning up was an egalitarian task on the *Golden Goose.* "Anyway, we'll be fine. Let's just hope things don't get too mucked up below."

Chicago poked her head in the door and looked over Shep's shoulder to the ominous blob on the radar screen.

"How's it look?"

"Like a bull." Shep slid over and let her look at the charts.

"If it keeps up like this, it will either pass by here or smack us directly tomorrow afternoon."

Alex leaned in with the bowl of snapper fillets he had just cleaned. Since his first successful strike a few weeks ago, he had become truly lethal with the sling spear.

"Oh, lovely!" Marty reached up to take it from him. Shep's lined face creased a hundred ways in displeasure. He hated fish. He hated fish in every variety and incarnation. Always had, always would. It was the reason he got out of the charter business, every damn meal was fish.

"Don't that damn boy ever miss?" he grumbled.

"Will you eat with us tonight?" Marty offered. "Might be our last real cooked meal for a few days."

Alex brightened. Eating dinner aboard the *Golden Goose* had been one of the best parts about this expedition so far. The snapper fillets were thick and white, so fresh they were practically still quivering.

"What do you say, boss?" he asked Chicago.

"Sure. I want to go over and feed Lassie first, though. Wodie picked up a couple of rats in town. They've been trapping them for me at the hotel.''

"Remind me not to stay there next time I'm hung over.'' Stan grimaced.

"We won't eat for an hour, you have plenty of time,'' Marty assured her.

Shep's finger absently traced a line connecting the jagged series of penciled X's on the chart.

"Have you decided what you're doing yet?''

"We've tossed it around all day,'' Chicago admitted, glancing at Alex. "I'm not crazy about Provo Harbor.''

"I wouldn't,'' Shep replied simply. "She's shallow, and every boat in the area will be squeezing in. If the weather's bad you won't even be able to navigate the entrance. Plus you would actually be sailing closer to the storm.''

"How fast was it moving again?''

"Ten, eleven miles an hour. Could pick up speed tonight.'' Chicago walked the calipers across the chart, measuring the distance to the storm. The path of a hurricane was unpredictable, but the current course had been pretty steady.

"Our other idea is going west.'' She traced a path with her finger. "And hiding out here, behind Crooked Island. We'll have the whole island between us and the storm, unless the damn thing pulls a U turn, and I've never seen one do that before.''

"Hmm, that does sort of make sense,'' Shep agreed.

"And, if we can't hold and drift, there's no reefs or anything to hit till Cuba,'' Alex added.

"Isn't that an awfully long sail?'' Martha said. "You're still going to get some blow.'' She had taken a motherly interest in the pair. Martha and Shep had lost their only son in Vietnam.

"Ten, twelve hours maybe.''

"You'd have to leave tonight?'' Stan asked.

"We'll need a few hours to ready the boat, maybe take a nap. What do you think?'' Chicago turned to Alex. "Set off around three A.M.?''

Shep nodded at the sense of it. "Good idea. If she does hit, the McGuires will most likely postpone their trip, so you'll have plenty of time to get back.''

# *TWENTY*

Annabel Lee lay awake with her stomach in a twist, kneading her toes against the footboard, holding her breath and trying to will her mother to change her mind. They were in the next room, arguing her fate.

"Jack, I don't care if you and that damn brother of yours want to drown in a hurricane, but you will not put my daughter in danger."

"It's not a hurricane . . ."

"I don't care what you want to call it. It's a bad storm and I'm not letting you take her out on that boat!"

"April, honey . . ."

Annabel imagined her father sitting her mother down on the rose bedspread, and patting her shoulder.

"It's already moving north. If it hits Mayaguana at all, it will hit tomorrow, and move on. By the time we get to Miami it will probably be long past."

"And if it's not?"

"Then we'll hear the weather reports and stay in Miami a few days. We won't even get to the site until Thursday." Jack didn't remember her ever being this nervous with the boys. But there was a ten-year gap there, long enough for her to have forgotten how it was, all the trips to the ER, all the panicky nights when they first started to drive and didn't come home on time.

Maybe it was the change of life. And the fact that poor Mizzy was a girl. April, for all her feminist ways, for all her nonsexist child rearing, her insistence that their sons learn to cook and sew buttons on their own shirts, had gone absolutely lacy over their daughter.

"And you've got her missing school."

"Only a week. What better education could she have, April?"

"Jack, she's just so young."

Annalee squeezed her eyes tight with frustration. She was too young for *everything* as far as Mother was concerned!

"April, come on. You know I would never do anything to endanger her."

In the end, her father managed to convince her mother that the storm was not going to pose a threat to their dive trip. Annalee breathed a sigh of relief. Not that she could sleep now anyway. There was just too much in her mind. Blue water, fish, freedom. A whole glorious week diving on a shipwreck. What would they find? Would Shepard and Martha be nice? Would they treat her like a kid? She had her own wet suit now, all her own gear. Would she remember everything? Parrotfish . . . eagle rays, maybe a shark. Madison to Chicago, to Nassau to Mayaguana to the *Golden Goose*. If they found a treasure, they could live the rest of their lives on a boat. Or buy lots of skeletons. An ostrich maybe. *Hope Mom didn't go through my suitcase and take out all my favorite old clothes. Oh, God, what if I get my period?*

The thrills and apprehensions of the trip jumbled through the young girl's mind, until finally the images and thoughts yielded to dreams.

# *TWENTY-ONE*

Mark Whitstone hurried upstairs to his tiny apartment, and before even removing his coat, crossed to the table and switched on the small television. The news was just starting. He sat on one of the straight chairs, still shivering, and pulled his coat tighter around him. The lead story was about the fighting in Bosnia. He got up, his knees surprisingly weak, hurried to the kitchen and took down the bottle of sherry, his hands shaking.

Did it really happen? It wouldn't seem real until he saw it there on the telly.

More world stories: Somalia, Israel. He waited impatiently for the local news. There—there was a reporter standing outside Charing Cross Station. Whitstone felt faint.

". . . The woman was identified as Margaret Haversford, twenty-four years old. The station is still closed, and police expect it to remain closed for another few hours. Early reports, however, seem to indicate that the victim fell, or was pushed onto the tracks when she struggled with a purse-snatcher. It was rush hour, and the platform was crowded."

"So there are witnesses?" The unseen anchorman's voice came through, and the reporter pressed his earpiece to hear him.

"Police are questioning witnesses, but as you can imagine, it all happened so quickly. Evidently the man tried to grab her purse. One witness said it had a long shoulder strap—it either caught on her arm, or she grabbed it . . . it's just too soon to tell. It's a tragedy. The young woman apparently worked at the Victoria and Albert Museum. She's originally from . . ."

There was a buzz in Whitstone's ears, and he felt lightheaded. The anchorman came back on the screen.

"Police recommend that you never resist a purse-snatcher or any kind of thief. Nothing they can steal from you is worth your life, as this dreadful accident has so graphically pointed out . . ."

Only yesterday she had been in his office, a lovely young woman. Bright, too. Whitstone shivered. She might have had a real future.

# TWENTY-TWO

The wind screamed and the rain slashed in a fierce horizontal torrent. Alex was soaked and shivering, drenched inside his slicker by a huge wave that had caught him by surprise. The sky that had been low and gray all morning was beginning to blacken. The *Tassia Far* was pitched so steeply that as Alex stood at the helm, he had one foot on the cockpit floor and the other wedged against the seat. The waves were huge and sloppy, coming from two directions, it seemed, so they often collided as they crashed over the port side in a one-two punch.

"How's it looking?" Alex shouted as Chicago struggled back up after going below to check the noon report. The cabin was stifling and her face was pale with sweat. "The transmission is breaking up," she reported.

"Could you make out anything?"

She nodded somberly as she clipped her harness to the brace behind Alex. She had to shout to be heard over the wind. "It's a little more westerly, but the center might already have passed. I couldn't exactly make out the latitude."

So far they were doing great, the *Tassia Far* charging on through the waves, her sturdy hull not even creaking. He glanced at Chicago, and she grinned. They were riding that exhilarating edge of danger. He knew tomorrow her beautiful tawny skin would be a mass of bruises from crashing around the boat, but four hours into the heart of the storm, they were doing well.

Chicago climbed up beside him and looked up at the sails.

"Maybe we should drop the main."

"You think? The wind speed isn't all that bad."

"It's the gusts I'm worried about. With these new sails, the fabric doesn't tear so easy," she explained. "The sail just keeps

88

holding on until the mast breaks.'' They had long ago reduced both the headsail and the main, and were still screaming along at seven to eight knots.

''That's a cheery thought—but the mast is new, didn't they make it stronger, too?''

''So the mast holds, but it tears right out of the hull—or pulls up the rigging. There's always a weak spot. But I guess its okay for a while. I'd hate to lose any speed.'' She pulled the collar of her slicker tighter as a wall of rain stampeded toward them. The *Tassia Far* could take a lot more than this. *They* could take a lot more. Easy.

The plan appeared to have worked. If the eye of the storm was truly north of them, this mess, nasty as it was, was only the hem of the swirling skirts. If they had been holding anywhere near their intended course, they should be coming up on Crooked Island in the next couple of hours. The approach was pretty straightforward. They would see the lighthouse of bird rock, then have to bear off to avoid the shoals, round Pittstown point, and find a nice protected anchorage.

It was a good feeling. Soon enough they would be dropping anchor and taking hot showers. Alex threw a weary arm around Chicago's shoulders and grinned. ''Crooked Island will be the perfect place to open that last bottle of good wine.''

''If it hasn't gone off by now.''

''Well, you know what they say,'' Alex couldn't resist the pun. ''Any *port* in a storm.'' Chicago groaned and punched him. They were together, still together. They fell silent for a while, the steady hum of the storm leading to quiet thought. Chicago wondered about the young Queen so long ago, sending her baby off across a sea as fierce as this one.

''Why don't you go below and warm up?'' Alex suggested.

''I'm not cold.''

''You shivered.''

''I was thinking about Mary Beatrice. Do you think you could do it? Just send your child off in the care of strangers?''

''To protect it?'' Alex's face hardened a little. ''I hope I never have to think about it.'' He saw once again the daily circle of women in Argentina: mothers, sisters, and wives of the *''disappeared.''* He remembered the face of an Indian woman in the

Andes who had brought him a basket of food for his journey, and hidden her infant in the bottom.

"History is full of it, though, from Moses on down."

Was she thinking about children now? he wondered with a bit of worry. They hadn't really talked much about it, except for the details of immediate prevention. He couldn't remember her ever going gushy over babies, but she was thirty-five. It had been a long time since he had ever thought of having children himself.

"Any sign of the lighthouse yet?" He was grateful for the transition.

"Should be sometime soon." Alex glanced at the compass. With the sloppy waves, they were doing well to keep the heading within ten degrees.

Chicago took the binoculars, hooked one leg inside the cockpit for balance, and leaned out to scan the horizon. She was just turning back, about to say something, when there was an explosive crack. The mainsail, caught by a sudden gust at a critical angle, snapped free of the reefing. The sail billowed out, catching the full force of the wind with such violence that the pulley track sheared off and the boom swung free. Suddenly, there was chaos. Snapped lines whipped across Alex's shoulders, and he felt the aluminum wheel being torn from his hands.

As if in slow motion, he saw Chicago's feet, her torn old sneakers pointed like ballet shoes, fly up in the air. She looked surprised, her arms spread, reaching in vain for something to grab as her body tumbled slowly backward. Alex lunged for her, but he, too, was flying through the air, grasping at empty space. His chest smashed on top of a winch with enough force to knock him breathless. He felt the roughened deck surface abrading his palms as he spun across the deck, grabbing for a handhold. His foot bounced off a stanchion, then slipped between the safety lines over the side of the boat. He was stopped by the sudden tug of the harness, the deck at a steep angle.

"Chicago!" Alex shouted. The *Tassia Far* was in real danger, heeling so far over that the starboard rail was underwater. Frantically he looked for her yellow jacket. There was a pile of snaking lines all around him, and he began grabbing at them, searching for her lifeline, groping wildly for the one that was taut with the weight of her. Oh, God—just let it hold. He snatched in the mess of ropes, oblivious to the pain in his own body as it was slammed around the deck. The loose sailcloth flapped over him, then snapped like a cannon shot as the wind filled it again.

There! His hand fell on the nylon cord taut with her weight. One end was still clipped to the cockpit railing, the other disappeared over the side. Alex pulled, every muscle straining, but the line did not move. He braced his feet against the gunwale. "Shit!" His own harness, clipped to the helm post, didn't allow him enough room to get to the side. Desperately he scrambled for footing, pulling himself hand over hand along the lifeline, pulling himself up the tilting deck until he could unclip it. Once freed, he slid back down, wrapping one arm in the loose lines to keep himself from going overboard with her.

There she was, the harness holding her suspended half in the water, her body slamming into the hull as she desperately tried to fend off the swinging boom. Another gust filled the mainsail, bursting it out like a spinnaker and jerking the boat even farther over. Chicago's head disappeared beneath the churning waves. Alex braced his feet and tugged on her line. She looked up at him, surprised and terrified, but still not panicked. She weighed less than a hundred twenty pounds, why couldn't he pull her up!

The mainsail filled with another gust, and the tortured boat dipped farther on its side, dragging Chicago under again. She was tangled, Alex realized. He fought his way forward to the mast, the clip of his loose harness clanking behind him like a ghostly chain, then he yanked at the cleat and freed the sheet that held the mainsail aloft. The canvas came rattling down, still flapping in the wind, but robbed of its power now with nothing to pull against. The boat suddenly stopped its horrible tilt and righted itself, bobbing crazily in the sloppy seas.

Alex vaulted back over the flapping canvas, leaned over the side, and grabbed hold of Chicago's jacket. It was slippery and stiff. Her eyes were huge with fear. And she made feeble swipes at the bunched sail, trying to work her way free.

"Hang on," he shouted, reaching for a better hold. He looped one hand through her harness and held her head above the water while he worked on freeing her. Finally, he hauled her up. They tumbled backward, landing on the mess of canvas and lines. Chicago screamed in pain, then let out a string of cussing that would have made a pirate blush.

"Hang on—oh, God." Alex crouched over her, breathing hard, shielding her with his body while he caught his breath.

"Oh, shit—oh, goddamn . . ." He was relieved to hear her swearing in his ear, relieved to see her head in one piece. "Hold on, babe, don't move." The boat was still pitching, the deck was slippery, and the swinging boom and flapping mainsail were still a danger. "We're just gonna slide up here into the cockpit. Okay?"

"Oh, shit! My shoulder."

"Okay. Hang on." As gently as he could, Alex pulled them both across the deck and into the cockpit where he laid her out on the cushions. His adrenaline rush was starting to fade, and his limbs were shaking. "Don't move—just rest a minute," he gasped.

"You need to . . . secure the boom," she commanded in a terse, painful voice. "And get the sail in."

Alex laughed at her commanding tone. "Aye, aye, skipper." He slid down to the helm. With the track ripped up, there was no good place to secure the boom and he had to settle for wrapping it around a winch. Once that was secured, he had to work his way back out to the mast, taking care to clip his lifeline this time, and haul in the acres of wet sail. It was a struggle in the best of circumstances, and he was still fighting against the wind and rain. Finally he had the sail strapped in place. He ducked back into the cockpit, and finding his knees too weak to support him, slid to the floor, one arm flung across Chicago's body.

"Hey, thanks. I'm sorry I . . ."

"Shush—it's okay."

"I should have dropped the sail—damn rigging—there's always a weak place."

"Shut up a minute." Alex unzipped his jacket, and steam drifted out. "It wasn't your fault. Now hold still—let's check your shoulder. Can you move your arm?" Chicago lifted her arm, but was seized with pain. "Damn it!"

"Okay. Okay." He reached one hand up under her jacket. She winced when he touched the area, but let him feel around. "I think it's dislocated," Alex announced. He swiped the water out of his eyes, breathing heavily, exhausted by the struggle.

Chicago was shaking with cold, and Alex realized they were

both in danger of hypothermia, Chicago acutely so. There were other needs, too. He had to find out their position and correct the course. Twenty minutes of bobbing in this storm and they could be anywhere. The weather was getting better, and maybe the autopilot would be able to steer now. Alex quickly did a little mental triage. Check the GPS for position, set the course, get them both warm and dry, fix Chicago's shoulder.

"Hey—" She smiled, interrupting his thought and curling her fingers through his. "Thanks for the rescue."

"It's okay—I owed you one." He brushed her wet hair out of her face and kissed her cold lips. "How are we fixed for painkillers?"

"What are you planning to do?"

"Pop your shoulder back in place."

"Just like that?"

"If we're lucky." She took a deep breath and tried to will away the nausea that gripped her.

"Yeah? How many times you done this?"

"Personally—never. That's what the hopefully was for. Morphine would probably be nice. We have some in the first-aid kit, don't we?"

"How bad will it be?"

"Well, hopefully, only about ten seconds of excruciating pain, then you'll just throb like hell for a few days."

# TWENTY-THREE

During a storm, it is said, the ghosts of those drowned awaken. Cold bones stir in the dark waters and those quietly resting are suddenly roused, tormented by the memory of air and light. Desperate fingers swirl out of the sand as pirate and passenger alike are wakened. The breaking waves give a path of escape, the howling winds a chance to launch their spirits toward the sky. The currents are sharp and strong, but the ghosts clamber for escape. Their cries career across the roiling sea. Long dead fingers clutch at the rudders of ships. Seabirds screech, dive, and drive them back, but now and then, one beleaguered ghost, stirred by a storm, fights through the turmoil and finds its spirit loosed.

And thus it was that as the storm roared northward across the Caicos Passage, it stirred the ghosts of the *Christiania*. A storm wave rolling in from the open Atlantic was funneled between the islands. The wave rolled under the hull of the *Golden Goose*, lifting and dropping it with terrifying power but doing no damage. The furious wave crashed against the shallow reef and tumbled its force downward, thundering down the reef wall, knocking huge chunks of coral loose in an underwater avalanche.

At the base of the reef, the wave churned up sand and muck. Stakes and strings that so carefully marked the excavation of the *Christiania* were crunched and broken. Some of the timbers, already tossed by the ravages of time, were further scattered. A cannon, recently uncovered and ready to be hauled up, was reburied. But chaos is an indiscriminate force, and a wave has no malice. As the storm wave destroyed some parts of the wreck, it uncovered others . . .

It reburied the old cannon, but uncovered an almost perfectly preserved iron cookstove. It swirled layers of muck over a carefully uncovered skeleton, but revealed a sailmaker's kit and a heavy brass looking glass. The leather sea chest, discovered only the day before, was tumbled and rolled and finally driven deep into a wedge in the coral. A large beam, which had rested undisturbed for three hundred years, was suddenly wrenched free and toppled end over end. And beneath it, finally uncovered after all this time, was a box. Six feet long, two feet wide, built of iron, it was a coffin befitting a king.

James Francis Edward was at last unburied.

# TWENTY-FOUR

To a storm-wearied sailor at the dark end of day, there is nothing so beautiful as the first faint sweep of a lighthouse beam on the horizon. At first you squint, suspecting tricks of imagination, of light and cloud reflection, but finally you allow yourself to believe; it is indeed the lighthouse and you have come at last to land.

When you are on the water, there is always the trace of fear that you will never see land again. It is not a conscious fear, but it is there. Even a lifetime at sea cannot completely erase it. Experienced sailors may go for days, watching the track of miles on the chart, knowing that all is well, and then, for no reason, the feeling will hit. It might come on the twilight watch, when the last red rim of sun drops into the sea. Or at four A.M. when the night has grown comfortable and the stars are bright, and there is nothing in the world but the peaceful sound of your hull cutting through the water.

There you are, fair weather, clear skies, content and free, in harmony with the tides and currents, when it comes out of nowhere, this cold creeping fear, small and hard as a seed. You fear that the ocean will have you this time, that despite the instruments, the engines and radios and beacons, the ocean can take you if it wants to, swallow you without a trace. But perhaps this is why we go to sea in the first place. We crave the taste of fear. We court the smack of God.

By the time Alex finally dropped the anchor, his bones felt like lead, and his skin was brittle with a crust of salt. He stood on the bow, leaning against the railing as the boat drifted back, making sure the anchor had a good hold. It was a good anchorage. Even if they did break loose and drift in the night, there was no reef

95

to crack against, no land to bump into until Cuba. They were safe. He went back to the cockpit and killed the engine. There was absolute silence.

Chicago roused a little. She was lying on the cockpit cushions wrapped in a sleeping bag and the sweet fog of morphine, her arm strapped to her chest. No bones seemed to be broken, though she had a nasty bump on her forehead, and an assortment of cuts and bruises. Alex hadn't assessed his own wounds yet, but with all limbs working and no blood pooling at his feet, he supposed there was nothing serious.

"Hey—how's it look?" Chicago asked sleepily.

"Quiet. A few lights on shore, probably the resort. No other boats. The bottom felt good, I think we're hooked. How you feeling?"

"Nice. Warm." Her brows wrinkled with concern. "Are you all right? What the hell happened to your face?"

Alex felt his cheek and found the skin tender. "Sliding across the deck, I suppose." She moved to get up, but he held her down. "Stay. I'll open the hatches and get some air down below, then we'll put you to bed."

"Check on Lassie, will you?"

"I'm sure she's fine." He doubted the snake was even aware there had been a storm.

"Hey, Alex . . ."

"Yeah?"

"Thanks again for the rescue."

"No problem."

"Really . . ." He was surprised to see her eyes misted with tears. "Hey, it's okay. I would have done it for any old girl. Besides, I owed you one. Remember? Hey, come on . . ." She was crying now, real tears, and he didn't know what to think. Chicago was definitely not a weeper. Perhaps the painkillers were making her sentimental.

"Hey, what's the matter?"

"It's my own damn boat. My own goddamn boat." Her voice was slurring. "Really pisses me off. I've never gone over. Never . . . I hate you . . ."

"You hate me?" She nodded solemnly, her eyes barely focused. Alex stroked her hair.

"Well, sorry . . ." He smiled.

"I hate you pulling me out. Now when you're gone . . ." She tried to turn away.

"Wait a minute. When I'm gone where? Where am I going all of a sudden?"

"You're going."

"Come on, you're drugged and dreaming. Let's get some sleep."

"But, Alex . . ." She squeezed his hand. "It's okay. We'll still see each other. You know, you can catch up with me sometimes. I might go to . . . I can't think of the name—the island with the statues . . . the heads . . ."

"Chicago, come on, let's talk about it in the morning." He eased her up and steered her toward the companionway. She kept babbling, in a soft slow murmur.

"It's been really really great all this. You being here. I never thought we could do it, y'know? Thought we might go nuts. Anyway, when you go . . ."

"I'm not going anywhere."

"Yes . . . but . . ."

"I'm not going anywhere!"

"Yes, you are. You have to."

# TWENTY-FIVE

"Boys—boys—what is all the commotion?" Harry and Wills looked up, surprised to see their father in the playroom. They quickly untangled themselves and sprang to their feet.

"What's this—are you having a row?"

"No, Daddy, we were playing," Wills told him.

"And what were you playing that requires you to be thumping your brother all about the nursery?" There was a guilty silence,

and Wills scowled. He hated for anyone in the palace to still call
this place a nursery.

"Well?" Charles smiled, he hadn't meant to be stern. "What
game is this?"

Little Harry finally spoke up. "Commoner, Daddy." His brother
glared at him for betraying the secret.

"Commoner?" The prince was half disturbed, half amused.

"Mummy, lets us play ..." Harry offered in their defense.
William surreptitiously kicked his ankle. That was a secret. Daddy
didn't like a lot of Mummy's games, though Harry was too young
to realize this. Daddy didn't really like *any* games and thought
their mother not strict enough.

"I see. Well. Holiday's over, and with you going back to school
on Wednesday, I thought we should ... Ah well, I've had some
videos brought up. We could watch one."

"Ninja Turtles?" Harry asked excitedly.

"I don't know, I asked Mr. Wentworth to bring a selection.
You can look through them." He hoped they weren't all confound-
edly stupid. But it would only be a couple of hours. It was difficult, trying to spend more time with his sons here in Balmoral on
a rainy January night. At least during the days they could ride.
Wills was getting to be a good shot, too. It was these confounded
evenings that he disliked. He loved his sons, of course, but children could be so tedious.

"Shall I call for some popcorn then?"

The boys selected *Terminator Two*. The prince didn't understand
it. He was distracted. He watched the flickering television light
reflecting off his children's rapt faces. Playing Commoner. At what
age did he clearly realize exactly what he was? And when had
the burden of the crown become so crushing, his legacy so bitter?

His life was a failure. He had tried, of course he had tried, but
he had been an awkward father. He knew they thought him cool
and aloof. Their mother adored them. For all her trying ways, she
had been a good mother. She had simply taken over the role,
overflowing with competency, filling up every space, nudging him
out not with a purposeful shove, but absently, with a sort of cruel
innocence, and the mildest disdain.

The boys sat on the floor, Wills leaning against the sofa, Harry
lying with his head in big brother's lap, ducking his face at the

scary parts. They had forgotten their father was even there. Who *were* these little boys? He was seized with a desperate unhappiness.

"Wills," he asked them when the video was over, "what would you like to be when you grow up, if you didn't have to be king?"

"If I didn't have to? Who would then? Would Harry?"

"I'm just saying pretend. Like your Commoner game."

"I'd be Terminator." Little Harry rolled on the carpet and blasted the room with an imaginary death ray. "Or a scarecrow. Or an astronaut."

"You can't be a scarecrow," Wills said. "People aren't scarecrows. We can't be anything." There was a sad resignation in his voice.

"Sometimes when I was a boy I used to think about it." The boys peered up at their father, clearly unused to such soul-baring. "I wondered what I would be if I didn't have to be king."

"But you're not king," Wills pointed out.

"Grandmummy won't let you be," Harry added. Wills shoved him, but the words had been said. The prince felt as if he had been punched.

"Where . . ." His voice caught and he had to cough to clear his throat. "Wherever did you get that idea, Harry?"

Harry, chastened by his brother's glare, just lowered his eyes. "Have you heard people say this, Wills?" The older boy nodded.

"She likes being the queen."

"Yes. Yes, and she's a very good queen." He didn't know what to say now. He felt a mixture of sadness and anger. These poor sweet little boys, these strangers with his own face; he was not a good father, but maybe there was something he could do. Maybe there was a way to save them yet.

"All right then, fellows," he said with forced cheer. "Off to bed with you now."

# TWENTY-SIX

The storm, as expected, gave the *Golden Goose* a good knock around, but with careful anchoring, and two on watch all night, they came through with only some tumbled cans in the galley and a few bruises. In the morning, as soon as things settled down, Stan and Marty went down to check things out. The water was murky, with ten-foot visibility at best, and it took some time before they realized exactly how much havoc had been wreaked down below. Markers were out of place, and snapped grid lines waved in the current like feeble streamers.

Swimming slowly, an arm length apart, they began to survey the area, noting the changes with a mix of excitement and dismay. All the carefully marked artifacts were jumbled here and there. The sea chest that Alex and Stan had marked had disappeared, but a good many new things had been uncovered. Stan stopped to tie a yellow tag on the newly uncovered cookstove. Martha swam a few yards away, and hovered a little above him, trying to get an overall view. The McGuires would be arriving in three days, ready for a complete archaeological survey. She and Stan and Wodie might at least get some of the grids reset today, and if Alex and Chicago returned by tomorrow, and the water cleared, well, it wouldn't be too bad.

She checked her watch, looked at Stan and signaled to return. Stan gave her an O.K. and they turned around. They almost missed it.

Alex awakened with a start, and sat up too fast, immediately feeling the pain of assorted aches and bruises. He eased back down and squinted as the light beamed in the open hatch. The cabin was already growing hot. He sat up again, slower this time, stretched his arms and swung his legs off the bed, remembering the good old days when a few simple crashes and smashes wouldn't even have left a dent. He was still in good shape, but maybe the years of abuse were beginning to show. Thirty-nine suddenly felt old and creaky.

He pulled on a pair of shorts, climbed slowly up the ladder and blinked at the bright day. It was disorienting, this clear sunny morning. It seemed like a week had gone by instead of just a day. Chicago stood by the mast, buttoning the sail cover in place. He didn't know how she had managed to get the thing on with one arm.

She looked fresh and rested and clean, her black hair glossy in the bright sun. She wore her usual baggy shorts, and one of Alex's shirts which was big enough to button around the sling. She winced as she saw him. "Ouch—I hope you're feeling better than you look." Alex scratched at his two-day growth of beard and ran his fingers through his hair. It stuck out all over. "Is it that bad?"

"Don't look over the side, you might scare the fish." She laughed. "Come on, I've got coffee ready."

Chicago had been busy. Their foul-weather gear was spread all over the boat to dry, the abandon-ship bag, the safety lines, and other emergency gear was stowed away, all traces of the hell sail gone except for the broken boom track. Alex shuffled forward, slipped into the cockpit and she poured him a cup from the Thermos. It was the best thing he had ever smelled in his life.

"You been up a while?"

"Sunrise."

"How's the shoulder?"

"It's okay. Sore." She kissed the side of his face above the scrapes.

"The track is a wreck, though. Sheared right off. I thought I might be able to bend it back in place, but I'm going to need a new part. As soon as you feel like it we can go ashore and try to call the marina in Miami to send us one. They have a resort here, they must have a phone." She fussed with things as she talked, a sign Alex recognized as a certain level of anxiety.

How strange this was, to know a woman this way. To know her habits and rhythms, the subtle signs of her moods, the gestures that she wasn't even aware of but he knew by heart. He had lain awake most of the night thinking about what she had said. Was he really thinking about leaving again? What would he do if he did? Her talk last night had been true, he was feeling the tug of something, but didn't want to admit it.

He was happy on the boat, yet more and more lately, he found himself getting restless, remembering the past with a certain longing. An undeserved longing, Alex always reminded himself, for he knew the dangerous luster cast by time and distance. There was nothing to go back to.

When they started on this voyage six months ago, neither of them had given much thought to the future. They were adventuring, escaping, exploring. Chicago had worked for years to save money and rebuild her father's boat, and this trip had been her goal for a long time, but for Alex it was spontaneous. He had had no goals for several years, no mission except perhaps to avoid any mission.

But working on the wreck had stirred up his sense of adventure. The same sense that had gotten him into trouble most of his life, he reminded himself.

"You ready?" Chicago had her sneakers in hand, prepared to go ashore to make the phone call. "Can you help me with the dinghy?" She was such a hardass. After all this time, and with her arm in a sling, she still wouldn't ask him simply to drop the dinghy himself, a task he could have easily done, but only to *help* her with it. They untied the inflatable dinghy and lowered it to the water, then lowered the outboard into it. Alex climbed in and secured it, then tried not to seem like he was helping her at all as he helped her climb in.

"I had a thought—Jack and Peter McGuire are flying into Nassau tomorrow anyway, I'm sure they could get the part and bring it with them. It will save time."

Phone calls were much easier on Crooked Island because of the resort. Alex placed the call, while Chicago went to see about getting some fresh water for the boat. When she returned in a few minutes, Alex had just hung up and was all excited.

"They found it! They just got the word."

"They found the coffin?"

"Stan and Martha dove first thing this morning to check on

storm damage. Apparently the waves turned things up a lot, and one of the things was this coffin. They radioed in a call. The McGuires are going crazy ..." Alex trailed off, and Chicago looked at him suspiciously.

"And?"

"And—they want us back right away to help with the excavation."

"Well, I need two or three days with the boat. I might be able to rig something to sail, if the winds are light, but the engine started running hot yesterday, and it's a long way to motor." She knew he had some other idea in mind.

"That's what I told him."

"And?"

"They're working under pressure now, and Stan wondered if we might just leave the *Tassia Far* here. The McGuires hired a float plane to meet them in Nassau, they could come by here and pick us up, take us right to the *Goose*, save two days of travel."

Chicago frowned and looked over the water to where her boat rested at anchor. It was her home, her life, and she was very protective of it.

"I told him you wouldn't want to leave it, but maybe we could find someone here to look after it."

"Maybe. But look, I'm not going to be much good diving for a couple of days anyway. You were right about the throbbing like hell." She rubbed her shoulder which was still swollen and tender. "I doubt I could put on scuba gear right now. Why don't you just go ahead with them. I'll fix up the *Tassia Far*, then sail over and meet you."

Alex shook his head. "Oh, come on, don't go chivalrous on me." She laughed. "It's an easy sail. I've gone much farther solo before. Go on, I know you're aching to."

# TWENTY-SEVEN

"They found it," Dunagh announced without ceremony when Teneby returned from a trip to the telephone office. "Storm seems to have unburied the old bloke. Wodie just dropped us a line, but we could have picked it up from their own messages anyway."

"They broadcast so explicitly?"

"No, they talked some nonsense about a package delivery, but you could hear it in their voices. Very excited."

"Have they brought it up?" Dunagh shrugged and shook his head. "Wodie couldn't tell me much, but I wouldn't think so. We know Shepard has been pretty conservative with the job anyway, and the thing has to weigh twenty stone or more. If they really do know what they have, or *who* they have, I should say, they'll probably be extra cautious. Especially now with the archaeologist on his way."

Teneby plucked his sweaty shirt away from his chest and stood by the air conditioner, his brow wrinkled in thought.

"The storm has knocked out the telephones. No overseas calls, maybe not for a few days."

"We do have the orders." Teneby was only slightly disturbed by Dunagh's eagerness. He understood the desire for action, when so much of this business was just sitting around and watching. But these were not orders to act on lightly. What the hell was Hayes thinking about?

"Those are confirmation orders. We can't act without Hayes's direct approval."

"In a contingency we can. You know what he said: the coffin is best not recovered at all. Cut the thing off at the root."

104

"Well, no need to act hastily. The phones could be up tomorrow."

"But the Americans arrive in three days. The fewer people around, the less risk. I can arrange for a boat tonight."

"That's too soon. The water will still be murky from the storm, and we don't know exactly where to find it."

"I'll find it. I'm good at that sort of thing."

"No doubt. But we need to do this quietly."

"How do you have a quiet explosion, mate?" Dunagh laughed. Blowing up the coffin! The idea was absurd.

"Look, if we work it right, by the time the thing is detonated, we'll be well out of sight."

"But you know the difficulties—just getting close enough without them hearing will be tricky."

"We go from upwind, cut the engine while we're still a ways out, and drift in," Dunagh offered. "I go down dark—it's only sixty feet deep, and I'll be able to see the lights of the *Goose* above to know whereabouts I am. Switch on my torch at the bottom—pow . . . there it is." He shrugged. "Simple."

"There's no need to rush." Teneby unrolled the chart they had obtained and studied the distance to the site. "We can set things up, let the water settle a bit, try again for confirmation. I'm thinking, we could get someone to take a ride out there, one of these government fellows, you know, checking their permits and so on, have him get a message to Wodie."

"To do what?"

"Draw us a map of the site, tell us precisely where the coffin is, maybe mark it some way to make it easier to see at night. Patience, man. We'll plan this thing. Wednesday night is plenty soon enough."

# TWENTY-EIGHT

"There it is! There's the *Golden Goose!*" Annalee cried excitedly, her face pressed to the plane window. They all strained to look. The boat looked so small and vulnerable out there. Jack had a slight pang of apprehension about bringing Annalee. If she had a diving accident, what would they do?

The pilot swooped lower and Alex saw Shepard, Stan, Martha, and Wodie on the deck. Martha was waving. The water was still choppy, and the wind gusty enough to make Alex, an experienced flyer himself, feel tense about the approach. The pilot sensed his apprehension. A middle-aged Bahamian in a pink nylon golf shirt that strained a little over his waistline. He handled the floatplane with the ease of someone driving a rider mower around a suburban lawn.

"Relax, my friend." He laughed in a rich, deep voice. "You ever land on de water?"

"Not on purpose," Alex replied, trying to suppress the sickening memory of a crash near Miami only a year ago.

"Well, I put her down in far worse." A sudden gust punched at the light plane. The pilot wasn't fazed. "Fah fah worse." He grinned, a huge gleaming grin like a new tile wall. "We're a little heavy dhat's all," he explained as they bumped closer to the sea.

"Can we dive right away?" Annalee begged.

"I don't know Mizzy," Jack replied tensely, his own nervousness putting a strain in his voice.

"We need a checkout-dive first, Miz," Peter insisted. "You haven't been in six months."

"I remember everything!" Annalee protested.

"We're all going, hon," Peter explained. "I'm sure we can all use a little warm-up before we hit the deep." He leaned over the

106

seat. "Is there someplace shallow we can do that, Alex? Around the sides of the reef?" Alex turned to be heard over the engine noise.

"The sides are pretty steep, but I know a few little patches in about twenty feet." Annalee frowned, and Alex wondered if she was about to pout. She didn't really look like a pouter, but she looked like something, some kind of trouble. Those eyes, dark brown, soul-boring eyes, Joan of Arc eyes. She fixed that gaze on him now, as if really sizing him up for the first time.

"Have you found any bones yet?" she asked.

"Excuse me?"

"Any bones in the wreck?"

"No. Not yet," Alex answered. "I wouldn't think bones would last three hundred years in the open sea."

"They might; the scientists said they could. Skulls anyway. And in a coffin they would," the girl replied with an excited gleam.

# TWENTY-NINE

"In the first place, how in God's name are you going to prove this body—if there even *is* one—is really the son of King James the second? It's three hundred years old! There's certainly nothing but bones left." Adrian Spencer was feeling cross. The office was too hot, and Hayes was getting on his nerves. Had this become some kind of obsession with him? Spencer watched the Director General closely, the way he moved his veiny hands over the blotter, crablike, as if feeling for something very small.

"The Russians dug up the czar's family last year, brought the bones to our chaps at the Home Office's forensic science unit," Hayes replied in an even voice. "They made a positive ID. They don't need but a few bits today for DNA testing. A scrap of bone, piece of hair even."

"Well, fine then. Still, so bloody what! Even if you round up every antimonarchist, and every one of those kilted kooks in the SNP, we do still have a constitution in this country. They couldn't oust the queen!"

"If the body in that coffin turns out to be the true prince, they may not have to."

"What do you mean?"

"I mean . . ." Hayes folded his hands as if consciously restraining them. "The argument has been made that King James never abdicated, never ceased his claim to the throne. He was deposed in a coup. The funny thing about the whole business back then is that there was never really a huge opposition to the poor chap," Hayes explained as if talking about an old friend. "He was never popular, but it wasn't like all of England was trying to run him off. It was apathy more than anything else. There's a good many people believe that the English went along with it all the time figuring James would be back in a few months. That they had no intentions exactly to depose him, but to teach him a bit of a lesson and maybe scare the damn popish ideas out of him."

"You've been reading up on your history," Spencer noted.

"Fascinating stuff. Makes one kind of long for the good old days when a backstab was really a backstab." Spencer was unsure what to make of this comment. The office was uncomfortably hot, and Spencer was growing irritated.

"At any rate, if they can prove the body in that coffin is his son, and if they have a flawless genealogy from there on, and MacClannon, or whoever it turns out to be, is within the criteria for royalty, he might well be able to claim the throne."

"It's been tried before, man!" Spencer said with exasperation. "Whether or not the prince was switched at birth or not, there were fifty some decedents with a better claim to the throne when they brought the Hanovers in, and they were all rejected."

"They were Catholic. We have baptismal records from Port Royal showing the young Edward joined the Church of England."

"I refuse to be the slightest bit worried about this, Hayes," Spencer said with disgust. "I just refuse. It is so preposterous. Regardless of anybody these Americans may or may not find, the fact is that the English clearly rejected James II, and his progeny, several times, and that should end it right there."

"I agree, sir. But, playing devil's advocate, I would contend that a true rejection did not happen, because . . ." and here he paused with the drama of a barrister about to make a brilliant point, ". . . because they were rejecting the wrong man!"

Spencer was momentarily taken aback. It was an interesting legal concept. A contract signed by a pretender would be invalid, a license issued under false pretenses void, what did it mean for a country to reject a prince who was not the true prince?

"Oh . . . poppycock." In any other circumstances, perhaps if the two were old friends drinking brandy at their club, there might have been a spirited pursuit of the idea, but Spencer, at this point, was fed up with Hayes and simply wanted the whole weird thing to go away.

"All right. Suppose—" Spencer pressed. "Suppose—by the wildest stretch of the imagination, by the most farfetched theory, suppose MacClannon is declared king of England. What happens?"

"What happens, worst-case scenario? Well, economic chaos for sure. MacClannon makes a claim on the fortunes of the House of Windsor, asserting that since the family fortune was based on ill-gotten royal wealth in the first place, the great chunk of it ought to be turned over to him. Never happen, of course, too much legal precedent there, but it could tie things up for years.

"Then, of course, he could dissolve Parliament. Don't look that way. There are some gray areas, some real arguments among constitutional scholars here."

"So you're saying that Cory MacClannon, as king of England, could dissolve the sitting Parliament?"

"I repeat—it has not been ruled impossible. You asked for the worst-case scenario."

"Even if he does, it won't do him any good. He can't just bring in his own supporters. There would have to be a new election, and you've said yourself, they've never polled over thirty percent. Say there is this tremendous groundswell of support among the Scots, even that . . . it would be counterbalanced with all the rest of the UK being bloody well tired of his nonsense by then." Spencer felt he had made an ironclad argument. "What else?" he asked with a touch of smugness.

"Well, the Royal Prerogative allows the monarch the power to declare war, make treaties and," he paused, "cede territory."

"Cede as in . . ."

"Give away. King MacClannon could give away Scotland to the Scots. Declare it an independent nation."

"Bankrupt the nation, dissolve the Parliament, and destroy the Commonwealth. My. Rather a busy man," Spencer said drily.

"But you need not worry, old boy. My lads have it all under control. It's obvious there is a very simple way to deal with the whole thing."

"And how is that?"

"We simply make sure the bones are never recovered."

# *THIRTY*

"Where is he now, Birdy?" Grace asked warily, nodding toward the living room as she came in with a case of whiskey. Water dripped from her slicker and misted on the dark curls that poked out from her hood. Grace, like all the MacClannon women, was easily strong enough to haul around cases of her father's whiskey, though in real life, she more often hauled around thick court files.

"He's just finished the brave Dundee's battle at Killicrankie," her sister reported. "We've two more skirmishes and Grey John's bribe before MacIan even struggles through the snow, it won't be half-four till the massacre." Grace glanced at the clock. "Well, I'm going to help Robert with the rest of this, then bring the truck up to the shed. Do pull Kerry and Tim out before he gets to the gnawing off her fingers bit, will you?"

Birdy laughed. She was the youngest, the only one still unmarried, and quite happy being just an auntie for the time being.

Fortunately, her brothers and sister had married and produced enough children by now to keep the parents happy

"He's go'in on longer today between the rain and the lager, luv," she reassured Grace. "He might not get to Glencoe till tea."

"Well, last time, Kerry had nightmares for weeks, and Timmy frightened his whole class talkin' on about entrails swinging from the rafters." Grace pried open the box, pulled out one of the bottles, uncapped it and took a MacClannon-size pull from the bottle. Scottish family gatherings got on so well, she firmly believed, because everyone had sense enough to tipple their way through them. "Why does he have to make it so bloody?"

"Oh, but that was always the fun part, don't you think?" Birdy chided her sister. "Remember how we used to sit right there like them now, wee small and terrified so ..." She opened the oven door and a rich smell of roasting lamb drifted out. "Besides, Scottish history is bloody."

"Well t'will be him is bloody if I'm up with Kerry's terror tonight." She opened the door and pulled her coat tighter against the rain.

"Speaking of bloody," Grace caught her. "Annie asked do you have a pot for the haggis?"

"In the pantry—the enamel one should be right."

"She's bringing two."

"Why, is the brave Dundee himself expected to show up with his army to help us eat the thing?"

None of the MacClannon children was particularly fond of this Scottish delicacy. Haggis was made from minced sheep heart, and other offal, mixed with blood and oatmeal, stuffed in the sheep stomach and boiled. Their father not only enjoyed the ritual of serving it, where he got to stab the black lump with his dagger, he actually relished the taste.

"Go on with ye now," Birdy said. "I'll snatch the young ones out before it gets too gory."

The Clan MacClannon had gathered in the country for the weekend to celebrate Cory's sixtieth birthday, which fell conveniently after Christmas. Although the name of the house, Inishail, meant "Island of Rest," there was little resting for Cory MacClannon, and he was always glad to get holidays over with in a bunch.

They sometimes referred to Inishail as "the croft," though the sprawling hundred-acre estate bore little resemblance to the small traditionally rugged farms of the Scottish Highlands. Still, the place was far from pretentious. The main house was 212 years old, and, despite renovation, bore little in the way of luxury. Built of stone and hand-hewn timber, it had settled over the years, so there was an overwhelming but endearing sense of crookedness everywhere one looked. "Suits old Cory, though," a friend had once remarked. "A bit off from every angle but all and all a sound chap."

It had once been an earl's estate, and there was still a little cluster of houses and a barn in the glen below that Cory was having fixed up to be a historical working farm.

Birdy looked around the kitchen one more time, and assured herself that everything was in order. There wasn't much to do, there were so many coming this year that they had hired a caterer, but her poor mother, still awkward with the trappings of wealth, had insisted on roasting the lamb and doing a few other dishes herself. She had gone to the village to pick up a special lot of bread and rolls she had ordered from the local bakery.

Birdy slipped out of the kitchen, through the massive dining room, with its eight-foot fireplace, and stood at the doorway to the living room. Her father was sitting in a gigantic overstuffed antique chair, the "throne" they called it, with the grandchildren gathered around him. Despite having heard his stories of ancient heroes and battles all her life, Birdie still enjoyed hearing him tell them again. He was so passionate, you could feel the hoofbeats and smell the fear.

"Now MacIan MacDonald was a stubborn-proud man, stubborn-proud even for a highland chief . . ." His voice had a deep, rich tone, and his blue eyes shone.

Birdy was always surprised to see this mob of children, otherwise so restless and rowdy, weaned on TV and video games, listening raptly to these historical tales. He kept them involved by having them boo the villains and thump the floor at the mention of the heroes.

"This impostor, this Dutchman, William of Orange [a chorus of boos] was brought in and made king, while the rightful King James, born a Scot and a brave man, was exiled. [A dozen small feet kicked against the worn carpet].

"This devil, William of Orange ordered all the clan leaders to come declare their allegiance to him not later than the first of January, but they only announced this around Christmastime, you see, giving them hardly any time to travel. Well, most of the chiefs finally went along, but MacIan MacDonald of Glencoe, not a man to be pushed around by this faker king William, waited for the last moment, then his long trip was slowed by a terrible blizzard. He was only a few days late, mind you, but William decided to make an example of him.

"He sent the treacherous Robert Campbell ..." The brood erupted excitedly with hisses and cries, for they knew Campbell was the worst villain of all. Injustice from government, tyranny from kings was bad enough, but was, after all, to be expected. Campbell himself was a Highland chief, and his betrayal was unforgivable.

"Campbell's men went to Glencoe under the guise of friend-ship, and spent eleven days living on the MacDonald's hospitality. They slept in their homes, ate at their tables, played cards and drank with them, for all these days. Then suddenly, one terrible night ..."

Oh, dear, here it was coming, and Grace not back yet to snatch the children away. Birdy gave a little cough and her father glanced up. The children turned to look at her, scowling as if she might be treacherous as a Campbell herself just for interrupting.

"I need the little ones, Father. Jim and Kerry and Gwen ..." She scanned the rest, wondering who else might need to be spared the grisly ending.

"Auntie Birdy!" The protest was immediate, especially from Jim, who at five and a half would clearly lose face to be pulled away when his six-year-old-cousin could stay.

"But I'm not through here, lassie!" Cory protested.

"I've a special job for them, Da." Kerry, who was a dreamy and fainthearted child anyway and not looking forward to the gut-ting of clansmen and dashing of brains on the stones, scampered to her aunt's side. "Is it time to do the cake?" she whispered. Birdy smiled, nodded, and put her finger to her lips.

Despite the protestations of the banished children, the sisters knew that it made the stories all the more exciting when they were slightly forbidden. No doubt, Jimmy would hear the details, probably worse, from the older cousins, but at least the lure of mystery would be kept alive.

"In the wee hours of the morning," she heard old Cory's voice lower to a suspenseful tone as she led her charges down the hall, "most of the village was asleep. Robert Campbell and two officers had dined with Ian MacDonald that night, and were still in the house, smoking their pipes and playing at cards. Ian got up to fetch another bottle from the shelf . . ." The older children knew what was coming and held their breaths, watching their grandfather as he got up and turned, reached toward the invisible shelf.

"Here he was, going to fetch them another wee dram . . ." Cory MacClannon paused for dramatic effect, glancing surreptitiously over his shoulder to be sure he had them all on edge. "BANG!" he shouted. His body jerked in imitation of the shot and the grandchildren screeched. "Campbell shot him dead. In the back. In his own home."

The story went on, no details of the atrocities left untold: women raped, children beaten, men butchered with knives, with bayonets and swords, their intestines strewn steaming on the snow. Cory ended, as always, with one of Campbell's men looting the bodies of the dead and unable to get the rings off MacDonald's wife's hand, ripping the finger off with his teeth.

Suddenly there was a great knocking on the front door, honking of horns in the yard, and ringing of the bell all at once. Birdy ran back in, alarmed, the children chasing after her, still with frosting on their fingers. Her brothers came charging down the stairs, all wondering what catastrophe might have fallen, but the faces at the windows were joyous faces, faces of friends, swinging bottles and jugs. Cory got up, puzzled, and the children scampered to open the heavy old door.

The raucous crowd swelled in, Kelly and Ewing, Mackay, Mackenzie and MacGregor, already, by the looks and smell of them, well into celebration, half-empty bottles of MacClannon whiskey swinging wildly in toast.

"Wha d'ye mean by this, ye rogues!" Maggie MacClannon, just back from the village, appeared behind her daughter, raincoat dripping, her muddy wellies still on. "The party's not for another three hours! Get off wi' your drunken selves now!"

"Ah Maggie, Maggie!" MacGregor staggered forward, his arms flung wide as if to embrace her. Maggie, a tiny scrap of a woman, shrank back at his approaching bulk, wielding her bags of bread in front of her. But MacGregor stopped, sank to one knee instead, and with a gallant sweep of one juggernaught arm, bowed so deeply he toppled to the floor.

Laughter erupted as Michael and Thomas went to drag the man up, and Cory, perplexed but enjoying the scene, put a protective arm around his wife's shoulders. "They've just come to wish me a happy birthday, luv."

She shrugged him off with a flinty glare and demanded that he throw the dripping drunken sorry lot of them out or she would call the dogs. Those who overheard this and were familiar with the MacClannon dogs—dotty old mutts rescued from the pound, half lame and a few toothless—laughed even harder.

"Here, here, MacGregor—away you go." Neil Swinny helped Michael steer the offending MacGregor away. "Settle down, lads, quiet now, show some respect after all! Ye know where we are now!" Swinny, always one to smooth the ruffles, was Cory's business partner, and a friend since childhood. His sobriety seemed a little more assured than the others, and he took charge of this raggedy lot with the same ease he had commanded both boardroom debates and dockyard strikes.

When the murmers and cries had subsided, and the staggering MacGregor propped carefully against the wall in a corner farthest from the porcelain, Swinny raised his hand and snapped his fingers. Two of the men came forward, holding crowns of gilded paper, birthday party hats from Woolworths.

"Now my friends, my clansmen, 'tis a great day for Scotland!"

There was a great shout of agreement.

"Swinny lad, it's a fine homage ye've brought me here," Cory said quietly, as he ducked the fiery darts his wife was shooting his way. "But do ye think they'd mind if we went round the back to carry on, eh? Me sweet wife here . . ." He finished the sentence with a universal gesture of man submitting to the face of household tyranny.

"Roond the back? Roond the back? God love ye Cory—we'll go anywhere ye say, won't we, lads? To the ends of the earth, to hell and back if ye ask, for we are your loyal subjects."

"Aye, that's right! We will! Aye!" another chorus of support. Swinny fished in his pockets and pulled out a folded paper, already soft at the creases from much handing around. Slowly, and with great ceremony, he opened the page, took a step back, and with a much more successful effort at a proper deep bow, handed the paper to Cory.

"Cory Fitzroy MacClannon, son of Geddes MacClannon, of the Clan MacClannon, recently discovered to be direct descendants of James Francis Edward Stuart, we are happy to proclaim you, sir, the rightful King of England!"

# THIRTY-ONE

It was Wednesday evening, after their first full day aboard the *Golden Goose*, and everyone was in a happy mood. They had done three dives that day, bringing up many of the artifacts that the storm had uncovered. The coffin would have to wait a little longer. Lifting it would be tricky, and then there were problems of storage. Jack wanted to be able to ship it off to a lab as soon as possible after getting it in the open air.

Alex was amazed at Annalee's diving. The girl seemed completely at home underwater. She was transformed, graceful, with no trace of the gawkiness she had on dry land. Peter kept her close at hand, but she seemed exceptionally mature, with an awareness that Alex hadn't seen it in a lot of older, more experienced divers. He imagined Chicago at this age twelve, and laughed. The two would like each other.

Right now, they were digesting all the new information Jack had brought. All they had known before was that they were looking for a coffin that had something to do with an old king. Now the search had assumed a new and fascinating angle.

"But why send the baby to Jamaica?" Martha asked logically.

"When they fled from England in 1688, Mary Beatrice didn't trust anyone," Jack explained. "She had lived too long in the midst of a duplicitous court."

"Maybe she really did send the baby to Italy," Peter added. "And the ship was captured, or ... who knows. But maybe she chose Jamaica and told Rizzini to throw him off as well."

"She was under severe strain remember," Jack broke in. "She was still weak from the birth, and probably suffering what we call postpartum depression, or a sort of hysteria. King James was suffering what seems now to have been a nervous breakdown. Mary knew she could not rely on him, could not trust any of his confidants. She assumed that everyone was plotting against her child."

"Didn't she trust anyone?"

"She knew that everyone had his own agenda. A different idea of how to deal with the situation. All she wanted right then was for her son to live."

"In her fever deliriums, she began to see images of a tropical paradise," Annalee interjected with a dramatic tone. "She imagined a place where her baby would grow up in fresh clean air, healthy and strong. He would splash in the sea and play in the sand and eat bananas and coconuts."

"Remember, that as a child, she would have heard stories about the explorations and discoveries in the New World," Peter added. "Jamaica was a British colony, a thriving island with a British government. Plus the governor owed the king a big favor."

"He was a pirate," Annalee explained. "Captain Morgan. Like the rum."

Shep groaned. He wasn't sure how many more twists the fantastic tale could hold. Jack noticed his look and laughed.

"I know, I know. But actually, that bit is true. Captain Charles Morgan, one of the most notorious pirates ever, was made governor of Jamaica by Charles the Second."

"The baby's uncle."

"Right."

"Morgan was a Welsh buccaneer who got in some trouble while plundering for England. Charles II gave him a royal pardon and made him lieutenant-governor of Jamaica in 1674."

"So Morgan owed the Crown a big favor."

"Exactly, and the queen decides to call in this favor. She sends her baby to Jamaica, to be placed under his protection."

"I'm still having a hard time seeing any mother sending her infant on such a trip," Martha confessed. "It would have been so dangerous!"

"No more so than trying to elude spies and blackguards throughout Europe," Peter pointed out. "But you're right, of course. We have no way to know how the baby wound up in Jamaica. Or really, even if he went there at all! All we have is the packet of documents that we are assuming went with the baby. These were found in the Port Royal excavation.

"It could be the papers were stolen, or lost and wound up there entirely by mistake. It could be that the baby really was smuggled to Italy, or hidden somewhere in France. Or that he was never switched at all, that it was all an elaborate ruse, with the documents intended to be discovered to throw the enemy off guard. There's no way to tell really. History is not a tidy business."

"But we do have an awful lot of evidence."

"Plus the coffin now! We just open it up, and if the bones are wearing a cross that matches our medallion, well . . ." Annalee smiled with anticipation. Stan stared at the girl, not yet used to her offhanded treatment of death.

"But the first medallion, the one you found in the fish's stomach two years ago, how did that wind up aboard the *Christiania*?" Martha quizzed.

"Oh, I can tell you that," Annalee said eagerly. "See, once they stopped trying to bring Edward back, well, he just went on with his life in Jamaica. He grew up, and went to school and everything, then one day . . ."


*Jamaica, 1710*

*"Edward! What are you doing? Where have you been?" Gene-vieve needed no answer to know where the boy had been. His hair was wet, his nose freshly burned, his tanned skin glowing.*

*"The guests are already arriving!"*

*"Yes, Mums." He grinned and kissed her on the cheek as he raced past her up the steps of the veranda.*

*"Hurry!"*

*"Yes, Mums." The boy laughed.*

*She followed him into the kitchen. "And how many times do I have to tell you . . . the English do not swim!" she shouted at his departing figure as he bounded up the back stairs. "Especially on their wedding days!"*

*Genevieve had no time for this, the minister's carriage was pulling up in the front of the house. She smoothed a hand over her graying hair and fluffed out the sleeves of her new silk gown. Genevieve had grown plump in her gentlelady life, and was huffing from the heat.*

*Outside of his penchant for swimming in the ocean and climbing about in the mountains, James Francis Edward had turned out to be a proper young gentleman, a strapping lad of twenty-two with a keen mind and a ready wit. Nothing like his father, she thought. God rest his soul. King James the second had died six years ago in France, a bitter old man, never resigned to his exile, driven mad some said.*

*The news didn't reach Jamaica for two months, but they had held a coronation the day they found out. It was a family party really, with cakes and punch on the back lawn, and a crown made of hibiscus flowers that Clarissa braided together for her beloved older "brother."*

*By that time, they had begun to believe the prince would never be returned to England, and that was fine with Genevieve and Richard, who had come to love him like their own son. Genevieve had borne six daughters and two sons of her own, but only three of the girls had survived. Though she still wrote to Mary Beatrice, the letters were fewer. Once, maybe twice a year. The time had simply been to great, the sorrows too deep.*

*There had been some talk of return, early on, then again when he was six years old and the reigning Queen Mary died, but it had been five years now since any serious effort had been made. Some Scots had come in 1703, after King William finally passed away, but Jamaica was in the grip of a plague, and they were not allowed to come ashore. Terrible fevers swept the island for months. Edward was stricken, nearly died. The ship sailed to Cuba to wait until he had the strength for the voyage; then it was attacked by buccaneers.*

*"Mummy, where is he?"* Clarissa saw the minister, smiled, and curtseyed politely. With a fierce glance, she managed to pull her mother away into the next room. *"Poor Catherine is about to faint! She's lying upstairs, wrinkling her gown, thinking her husband to be has been devoured by sharks!"*

*"He's here."* Genevieve smiled and waved at the Thistlewaites as they strolled by. The best of colonial Jamaica was here for the wedding. The bride herself was daughter of a judge; had uncles back home in Parliament. *"He's getting dressed. Tell the girls to get the flowers ready and I'll send your father to hurry him up."*

*"I'll hurry him myself. The beast!"*

Upstairs, James Francis Edward had combed his hair and struggled into the hot, constricting suit. It was a mark of British society to maintain old-world decorum, especially in dress and manner, no matter the conditions, but Edward thought it ridiculous to wrap his neck up when it was this hot. Satisfied, or at least sure every button was fastened, he hurried out into the hallway and ran directly into the harried Clarissa.

*"Edward—you are awful!"* He laughed and hugged his stepsister.

*"Clara, you look like an angel. Where's Catherine?"*

*"She's in my room, in a panic!"*

*"Good."* he kissed her on the cheek. *"Stall Mums a few more minutes, will you?"*

*"You can't ..."* He turned and winked, then ducked down the hallway. He found his bride sitting by the window, looking uncommonly pale, her hands wrenching a handkerchief. She burst into tears.

*"Ah, Cathy ..."*

*"You're horrible!"*

*"Oh, sweetheart—you knew I would come."* He knelt by her side. *"I'm sorry. Don't cry. Look—I've something for you."*

*"I thought you had drowned."*

*"I'll never drown. Drop me to the bottom of the sea and I'll come back for you somehow!"* he declared passionately. *"Come on now—can't marry a king with a snuffly nose."*

Catherine laughed and wiped her eyes. She was so pretty, even crying. He had loved her the first time he had ever seen her, her red hair shining in the sunlight.

*"Look here."* He handed her a little box tied with a ribbon. The young bride opened the box and saw a medallion resting on a piece of satin cloth. The piece, obviously old, was not a particularly pretty one.

*"Well, it's lovely, Edward!"* she said doubtfully, gazing at its odd shape.

Edward laughed. *"Oh, it is not."* Then he grew more serious, and took the medallion from the box.

*"Look on the back,"* he said. There was a loud knock on the door; Clarissa was bidding them to come now, Mums was about to have a stroke, and the cake was melting in the heat. Edward just grinned and turned it over in her palm. Catherine saw the partial inscription on the back, traced the outline of a little cross that had been carved out of the metal.

*"It's like yours!"* she realized, reaching to touch the little cross that hung around his neck.

*"It matches exactly,"* Edward said proudly. *"My mother had it made when I was an infant, and Genevieve has had it all these years. Now she says it is yours."* He stood, and fastened it around her neck, then lifted her thick hair over the chain. *"It's so everyone will always know that you are mine!"*

Fresh tears sprang to the girl's eyes. *"Oh, my love, I will never take it off!"*

Annalee clasped her hands in a melodramatic pose of rapturous love as she finished Catherine's dramatic pledge. Martha applauded, surprised to find herself so caught up in the tale.

"And they lived happily ever after, and had a baby of their own, but then he died," she concluded. "Edward, I mean."

"So that's the story of the medallion," Jack McGuire explained. "Or at least, one of the versions we've concocted over the long winter months. There's really no way to know how it came about."

"Well, it's a lovely story." Martha hugged the girl and Annalee was so content she offered no resistance. "But you've talked us terribly late here, and I for one am ready for bed."

"We'll try and get back on our regular dive schedule tomorrow," Stan explained. "We usually start at five A.M., do our first dive as soon as it's light. That way we can get in four, sometimes five, dives a day with plenty of time in between to off-gas. You know what that means, kid?'' Stan had not been exactly thrilled at the idea of having a twelve-year-old aboard.

"Letting the nitrogen out of your tissues,'' Annalee said with more graciousness than Alex would have expected. "I passed the exam. If you want to test me I'll get my tables.''

"Oh, don't be such a drill sergeant, Stan!'' Martha reprimanded him. "You saw her in the water. Come on now, Annalee, I'll get you settled in your cabin. Tomorrow will be a big day.''

# *THIRTY-TWO*

Teneby killed the speedboat's engine when they were still a half-kilometer from the anchored *Goose*. There was a good, steady breeze, and he was counting on it to blow the small boat closer under cover of silence. It was a moonless night, and though he would have welcomed clouds to shadow the bright stars, it was still dark enough.

Teneby lifted the night vision scope and watched the *Goose* for several long minutes while Dunagh silently readied his gear. The treasure boat rocked gently at anchor, and Teneby saw no movement in the eerie green field.''

"We're about two hundred yards now,'' he whispered. "I don't want to get much closer. How long do you need?''

"Give me fifteen minutes to swim over and find the coffin. Another ten to rig things up.''

"You can't come straight up after it's wired, you'll be too close to the boat.''

"It won't really matter, they'll hear you anyway once you start the motor, but if you like, I'll kick out twenty yards to the starboard side of the boat. Just get me quick once you see my signal.

I'd rather not be in the water when it goes off. Going to be a nasty shock wave.''

Teneby picked up the sack of explosives, and was surprised by the feel of it. He opened the bag, looked inside, then looked suspiciously at Dunagh.

"What the hell is this?"

"Bombs, mate—what d'ye think?"

"Where did you get a HICER shell?"

"Supply, of course. They've been wanting a field test."

"It's not authorized yet!"

"Neither is this op." Dunagh shrugged and took one of the shells from Teneby. It was a smooth, shallow cone shape, with a powerful magnet all around the rim. A byproduct from the aerospace industry, HICER stood for hi-intensity ceramic. An unusual fuse of ceramic and polymer fiber made it extremely tough and resilient. It was virtually unbreakable under ordinary conditions, yet when subjected to extreme force, such as explosives, it would pulverize into dust. While this "flaw" had prevented its use as an exterior protective tile for space crafts, some clever chap in munitions had realized another potential. The ceramic was strong enough to concentrate and intensify the magnitude of an explosive, but ultimately left no trace of itself.

With sophisticated techniques these days, almost any bomb or explosive could be identified after the fact, and thereby often provided clues leading to the bomber. The HICER shell so effectively magnified the explosive impact that detonation mechanisms, and even residue, were destroyed beyond identification. It also made a quick and secure shield, preventing anyone who might find the device from getting to it to diffuse it. The HICER shell could be slapped on in seconds. It was . . . was the Post-it note of explosive technology, a covert operator's dream.

"But the coffin is most likely lead or iron," Teneby pointed out. "The magnet won't work."

"I'll bury it in the sand beneath the thing. Just like to see how she does."

Dunagh held a small flashlight to the dial of his compass, charging up the luminescence, then took a bearing on the *Goose*. This would be almost too easy. They went over a few last details, then Dunagh strapped on the scuba tank, tugged on his fins, and slipped

quietly into the black water. He held on to the side of the boat
while Teneby carefully handed him the package of explosive.
Dunagh dropped quickly to a depth of fifteen feet, and with only
the faint green glow of the compass dials for light, began to kick
toward the *Golden Goose*.

# THIRTY-THREE

Chicago was tired but could not sleep. The wind made her restless.
It would be a great night for sailing, but she was reluctant to do a night
sail alone, with her injured shoulder. The repairs to the *Tassia Far* had
taken less time than she expected, so she had decided to leave this morning, breaking up the return trip into two parts. Now she was anchored
behind Plana Cay, halfway back to the *Golden Goose*.

The *Tassia Far* rolled slowly from side to side as long swells
moved under her hull. The sailing guide had warned that this
anchorage could be uncomfortable, and it was right.

She tossed for a while longer, switched on the light and tried
to read, then finally she got up. The bed seemed gigantic now
without Alex. She went to the galley for a drink of water, then
wandered restlessly through the boat. Lassie, who had been hiding
under the bow berth since the storm, had finally emerged, and
draped herself on a narrow shelf in the salon. Her body was
smooth and evenly thick, the bulge from the rats she had swallowed a few days ago now thoroughly digested. The boa picked
her head up as Chicago passed, her shiny black tongue licking the
air, and Chicago rubbed her head fondly.

The rolling of the swells had toppled a few paperbacks out of
the shelf and sent the ruler skidding off the chart table. She picked
these up and put them back in their places. What else could she
do? Everything was clean, nothing needed tinkering with, she was
just restless. The bathroom door was banging, and she went to
shut it. She saw Alex's toothbrush on the floor, forgotten.

She picked it up. They had bought these new toothbrushes at the same time, used them about the same amount, yet his was beaten down already, the bristles worn and crushed. She missed him, she missed the mass of him, the arms and legs and neck and weight of him. She missed his hard-brushing hands, and the way his body sank into the bed when he slept, as if gravity tugged harder on him than her.

Sorrow hit her like a wave. Everywhere she looked or touched was a reminder of him. When had this happened? When had this man become such a part of her life? After so long alone, to have a man so close, as if he were a vine around her heart. When had the roots gone so deep?

And after living so long alone, here they were tangled. There was his towel on the door, his toothbrush by the sink, his underwear all mixed up with hers in the hamper. She would read a book and see the pages he had turned down. He made little marks in the margins, almost invisible dots next to passages that he liked. She had discovered this by accident one day, and had never told him that she knew, but secretly, she had paged through all the books, looking for his marks, silently loving him more.

She went to the radio, trying to think of some reason to call the *Golden Goose*, just to hear his voice. Chicago couldn't believe she was being so sappy. She who had lived and worked with men all her life, and was so immune to the follies of love. It was eleven-thirty. They would probably be asleep. Anyway, she would see him tomorrow.

# THIRTY-FOUR

Dunagh found the shipwreck site with ease. By now, with so many string grids and colored flags it would have been hard to miss. He kept the tiny flashlight cupped in one hand. It was doubt-

ful anyone on deck could see the glow, but he wasn't taking any
chances. Dunagh never took chances. Well, almost never.

The business with Griffith had been a bit dicey. He had to drive
the car himself, and manage to cause the accident without breaking
his own neck, but fortunately it had come off just fine. Dunagh
was happy the man had only broken a few bones, but he wouldn't
have lost sleep over a more serious outcome. The agent had to be
removed so that Dunagh could take his place.

He kicked slowly over the ribs of the ancient ship. Halfway
down, then south of an orange flag about ten kicks, there it was,
just as Wodie had reported.

He patted the coffin, as if to reassure the long-dead king inside
that everything was going to be fine. He checked his watch. He
felt that the bag of explosives was in place. Time to do it. Time
to change the history of the world. Slowly, holding his packet of
explosives, Steven Dunagh began to swim up. Up through the still,
dark water. Up to where the vulnerable hull of the *Golden Goose*
floated, like a leaf on the surface.

Alex wasn't exactly sure what wakened him. Some faint sound,
some instinct. He lay still and listened, not wanting to risk movement until he had a better idea of what was going on. He had
slept on deck since their arrival, partly because he preferred the
open air, and partly because experience had taught him that bad
guys didn't often come parading in at high noon with trumpets
blasting. Two Bahamian officials had come out to the site that
afternoon, ostensibly to check on their permit. It could all be perfectly legit, but Alex's instinct had been pricked.

There it was again, a ripple of water, a slight clink. Someone
was out there. He rolled over, and, keeping low, peered out into
the dark water, searching for the darker shape of a boat. Nothing.
He grabbed the flashlight but didn't turn it on. Crouching low, he
glanced over the stern, then began to work his way up the port
side. Still no sight or sound of a boat. Alex knew if there was
one within a hundred yards, there would be some sound, if only
the gentle slaps of its hull in the water. Six months at sea had
tuned him to the sounds.

*This is gonna be real bad, or nothing at all,* he realized as he
assembled possible scenarios. The bow lights cast a pale gleam

on the water, just enough that he could make out bubbles. There was a diver under the boat. With such stealth, and no sign of the boat that brought them, this was beginning to feel real bad.

Alex scrambled back, swung down into the salon, and jerked open the door of Stan's cabin. Stan sat up immediately, his seaman's instinct recognizing an emergency.

"Get up and stay quiet," Alex said calmly. "We've got divers under the boat. Wake everyone and get on deck, but keep 'em quiet. I'm going in now. You got a spear gun somewhere?"

"Port locker. I'll go with you." Stan was already out of his berth.

"Cover us up here first. Does Shep have any weapons?"

"Couple of shotguns, I've got a pistol."

"I can't see their boat, but it must be around somewhere. Get Shep on deck with a gun."

"Shep, hell!" Stan smiled grimly as he pulled on his shorts. "Marty's the sharpshooter. National champion three times back in the sixties."

A thirty-year-old target-shooting award didn't give Alex much comfort as he climbed back up on deck, grabbed his mask and fins. There was an assembled scuba tank ready by the stern, kept there for emergency decompressions or rescues, and he pulled it from the rack. As he climbed down the dive platform, he saw the faint white shape of a boat about twenty yards away.

Stan appeared at the railing above, ready with his own gear. Alex pointed to the boat.

"Shit!" Stan laid his tank down. "That's our skiff!" Alex realized with horror that it was indeed the transport boat that they used to ferry back to Mayaguana, now cut adrift.

Stan pulled on his fins.

"Let it go."

"We need it," Stan said tersely. "If something happens, we're gonna need that skiff." Alex recognized the sense of that. Stan pulled his fins on.

"Wait till I'm under," Alex ordered as he tossed the tank on over his head and pulled the mask into place. "No use tipping them off." Alex saw Shep and Marty quietly taking positions on the bow. Jack McGuire, still groggy with sleep, stumbled on deck with Annalee.

"Life jackets," he ordered tersely. Alex picked up the speargun. This was not the little three-pronged sling he had been fishing with, but a real spear gun, a stocky weapon with double rubber slings, a gun for blue-water fishing. He looped the underwater flashlight around his wrist. There was no way to slip in silently, so he opted for speed over surprise.

Dunagh turned at the splash, froze as the beam of light hit him . . . but quickly recovered. He had already affixed the bomb to the hull and set the timer. Now he slapped the HICER shell over it all. Done. There was no stopping it now. His only goal was to get out of the water before the explosion. Dunagh turned and saw Alex charging toward him, spear gun raised. He reached for the dive knife strapped to his leg, dodged, but clamped his teeth in pain as the spear sliced down his side and gouged his thigh.

No time to reload. Alex dropped the speargun. Dunagh lunged for him. Alex met his attack and twisted away, sweeping his arm toward the man's head, hoping to catch his regulator hose or mask. Bubbles boiled around them as they wrestled. Alex's fingers touched a strap, fumbled for a grasp. His light swung crazily. The attacker grabbed his hand. Alex pushed him away, twisting free, groping in the darkness.

He felt a sting on his neck as the knife slashed out at him. Alex grabbed the arm and twisted it down. There was a tug on his shoulder straps, and he realized the attacker had hold of his scuba tank. Alex rolled and reached behind, up over his head, and grabbed the man by the neck, yanking his face down hard against the tank valve. His face mask shattered, choking on the blood in his mouth, Dunagh scrambled for the surface.

"There! There!" Peter was on deck with the spotlight. Martha shouldered the shotgun and aimed.

"Wait—don't shoot!" Shep shouted. "Where's Alex?" Dunagh's eyes burned, and he could not see for the blood. He fumbled for his flashlight, unsure the direction in which to swim, hoping to hear the motor of Teneby racing in to fetch him.

Some hundred yards off, Teneby had been watching the commotion on deck with the night scope. What the hell was going on? He scanned the water, looking for Dunagh's signal.

"Do you see him yet?" Martha kept the gun trained on Dunagh as he swam away from the boat.

"No."

Back at the stern, Jack checked the straps on Annabel's life preserver, his heart racing. God, he had never expected this! This was crazy!

Alex cleared the water from his mask. He had lost his flashlight in the struggle, but the bright glare of a Q beam spotlight swept the surface and made a milky green glow underwater. Guided by the light, Alex swam back toward the boat.

Teneby saw the light as well, and realized Dunagh had been spotted. He turned on the engine and roared toward the scene.

"There he is!" Shep shouted as Alex's head popped up next to the boat. Martha fired at Dunagh.

"It's a bomb!" Alex shouted. "Get me a crowbar, be ready to abandon ship!" He jammed his regulator back in and ducked under.

Alex had heard of the HICER shell, though he had never seen one. He ran his hands over the smooth surface, trying to shift or pry it off. It didn't move an inch. He heard rapping on the hull and swam up. Shep handed him the crowbar, then ducked as a volley of bullets hit the wheelhouse.

Peter, Jack, and Annalee worked to launch the life raft while Martha fired from the bow. She was a frail-looking warrior. Over her jeans flowed a pink silk nightgown and robe, the gun strap rumpling the lace collar. Wodie, panicked and terrified, jumped in the water and began to swim away from the doomed boat.

Teneby shoved the throttle up and roared close to the *Golden Goose*. They had brought guns, but he didn't want to kill anyone he didn't have to. He saw Dunagh's light waving and spun the wheel, whirled over and slowed to pick him up. Dunagh had ditched his gear and vaulted easily into the launch.

"What the bloody hell is going on!" Teneby shouted as he reached for the throttle. Dunagh didn't answer. He just sprang up, and plunged his knife into the man's back. Teneby turned. Dunagh thrust again, up under the ribs, a killer's strike. Teneby crumpled. Dunagh caught his arm and pitched him into the sea.

Alex sweated as he worked the crowbar around the edge of the shell, searching for a niche. But time after time, the bar slipped harmlessly away. The HICER was smooth as a spaceship, with no lip to wedge under. Alex tried a different approach, chipping at the edge to break off a piece of the housing. Working underwater, there was no leverage, nothing to brace against. On deck, there was a controlled chaos as Jack and Peter tried to deploy the life raft.

"Get that strap."

"Stand back—watch out!" Peter was frantically reading the directions. "Grab that end and lift. We throw the whole thing over."

"You have to tie the ripcord!" Annalee shouted, her voice thin with fear. "Shep told me. Tie it to something, so you don't lose the raft." Once in the water, the raft would tug against the cord and inflate, while still tethered to the boat. "Okay—look out! Shit!" Something went wrong, gas charges exploded and the boat began to inflate on the deck.

Alex slammed the crowbar against the shell. How long did he have? There! A sliver of the smooth housing chipped off. He jabbed the tip of the crowbar under it. He pulled but it did not move. He swung his feet up and braced them against the hull, but at this angle, the bar just slipped free. He almost dropped it. He shifted his body and tried again. He heard the sound of a motor. A high-pitched whine, a high-performance boat, not the battered old skiff Stan had gone after.

Dunagh grabbed the wheel and turned back toward the *Golden Goose*, firing wildly.

"Marty, get down!" Shep screamed, and ran toward his wife. Marty aimed again and fired. Dunagh fell, clutching his leg, but raised the gun again.

"Marty!" Shep screamed. Annalee turned in time to see it all: the old man reaching for his wife, his leathery hands spread wide in surprise as the bullets raked across his body. Martha spun around in slow motion, her pink dressing gown swirling around her legs like Ginger Rogers. A shower of blood spattered against the cabin and she fell, still clutching the shotgun.

Jack threw his body over his daughter. Bullets whined over head, smashed into the cabin house, zinged against the scuba tanks. Jack prayed, Annabel Lee was silent, her thin shoulders shaking uncontrollably.

Alex heard the gunfire, looked up and saw the wake of the speedboat arc around the anchored *Goose*. He heard a whipping sound, like something caught in a fan. Bullets. They had seen his bubbles and were shooting at him. He piked and began to swim down into the black depths. With a blinding flash, the bomb exploded.

# THIRTY-FIVE

The shock was like hitting a wall. Hitting a wall with a sack of bricks inside his gut. Thunder echoed inside his skull. His mask crushed against his face. Alex sank. As if in a dream, he saw the *Golden Goose* sinking with him. Slowly, ever so slowly they fell, as if in some strange ballet, the lights of the *Golden Goose* twinkling out one by one.

It was almost beautiful. Alex felt a numbing peace. The water was thick and heavy. There was water in his mask. No, not water, *blood*. The sound of his own breathing was loud, echoing inside his head, his blood rushing loud as waves, pounding at his ears, in his head. Dazed, he could not tell how deep he was. He reached clumsily for the inflator hose but couldn't find it. Of course. He had grabbed the emergency tank, set up with only a backpack, no inflatable vest. Drifting, falling, pressure on his ears, but was it from descending or from the explosion? He pinched his nose and blew gently. The pressure stopped. Good, something worked. Softness brushed his leg, and instinctively he recoiled. Just sea grass. Solid ground now. He was on the bottom. Okay no problem, just kick. It was only sixty feet. But what a long sixty feet. Rest a minute, he told himself. Stop, breathe, think, act. How many times had he heard Chicago drilling that into her scuba students? Would he ever hear it again?

Alex was surprised when his head broke the surface. There was a soft yellow glow, a fire. Chunks of the cabin were still floating, burning above the water. Debris, too, floated all around, and the clear night air was tainted with the smell of diesel.

Someone was crying. Alex swam toward the sound and found Annabel Lee clinging to her father. She saw Alex and screamed.

"It's me," Alex called out.

"It's okay, honey. It's okay. It's Alex, not the bad men. They're gone." Jack calmed the frightened girl. Another figure appeared, Peter, his head bloody, unconscious, the life jacket holding his head above water. Alex caught the man and towed him over.

"Where's the life raft?"

"It only opened halfway." Jack's voice was controlled. "Got hung up on something." Alex pulled off his mask and washed the blood out of it. There was a steady throb in his head and a ringing in his ears.

"Where's the rest?"

"Shep and Marty are dead. Shot. No one's seen Wodie or Stan."

"Stan went after the skiff."

They all looked, but saw only empty water. No one spoke, but they all knew. Certainly if he had reached the boat he would have come back for them. Certainly if the attackers had seen him, they would have shot him.

"Is he breathing?" Alex looked at Peter. Jack nodded.

"Okay, then." Alex pulled up his pressure gauge and checked the air. He had about half a tank left. "I'm going down to get the life raft. I don't guess anyone has a flashlight."

"Yes." Annabel Lee spoke in a small scared voice. "I thought it would be a good thing to have." She held out a trembling hand, and Alex unlooped the small dive light. "Good job, hon." He would have liked another few minutes to rest, but they were quickly drifting away. He pulled his mask back on, and found his regulator. "Don't go anywhere."

The shattered *Goose* lay on her side almost on top of the wreck of the *Christiania*. Trapped air bubbled up from a thousand small cracks. Two of the running lights, amazingly, were still working. The small flashlight beam was weak, and Alex located the life raft mostly by feel, pulling himself along the stern railing to where he knew it had once been fastened. The shell had twisted off its hinge while deploying, trapping the inflatable raft under the winch cables. Alex had to work it free by inches, pushing down on one end to shimmy it under the cables. But once freed, the boat sprang open and shot up toward the surface. Something hit Alex on the arm. Huge, shiny raindrops were falling from the life raft. Heavy, square raindrops. Cans. The life raft was equipped with emergency provisions, canned water, packaged food, all of which were now spilling out over the ocean floor as the boat rose.

They would be rescued soon. They would not drift long. But they might. A day maybe. They would need water. He should collect some of the cans. It was hard to think. Where would he find a sack? Alex tried to picture the layout of the *Goose*. Everything on deck would have floated away. He pulled himself along the railing, but found only twisted wreckage. Frantically, he tried to think, strafing the area with the tiny light, looking for anything. There! There was something. A big piece of cloth was snagged up by the bow. Alex swam over and pulled it. It was caught on something. He tugged harder. A mangled sheet of metal gave way, and Martha's dead body floated toward him. The cloth was her pink robe.

Alex jerked away in horror. He took a deep breath and swallowed the bile that had leaped to the back of his throat. There had to be something else. But what? Desperately, Alex searched for a bucket, a plastic bag, anything, but found nothing. What else could he do. Alex pulled the robe off Martha's dead body, carefully slipping each arm through the fabric. He buttoned up the front of the robe, tied the sleeves together and fashioned a knot in the neck end, then began salvaging the cans of water.

Soon the pink silk sack was bulging with seven cans of water and a few silver packets of food. He was searching the bottom with the little light, looking for more, when his breaths started coming harder. He did not need to look at the gauge to know he was low on air.

The sack was heavy, probably ten pounds. Sixty feet down, without a BC, it was all he could do to get off the bottom. Up into the black water, Alex kicked hard, draining every muscle. His legs began to cramp with the strain. He could not even tell if he was ascending. His lungs worked to pull the last breaths from the tank. Finally, he felt the slight shift in pressure and knew he was near the surface. The air stopped. Alex closed his eyes and summoned every last once of strength and broke out into the night air.

Jack and Annalee had climbed into the life raft, and were dragging Peter with them. They had drifted probably twenty feet. It might well have been twenty miles. Alex gasped a breath and struggled to stay afloat, but the weight of the cans dragged him down. His fingers dug into the nightgown, and suddenly he thought of Chicago, of them being old together, as old as Shep and Martha. He pulled himself up, gulped at the air, but felt the weight pulling him down again. No, it couldn't happen. Chicago hated nightgowns. She hated pink. She would never wear a pink robe. He would never see her again.

As he sank, Alex saw Chicago standing on the deck of the boat in a filmy pink nightgown. She called out to him, reached a hand for him. There was a splash. She was coming for him. The hand caught hold of his arm, pulling him to the surface.

"I got him! I got him!" Jack treaded water, holding Alex's head above water as Annalee tried to paddle closer.

# THIRTY-SIX

Chicago scanned the horizon through the binoculars. She should have seen them by now. Hell, according to the coordinates, she should be right on top of them. She scrambled back to the cockpit, swung down into the salon, and checked the GPS again. The readings were good. She was where she should be. Where was the *Golden Goose*? She picked up the radio again. *"Golden Goose, Golden Goose, Tassia Far."* Nothing. *"Golden Goose,* this is *Tassia Far."*

Could she have written down the wrong coordinates? Even so, she should be able to see the anchored boat. She walked around the deck, a nervous clench taking hold in her gut. She went out to the end of the bowsprit and stood with one foot on each rail, holding on to the halyard. The wind had died a little and the genoa was beginning to flap. There was nothing here. The water was calm, flat, shimmering in the afternoon sun.

Shimmering strangely, she realized. Chicago ran to the side and looked down at the water. All around were rainbow puddles floating on the water. She was sailing through a spreading pond of diesel fuel.

She dashed back to the cockpit, grabbed up the winch handle, and cranked in the sails. Her hands were shaking as she pushed the anchor over. "Oh, please God, please," she whispered, always slightly uneasy at beseeching divinity in times of trouble, when she basically ignored it the rest of the time. She tossed her mask and fins into the zodiac. Maybe it wasn't so bad since the prayer was for someone else. Many others, in fact. "Please, God, don't let me find this."

She yanked the starter cord three times and nearly flooded the motor, but finally she had the outboard running. She steered out into the oily path. Down here she could smell the diesel, a sickening stench. She steered out of the filmy trail into clear water, put on her mask, leaned over the edge, and looked underwater. Nothing. The water was pretty clear; she could easily see the bottom. She twisted the throttle and moved on, stopped, looked again.

For twenty minutes she puttered back and forth like this, trying to fan a faint hope, trying to imagine what else could have happened. But Chicago had seen enough of life's cruel fates, and when the time came when she put her face mask in the water and saw the *Golden Goose*, so freshly killed it seemed almost in pain, there was little surprise.

# THIRTY-SEVEN

Annalee turned over and leaned on the pontoon.

"Are you getting seasick, Mizzy?" Jack touched her tenderly on the back of her shirt. It was damp with sweat.

"It's just hot."

"Move over here, honey, I think the shade is getting longer." The life raft was designed with a canopy, to make it essentially a floating bubble, but the canvas roof had torn in the struggle to free it, leaving only patches of shelter from the sun.

"Here, drink some water." She shook her head. "There's plenty."

"We're getting blown out to sea." She turned and looked from her father to Alex, challenging them to contradict. "I looked at the compass."

"The wind will die down. The noon forecast yesterday said one to two knots, and southerly, honey. That blows us right into the Turks and Caicos. And there are plenty of boats around to find us. We'll be rescued in no time."

Annalee turned her questioning gaze back to Alex, looking to him for the truth her father was shading, hoping he wouldn't give it to her. It was five o'clock and the sun was starting to lose its intensity. They had been drifting for at least eighteen hours; Alex wasn't sure what time the chaos had started last night.

"Chicago knows exactly where the *Goose* was anchored," he offered. "She's probably there already."

"She won't know what happened. She might think we just left."

"She's pretty smart."

"She might think we're all dead."

"I don't think I can get away that easily." Alex smiled.

136

Annalee looked skeptical. Peter McGuire was still unconscious, lying diagonally in the bottom of the raft. His pupils were reacting to light, which was a good sign as far as the head injury, but there was a growing distention in one side of his abdomen, and Alex suspected there was some internal bleeding. He had been almost directly over the center of the explosion.

"If we had a bottle we could write a letter to Mom. No one might find it for years, but someday maybe they would, and she would at least know . . . you know, like we said goodbye and all."

Jack felt sick inside, a rotten sinking pain. "Honey, we don't need to write her a letter. We'll be home in a few days. Someone will find us."

"She thinks I don't like her very much." Annalee's voice was trembling, and her brown eyes welled up with tears. "I really do though."

"Of course you do." He pulled his daughter into his arms and hugged her as she sobbed. "She knows you love her. She just doesn't always understand you, that's all."

Why had he brought her? Why hadn't he thought more about the danger? He should have thought something might happen!

From the moment she was born he had done everything wrong. She rolled off the bed when he was changing her diaper. She choked on a grape when he should have known to break it in half. He had forgotten all the baby things in the eight years between the last child and this one.

It was a bitter flood of guilt that soured his heart now, a dark wash of parental failure as he stroked her tangled hair. He shut the car door on her fingers, led her through poison ivy, left a cufflink where she could swallow it. He once used her party dress to open the cap on an overheated radiator. He thought it was a rag. He did not shake it out and see the ruffles. It was in the backseat, on the floor, fallen there, he later learned, out of April's bag. She was meaning to take it over to her mother's to use the sewing machine to mend a torn sleeve but didn't have time that day, and had left it in the car so she wouldn't forget it . . . God, children were so complicated.

He could not even rescue her goldfish. They were cleaning the bowl and the stupid fish wiggled out of the net, flopped and slipped on the porcelain, its eyes bulging. Annalee had screamed

in his ears, her small hands grabbing at the fish, about to topple
the chair she stood on. Jack had reached for the fish, for his
daughter's balance, feeling the tiny scratch of her nails on his
hands, watching the stupid fish, its gills flapping, cold and slimy,
leaping through his clumsy fingers down the drain. Gone, all gone.
Wittingly or not, he was a horrible father, a stupid, bumbling
helpless man. His eyes felt hot with tears and he gulped a breath
of air.

Annalee finally pushed away, the crying over, her composure
regained—or the pain shut away, Jack couldn't tell which.

"Do you think Shep and Marty's bodies were eaten by sharks?"
she asked. Jack gave Alex a quick look of desperation. Alex did
not have any consoling words to offer. He remembered Martha's
body, trapped in the wreckage, the pink robe flowing around her.
Pink silk. The extravagance of it. No one wore silk on a boat,
except this elderly woman still so in love with her husband.

"What do you think, honey?" Jack spoke in a calm, steady
voice.

"Probably."

"Well, I don't think they suffered."

"No. I saw it when Martha got shot. It was fast. What do we
do if Uncle Peter dies?"

"He won't die, sweetheart," Jack said quickly. Though his
voice was steady, Alex saw a sort of panic in his eyes. "He's
strong. He's very healthy."

"I think it would be kind of cool to be eaten by sharks," she
continued in a small, flat voice. "I mean if you're dead anyway.
Something's going to eat you."

"No one is going to die, honey."

"Sharks or worms. Sharks are better."

"We're going to be rescued soon. They'll send a helicopter and
take Peter to a hospital."

"Were you in the war?" Annalee asked, switching subjects
again, staring at Alex's scars. "In Vietnam?"

"Yes," he answered, though the scars had not come from there.
"For a little while, near the very end."

"We studied it in history last year." She gazed beyond him
now, out over the still sea and the endless empty sky. "Did you
ever think you were going to die?"

"Not really. Not then."

"Mizzy . . ." Jack chastised her. She turned away, resting her pointed chin on her arms on the pontoon.

"I'm just asking."

# THIRTY-EIGHT

"Mayday, Mayday, Mayday, this is the *Tassia Far*—location twelve miles south-southeast of Mayaguana—reporting a sunken vessel—possible survivors. Over." Chicago waited for an acknowledgment of her distress call. In all her years at sea, she had never had to make this call. Her voice was steady, though the microphone shook in her hand.

"*Tassia Far, Tassia Far*, this is RBDF. Received Mayday—sunken vessel possible survivors. Request exact position."

Chicago had already thought about this. Giving an exact position would alert every local with a boat and a scuba tank to speed out for salvage on the *Golden Goose*. It would also lay the *Christiania* wide open to plunder. An exact position wouldn't help the search effort, either, since they would have been drifting for at least twelve hours.

"No exact coordinates at this time," she said steadily, then gave an approximate longitude and latitude. "Requesting status on EPIRB signal—request search alert for possible survivors." The Emergency Position Indicator Radio Beacon was required safety equipment, and she knew the *Golden Goose* carried one. It should have floated free as the boat sank, its signaling device triggered by the water. Its signals should have been picked up by satellite. Perhaps the explosion had crippled it.

The officer at the Royal Bahamian Defense Force repeated her location and reported that no beacon signals had been received. Chicago's optimism took a free-fall.

"*Tassia Far*—has a life raft been deployed?"

"Life raft status unknown," she explained. "I'm about to dive and find out, though." RBDF promised to alert the US Coast Guard in Puerto Rico, and to issue a watch order for the entire Caicos passage east of the wreck site. Chicago promised to radio again after her dive with more information. As long as there was something to do, some action to take, she could hold all emotion at bay.

Her hands shook as she screwed the regulator valve on the tank. *Let me not find a life raft. Let me not find any bodies.* She pulled on her wet suit and buckled on her weight belt. She clipped one high-powered underwater light to a buckle on her BC and slipped the lanyard of another over her wrist. She barely had enough spit to defog her mask.

The sun was low, casting a peaceful golden path over the sea as she slipped in and dropped beneath the still surface. The *Golden Goose* lay almost upright, tilted to starboard. It rested almost squarely in the middle of the excavation grid, and Chicago could see the exposed timbers of the long-sunken *Christiania* resting alongside, like some cruel shadow. From a distance, the *Goose* looked like a child's toy, a toy that had received some rough play. A jagged hole, eight or ten feet in diameter, was ripped across the bow.

Everything on deck that had been loose had long since drifted away, but there were bits of tangled debris, a windbreaker, a length of rope, still waving in the slight current. A rescue ring had come uncoiled and had drifted up thirty or forty feet, where it waved in the current like a child's balloon. It seemed pathetically hopeful. The diesel fuel was just a trickle by now, a thin oily column rising to the sky.

There was a school of yellow-striped grunts swarming around the bow, industriously picking away at something. Chicago took a deep breath and swam over, steeled at what she might find. It was unlikely they were feasting off the ship's larder.

With the sixty-foot depth and the sun so low, she needed the flashlight to see much beyond shapes. She switched it on and waved the beam over the scene. The grunts darted away as she swam closer. There was a bicycle still strapped to the bow rail, and clinging to the gears and pedals were a few shards of fabric, denim and pink silk.

Something small and white caught her eye. The grunts, bolder now, had swarmed back around it, and she had to wave her hand to shoo them away. It took her a minute to realize what she was looking at. Flesh and bone. Pale streamers of shredded flesh clung to part of a rib cage.

She felt nothing at first. There was a curious aseptic quality to the remains, a bloodless purity, unreal and disarming. It was horrifying, but she had to quell a flicker of joy, too, for it was not a man's body. This body had been wearing something pink, a nightgown maybe. The girl or Martha. How horrible to have to choose who she hoped was dead! But that was stupid. Choosing wouldn't change things now.

She strafed the sand nearby with the light and saw another piece of bone, a human jaw, with fine even little teeth, two fillings. It was not Alex. She began to shake. No time for feelings yet, she had to search the rest of the boat. Slowly, methodically, she swam up around the bow and down the other side. A small green swimsuit was still looped around the railing on the starboard side, waving like a merry flag in the slight current. What was the young girl's name? Ann something. Alex would have tried hard to save a child.

She reached the stern and stopped. Even without the flashlight, she could see what she had hoped to find. Mounted to the deck near the stern was a frame for a life raft. Empty. She closed her eyes, and tried to suppress the quake in her chest. The life raft was gone, but that didn't mean there had been anybody in it.

Chicago checked her air and the time and found she had plenty of both left. She pushed open the cabin door. Once inside, she pulled off her fins and wedged them securely beneath the chart table. It was dark inside the sunken boat, and she took a few seconds to remember the layout, then began a quick survey of the main salon, checking first for alternate escape routes.

A wrecked ship, especially one sunken so recently, could be very unstable. The *Goose* seemed to be securely settled on the bottom, but there was no way to be sure. Her weight in the wrong place could upset the balance. Exhaled bubbles could gather in one place, forming enough of an air pocket to cause lift and some dangerous shifting. But there were windows on each side of the salon big enough to escape through, and, of course, the huge rip in the hull would serve as an exit as well.

Still, she moved carefully. The darkness and potential for gruesome discovery was enough to make her stomach churn. She opened door after door, searching each cabin, the galley, the heads. The water was full of debris, books, clothing, cans of food, and she had to move carefully. Finally, she came to the last door, the bow cabin. She turned the handle and pushed the wooden door with her foot. Her flashlight was failing, and this was the darkest part of the wreck. As she reached for the backup, Chicago felt something soft and fleshy brush past her neck.

She screamed and a burst of bubbles escaped, clouding her vision. Then she ducked and flailed her arm. The flashlight crashed against something and went out. Once again she felt the spongy flesh. It was smooth and warm, an arm or leg? Or more horrible. Her scuba tank banged against something. It was black in the cabin, with unseen objects bumping all around her. Chicago forced herself to be calm, grabbed hold of the backup light. There. Still shaking, she turned on the good light and slowly, mustering all the courage she could, aimed the beam in the direction of the fleshy object.

At first she saw nothing. The water in there was murky. Sheets billowed up like parachutes, and cabinet doors hung open. Carefully, she reached behind her, feeling for the doorway, no longer caring to see what touched her, only wanting to escape. Alex wouldn't have been sleeping here—too claustrophobic. She found the door, and slowly backed through it. Then at the edge of her light, she saw it again, something moving.

Long, sinuous, green. She almost laughed with relief. It was only a moray eel. Of course, had she not been thinking about dead bodies she would have recognized its touch. It had probably come scavenging like the rest of the creatures, and found this dark labyrinth to its liking. She cast the light full on its face, and saw that her relief was premature. Hanging from the eel's mouth, held fast in its strong jaws and needle-sharp teeth, was most of a human hand.

She began to gag, and tried hard to control it. She took a deep breath, swallowed hard, and worked her way back out of the boat's interior. Chicago held on to the roof of the boat and waited for her heart to slow down. An eagle ray swam slowly across the bottom, its spotted "wings" flying gracefully. A school of vivid blue chromis darted around a chunk of coral, all turning in unison, like a blue-suited marching band. Twilight underwater is a beautiful time, with subtle shiftings of light. Cautious night creatures were starting to emerge, while the daytime fish began to retreat to the safety of the reef.

But right now it seemed indecent, almost a sacrilege, for any beauty to exist in this place. A pair of huge angelfish swam by, exploring for a possible home in a nook which was once a hutch in the galley. With emotionless practicality, the sea was already beginning to claim the wrecked boat.

What should she do about the bones? She couldn't bear to have them aboard the *Tassia Far*, but didn't want to leave them scattered like this. As the water began to darken, she finally decided to gather up what she could find, and secure them inside one of the storage holds. She pulled a mesh bag from her BC pocket and swam back to the bow, where by the deepening blue light, she began to collect the remains of the dead.

# *THIRTY-NINE*

The sun set with a scarlet flourish, a spectacular display, brash and flouncy as a dance hall girl. Alex, Jack, and Annalee watched silently, the generous display a soothing balm. After the last of the color faded away, they passed around a can of water. The provisions Alex had managed to salvage, weighty as they were at the time, were meager. Seven cans of water, and four foil-wrapped bricks of unidentified food substance. They had shared one that afternoon, and now, with great fanfare, Jack unwrapped another.

"Ze specialty of ze house—Le château flambé crepe de chapeau de la ... eh ... *Chien!*" he declared as he spread the gray brick out on its foil wrapper. "Our chef has meant to prepare ze special sauce from ze very expensive truffles, but we were ... ah ... afraid to let ze pig dig under ze raft ..."

His antics were so funny that even the morose Annalee laughed out loud. The light mood lasted until the last of the light faded.

The life raft felt smaller every hour, as if the ocean were compressing it. Peter still had not regained consciousness, and no longer even moved. His breathing was shallow, his color bad. They tried to get water into him, drop by drop, but Alex knew this was futile. At this point, he was hoping simply for a chance at a decent burial. They certainly couldn't keep a dead body here for very long, and he knew that despite Annalee's casual talk about getting eaten by sharks or bugs, she was a sensitive child. She had a vivid imagination, and did not need to carry around for life the image of her beloved uncle being devoured at sea.

The sun had dried them out pretty well, so aside from being a little salt-crusty, they were all fairly comfortable. Certainly, by morning, they would see the rescue planes.

# *FORTY*

Dunagh woke suddenly, panicked and disoriented and horribly thirsty. He tried to get up but was stopped by a searing pain in his shoulder. He fell back on the bed and took a few deep breaths, waiting for consciousness to fully bloom. Outside the hotel-room window, the sky was a deep turquoise. Dawn, or twilight—he wasn't sure which. Quickly the events began to come back to him.

There were two gunshot wounds, one a graze on his side, one clean through his shoulder. He had lost some blood, but not too much. It had been a rough ninety minutes getting back. The spear wound on his thigh was nasty, but he had scrubbed everything out thoroughly, biting a washcloth against the pain. He felt the bandages. They were dry. Slowly, he sat up. A little dizzy. He reached for the water bottle and took a few deep swallows. It was sunset, he realized; he had slept away the day, certainly aided by the now-empty bottle of rum on the floor.

But everything had gone okay. Well, mostly okay. Why hadn't they found out the damn archaeologist had come early? That was a stupid mistake, no need for so many dead. But it couldn't be helped.

He dressed slowly. What time was it? Were the phones working yet? He had to call Scotland. McKay should already be here, or on his way. So many details. First . . . no, first he would find out if there was any talk of the explosion last night. No one should know for a couple of days at least, but there was always the chance a boat passing in the distance might have heard and reported something. He went downstairs, across the street to the bar.

"Hey, Sam—what's up. Anything edible tonight?"

"Fish," the bartender replied as he always did. His family owned two fishing boats. "Conch fritter." They also had no compunction about using scuba to illegally pick up conch.

"Okay then." Dunagh smiled. "How 'bout some fish and some conch. And a Red Stripe." The man set the beer down and gave him a glass. Because he was still convinced that Dunagh was a rich land developer, interested in building a resort on the island, the glass was clean.

"So anything new around here?"

"Besides the boat sinkin'?"

"What boat?" Dunagh poured the beer slowly into the glass.

"Dat treasure boat been out da far reef couple a' week now. Mayday call just come on da radio."

Dunagh controlled his surprise. A mayday call? Who the hell . . .

"So the people on board were okay?" he said casually. "I guess they had to be to radio in, huh?"

Sam shook his head and polished a knife and fork. "Was two boat out dere," he explained. "One left from da storm, just come back an' find the *Golden Goose* gone. It sunk on the bottom. She call."

"Shit. No kidding. So what do they think—someone after the treasure or something?"

Sam shrugged and went to pick up the plate of Conch fritters.

"But the people on board—they got off?"

"Don't know. She say the life raft gone. They start a search come daylight."

"Bloody hell. That would be rotten, eh? Floating around in a life raft." He'd have to move fast now. It wasn't a serious setback, but it did put a crimp in things. He needed McKay in Provo soon. They would need to hire a boat, a plane . . . It had been difficult to arrange things from here, what with Teneby always hanging around and so little time, but it could all still go smoothly.

"Are the phones working yet?"

"I tink so, yah. Where you friend tonight?" Sam asked.

"Oh, he wasn't feeling too well." Dunagh smiled. "Just a little bug. Be up in a day or so I'm sure."

# *FORTY-ONE*

By the time they reached the standing stones, Cory MacClannon was sweating heavily, and Neil Swinny was beginning to wonder at what point he should have stopped toasting last night in order to feel just a little less like death's practice dummy today.

"Well, too bad I didn't turn out to be king of Siam or someplace where they carry you around in one of those chairs . . . what do ye call 'em . . ." He laughed and mopped his forehead with a very ordinary cotton handkerchief. "Though I remember precious little of it, I suppose the birthday must have been for real, because I'm feeling old today." He leaned his gun against one of the stones and sat next to it.

The ground was still wet with morning dew. Swinny rested himself on another slab of stone, a long flat rock that once topped two others to form a portico. It was one of the hundreds of remnants of those ancient druid circles that dotted the countryside of England and Scotland. This was a small and undramatic circle, a distant relation to Stonehenge, a country chapel to its cathedral status. MacClannon had found it years after he bought the estate, and only then because a deer had led him there.

They were after birds today, pheasants and grouse, though neither MacClannon or Swinny was much of a hunter. They liked to tromp the Highlands, and if something presented itself to be shot for supper, why, so much the better—and if not, well, there was always something in the freezer at home.

"So what shall we do about it now, Cor? Have you giv'n it any thought?"

"Do? Do about what?"

"About you being king, of course, what do ye think?"

"Oh, blow off. It was good for a bit of fun last night, 'at's all."

"Cory, it's the truth. You saw the evidence!"

"I heard a bit of a tale."

"There's more."

"Oh, baghhhh!"

"Where did the Clan MacClannons arise from, tell me. Who's your ancestor?"

"Edward Stewart MacClannon—"

"—Who was born in the colony of Jamaica, to James Francis Edward Stuart, true son of King James the second."

"Swinny old boy, has your missus got you watching one of those shows, those eh—miniseries on the telly lately?" MacClannon smiled, then reached in his jacket pocket and pulled out the flask. He took a small swig and handed it to his friend.

"Is that someone coming?" He squinted into the distance and saw two figures approaching.

"Aye," Swinny answered without looking. The men walked purposefully, carrying shotguns but not looking for birds.

"Someone you know?"

"Party members, Cory. We've asked you to a meeting."

"Have you now?" Gray clouds rolled over the hills and a light wind ruffled the heather.

"I know most of the Party an' I don't know these lads," MacClannon said quietly as the pair got closer.

"Ye won't know them, Cory. Sit down now and listen to wha' we have to tell ye."

It was a fantastic tale, not told as well as MacClannon might have shaped it, but riveting nonetheless. A tale about how three hundreds years before, a few survivors from the Glencoe massacre had escaped through the snow into the hills, about how they formed a band and vowed revenge.

They joined with other Scots still loyal to King James. Over the years, their hatred of the English flourished, and with good cause. Scottish ships were denied rights to English ports, tariffs were levied, property taken. On and on, the injustices mounted. Opposition to the English peaked when King William left thousands of Scottish settlers to die in Panama.

"Things began to really boil after King James died," the one man explained. Neither of the two had given his identity. This one was a tall thin, dark-haired Highlander, whose speech marked him from the far north. The other was of a stronger build, red-haired and heavily freckled, with a fisherman's hands, and watery blue eyes.

"The Jacobites had kept in contact with the exiled king," the thin man continued. "And were working to restore him to the throne."

"It was the strength of the Jacobites that finally proved our downfall," explained the red-haired man. "For the English were frightened, and so offered concessions. England was at war with France, and did not want to fight Scotland as well."

"We were sold out," the thin man summed it up. "But not all of Scotland agreed," he said bitterly. "Not the Jacobites. Not then and not ever after."

"My friends, you know *I'm* no friend of the English," Mac-Clannon offered lightly. "And I work to see the day we're rid of them, but this . . ." He almost laughed, but didn't. These men were not only serious, there was a touch of the sinister about them. "I don't see as we need an old grudge to validate our cause. What does it matter who should have been king three hundred years ago?"

"Because the Hanovers established a dynasty that has held

power since then. A dynasty that was rightfully the Stuarts. And they grew rich because of it."

"Well, fine then, let the however many great-grandsons of the Stuarts sort it out." MacClannon was feeling testy. He had walked far over the moor and his legs ached from the sitting.

"But that is exactly what we are trying to tell you, sir. You are that many times great-grandson."

"And the rightful king of England."

"Well, fine," Cory stood and picked up his gun. "I'll just go ring up the queen and challenge her to a duel."

The two strangers scowled, and Swinny gave them an apologetic look. He knew this wasn't the way to approach MacClannon, but they had insisted. He knew his friend, devoted as he was to the SNP, had little tolerance for zealots.

"Look, Cory, you yourself have heard the stories that the true prince was switched and hidden away."

"Yes, and I've heard tales of Nessie and other Ferlies."

"You know our history man," the thin Highlander spoke now.

"What is it you want me to do?" MacClannon asked with a touch of exasperation.

"To claim the throne, of course, restore the royal fortunes to those from whom they were plundered, and then to cede our country back," the thin man answered passionately.

"But in the meantime," the red-haired man smiled, "we simply need money. Our man called from the island early this morning. We're ready to move. We need to hire a boat to recover the coffin, and a plane to fly it home."

"The damned coffin again. I just can't believe it, lads."

"The MI5 believe it!"

"How do ye know that?"

"They sent a team to blow it up! That's how much they believe it."

"Only we had one of our men along. He changed their plans."

"Changed how?"

"He—diverted the explosion."

"Christ almighty—what are ye tell'n me?"

"You don't have to know the details, Cory. Just give us the money we need to bring the king's body home."

"How much."

"Fifty thousand."

"Fifty! You're mad. Even the king can fly commercial."

"We need to get it out of there fast," the shorter man explained. "If the English get a hold of it, you can be sure we'll never see it again, and no truth will come of it."

"What say, Cory?" Swinny pressed.

MacClannon felt confusion as he had never known before. There were practical concerns of legality. He did not trust these men, these Jacobites. What did that mean, "divert the explosion?"

"What's your place in all this, Swinny? Are you telling me you're one of these Jacobites?"

"Aye. And me father before me, and his before that. There's more than a few in the Party."

"God in heaven! Don't you realize what something like this could do to discredit us all? For the first time in a century the SNP is starting to amass real political power and be taken seriously, and now you come out with a damned secret brotherhood, smuggling out coffins. It's daft!" He picked himself up and strode off across the moor. "I won't be a part of it. And I won't let it ruin the Party!"

With that, MacClannon turned his back on the men and strode off alone. He and Swinny had driven around in the Range Rover and come in from a shorter way, but it was only three miles back if he cut across the glen. He was glad for the hike, and by the time he reached Inishail, he had settled his thoughts. A secret organization within the SNP could not be tolerated. He would ring up the leadership and they would decide what to do about this. At the very least, they had to distance themselves, clearly and immediately.

"Maggie? Maggie, are you home?" he called as he walked through the kitchen door.

"She's taken the kiddies to the barn," Birdy explained as she hurried in. "Aeowulf's having pups. And there's a message come for you." She handed him a heavy, cream-colored envelope. "A chap delivered it in person. You see where it's from . . ." The envelope bore the royal crest and the seal of Balmoral Castle.

"Hmmmmm." MacClannon frowned as he read the card inside.

"Come on—tell!" she leaned over his shoulder.

"It's nothing dear, just the prince of Wales asking me to tea."

"Just you? How rude. Oh, well, I'd lots rather go watch the pups anyway, and I didn't bring a thing to wear. When's it for?"

"This afternoon," He glanced at his watch. "Half-three."

"Awfully sudden. Does he say what for?"

MacClannon slipped the note back into the creamy envelope. "Probably wants to tell me happy birthday and bugger off."

# FORTY-TWO

"We don't know when Mary Beatrice first told anyone about the switch, or who she told." Jack's voice was hoarse by now, his mouth dry. It seemed a little absurd, to be discussing English history while bobbing around in the middle of a vast ocean, but it helped pass the empty hours.

"There is evidence of contact from Jacobite sources over the next decade, but as I said, nothing definite. There were lots of Scots all over the New World by then. My guess is that the story of the switch and the identity of the prince became more of an open secret. It seems likely that they would have tried to return him to England in 1702 when King William died, but obviously it didn't happen. We don't know why. Certainly the false Prince Edward, if he knew about his situation, eventually may have had some play in matters. It had to be terribly complicated."

It was late morning of the second day and the sun was already hammering down on the life raft. They had passed a comfortable night, and a visiting school of dolphins had put everyone in a good mood, but the prospects of another long day were beginning to have a sobering effect. Peter still had not regained consciousness, and though they talked optimistically, it was clear that his condition seemed worse. His color was bad, his breathing shallow and slow. Alex and Jack had taken turns sitting awake with him all night, dripping water, drop by drop, into his mouth, but there was no response. No sign of rescue, either. They had seen no other boats, and heard only once the drone of an airplane far above the clouds.

Sit in the lifeguard chair of an olympic-size pool and try to spy a daisy petal floating on the surface. That, Alex knew, was the challenge facing a search plane as it scours its territory. The pilot would be looking down on a vast expanse of blue, straining to see a fleck of orange.

"When you say they were planning an uprising, are we talking about armies storming the gates here? An actual war for the throne?" Alex asked.

"Possibly, though a good show of force may have been enough."

"But if they did go to war, they also were hoping that the real prince would turn out to be less of a wussy than the one they had on hand," Annalee commented.

"Don't be mean, Mizzy," Jack reprimanded. "He was hardly a wussy. Made a few brave efforts, as a matter of fact, to regain the throne. He just seems to have been a bit of a dud personality wise. This Edward was a somber, brooding fellow. They called him Old Mr. Melancholy. At any rate, by 1714 the Jacobite cause had weakened. The Highland clans were still pretty rebellious, but the lowlanders were learning to live with England, and even profit by the union. If they were to be roused up out of their complacency, a more inspiring leader had to be found."

*April 1714*

"*It is our last chance.*"

"*It is preposterous. After all this time. You have no idea what the man is even like.*"

"*How can he be worse?*"

"*How, indeed. He could wonder each morning which side of his bread to butter . . .*

"*Or whether, indeed, to have bread, or a roll, or a pastry . . .*"

"*. . . Or porridge maybe.*"

"*Porridge? With cream? Or . . . or . . . no . . . with honey?*"

*The men erupted in bitter laughter until John Erskine's silent scowl brought them back to the business at hand.*

*"If we cannot return the true prince we must be ready to swear alleigence to the one at hand," he reminded them. "Imperfect as he may be, this is, most likely, the last chance to restore the House of Stuart."*

*"And to save our heads," Harley added grimly. All the men knew that even if their planned uprising never came about, they would be considered traitors merely for discussing it. At this stage, if the plot failed, the best they could hope for would be a brief stay in the Tower of London, and a deft stroke at the end.*

*They had begun to plan a year ago, first just Erskine and the Viscount, then the others; Simon Fraser, the duke of Ormonde, and finally Robert Harley first earl of Oxford. They were powerful men and they commanded supporters in Scotland and England alike, all steadfastly allied in support of the deposed Stuart king.*

*"How much longer would you give her, Harley?" the duke asked. "I've heard she doesn't leave her bed there days."*

*Though official reports from the palace continued to speak of the Queen's good health, it was widely rumored that Queen Anne, after a twelve-year reign, was on her deathbed.*

*"A few weeks, a few months—who can tell?"*

*"All the more reason we must act quickly," Erskine reminded them. "She may yet name Edward . . ."*

*"She will never . . ."*

*"He is her half brother!"*

*"And she has spoken privately of reconciliation."*

*"She can't name him," Harley pointed out. "Even if she wanted to. To recognize Edward as rightful king now would spurn her sister's legacy. You cannot say on the one hand that William and Mary were right to take the throne, then on the other that now we will let the banished one rule. When Queen Anne dies, George of Hanover will be named the successor by virtue of the Act of Settlement."*

*"But everyone knows that Edward has a far more legitimate claim."*

*"If he would renounce the pope, perhaps," Harley muttered. "Right now the average Englishman sees it as a choice between*

*the German or the Pope. At least with George, the peers will retain some control.''*

*"Will he renounce?'' Fraser asked.*

*The men all looked to Erskine for the answer. He was the only one close to the exiled court in France. It was to him, three years ago, that Mary Beatrice had confessed the switch, and with him she had pled for her true son's return. He, in turn, had begged her to persuade the prince to convert, or at least to quiet their Catholic zeal, but she had refused. "Then issue a decree renouncing any church interference with matters of state,'' he had begged. "Convince your people that England will not be ruled from Rome, and I will return your son to the throne.'' She had refused.*

*"He will not renounce,'' Erskine reported with a terseness that told the others that further discussion would be useless. "Which is another reason for us to approach the true son now. He has grown up free from the pernicious influence of the Catholic French.''*

*"So you think he would convert?''*

*"More likely than the impostor, if he hasn't already. At any rate, we must strike while the iron is hot! If we are to restore the Stuarts, and hold our power, we must take this chance now. We have good sums promised from the Jacobite supporters. There is a ship that sails in two days for Jamaica. If all agree here today, one of our men will be on that ship, bearing letters for the true prince, and monies for hire of a schooner to bring him back. With all well and fair weather, the true prince could be home as early as August.''*

*"If Queen Anne holds out that long, we may have a chance.''*

*"Do you really think he could do it, sir? He will know nothing of the court, none of his supporters.''*

*"Exactly!'' Erskine's eyes shone. "Mary's true son, switched in the cradle and raised across the sea, will be free of all his prejudices and allegiances. Free from the influence of the French court, and from those whose interests . . . differ from our own.''*

*While each man there believed his actions were for justice and the good of England, it was a simpler and more parochial interest that really compelled them to this drastic action. With George of Hanover on the throne, they lost power. With the Stuarts, they prospered. With the true James Edward, a young man of twenty-*

*six raised in the primitive backwaters of the Colonies, they would have a puppet and they would flourish.*

"But wait a minute," Alex objected. "These are grown men now, not babies. Certainly people could tell the difference."

"Those close to him could, of course, but remember he had been in France all these years, and there were no photos back then."

"*Paintings* then. He was a prince, he would have had a portrait done."

"A romanticized painting," Jack reminded him.

"They all look alike," Annalee said. "We looked at thousands of paintings, and when they're in wigs and stuff, you can't hardly tell one guy from another. They all had the same lips." She puckered her lips a little, trying to simulate the full cupid's-bow shape that had been favored by the eighteenth-century portraitists.

"Okay, so the Jacobites go to Jamaica to return the prince in time for this uprising, and hire the *Christiania* for the voyage."

"Right."

"With the pirate Henry Avery at the helm?" Alex asked skeptically.

Jack smiled and shrugged. "Hey, winter in Wisconsin is long, cold, and dark. Don't begrudge us our imaginations. But why not? Avery seems to have retired from piracy in the early 1700's and not a lot is known about his later years. Jacobites were outlaws anyway, they would have got on easily with a buccaneer."

"So these Jacobites hire Avery to carry the real prince and his new family back to England, only James Edward had died."

"He was swimming and the waves were strong," Annalee said sadly. "The waves tumbled him into some coral, and he cut his leg. They didn't know about coral cuts back then, how easy they get infected, so the little wound just got worse and worse. His whole leg swelled up and he got gangrene." Annalee shifted into the slight patch of shade that remained from the tattered canopy and went on with the story.

*For a week Edward lay delirious, writhing with pain and burning with fever. Two slave boys stood by his bedside night and day, fanning away the flies and trying to cool his sweats. English doc-*

*tors could do nothing. The infection had spread so rapidly that even amputation would not contain it now.*

*In desperation, Catherine had asked one of the house slaves for advice. The natives were always playing in the water, surely they must suffer cuts. What did they do? A plant perhaps? Catherine stared into the thick tropical fringe beyond the sugarcane fields and imagined that somewhere in that steamy woods was the magic plant that would save her husband. But the slaves offered no cure. Most were as recently arrived as the English, and the plants of Jamaica were different than those of Africa. Finally they did find a fisherman who knew how to treat a coral cut, but it was too late.*

*"You maast cot first 'ting when it hopp'n," he explained sadly, demonstrating how they would use a knife on the wound. "Scrape an' scrape de poison. But now too long time pass . . ."*

*But Edward was liked in the slave community, and as news of his illness spread, they came one by one, secretly leaving charms at the door of his room. Catherine would come in to find a small bundle of leaves tied with blue thread, or a scrap of cloth burned around the edges. A little pouch of ashes and stones, a string of shells. Sacrilege, all of them, demon worship, but the Christian god was not showing any favor, so she kept the heathen charms.*

*An English indigo merchant suggested moldy bread. The minister brought a milk poultice. A ship captain insisted that a brew of cloves and pepper would drive out the poison, while another insisted the wounds be bathed in urine.*

*Catherine sat on the veranda, watching the baby who was just beginning to pull himself up and try to stand. He looked at her, wobbling like a drunken sailor and crowing his delight, and fresh tears began to flow. He would never know his father. How could she tell him what a good man he was, how handsome, how strong. How could she explain the expressions she knew so well, the passions of his heart, the reach of his mind, the way he made her laugh. Her thoughts were disturbed by the sound of carriage wheels, and she looked up to see Genevieve's team trotting up the gravel path. There was a man in the seat with her, a stranger, another doctor perhaps, maybe one who could really do something.*

*"Catherine, sweetheart, is he any better?" Genevieve kissed her flushed cheek and pressed her hands. She looked even more*

*distraught than usual. Catherine just shook her head. The baby*
*gave a squeal of joy to see his grandmother, and began to crawl*
*toward the steps. Catherine ran to catch him.*

*"This is the child?" the man asked, surprised. "Edward's*
*son?"*

*"Yes. What is it?"*

*"Nothing—his eyes—so like his grandfather's!"*

*At mention of King James, Catherine felt a chill and clutched*
*the baby tighter, looking to Genevieve for explanation.*

*"This is Sir John Morningside. He has come from England.*
*They want to bring Edward back."*

"We do know that in 1714 the Jacobites began to plan a major
uprising." The sun had passed its zenith, and the wind had picked
up, a cooling breeze but one that was blowing them farther out to
sea. They had told the story off and on all day, each elaboration
filling up the hours they would otherwise spend worrying about
their fate.

"When the Jacobite emissary got to Jamaica and found Edward
dying, he didn't know what to do." Of course, we don't know
the true nature of Edward's illness. It could have been smallpox,
malaria, or any number of tropical fevers."

"But they might be able to tell from the bones," Annalee explained. "They can tell a lot of diseases from bones now."

"Queen Anne died on August first."

"This was Mary's sister?" Alex was having a hard time keeping all these royals straight.

Jack nodded. "Right. James's younger daughter from his first
wife."

"So how was George connected to the Hanovers?"

"A distant cousin named Sophia had married him."

"He didn't even speak English!" Annalee offered.

"That's true." Jack smiled, glad the girl was still involved in
the story. "When Edward finally died, we suppose the emissary
decided that the baby son should be brought back anyway. He
was legitimate and, very important here, not a Catholic. We don't
know if Edward ever converted, but the baby had been christened
in the Anglican church. Even with the father dead, with his son
they still had a good chance to reinstate the Stuart line."

Jack shifted. They were all beginning to develop sores from sitting in the damp boat. "No doubt several Jacobites would have been particularly happy to have an infant on the throne, and their own hands on the scepter."

"But they had to bring back the father's body as well," Annalee said. "To prove that he was indeed the true prince, James Francis Edward."

"Exactly. The chain, fastened around his neck as an infant, was still intact, with the special triptych charm. We hope. The coffin was sealed and loaded on the ship—"

"Did you know that it happened a lot back then that people got buried alive?" Annalee interrupted. "They would go into a coma, but no one knew about comas, so they thought they were dead. Then they would wake up underground in a box."

"But James Edward was completely dead," Jack reminded her.

"We don't know that . . ."

"He was, Mizzy. Trust me." The girl picked up her uncle Peter's hand and began to stroke it. Jack felt a new wave of desperation at the sight.

"And there you are," he finished, his voice finally breaking. "The storm, the reef, the wreck of the *Christiania* and rescue of the baby."

"That part you know?"

"We have some good records. But honestly, I suppose we really don't know a thing."

"Well, maybe not, but someone does."

"What do you mean?"

"We aren't floating around out here by accident."

It was then that Jack noticed Annalee. The girl sat stiffly, eyes unfocused, face ashen, her thin body trembling.

"Mizzy—what's wrong?" Jack grabbed her, but the girl broke away. Then he noticed her eyes, huge and full of tears, staring past him, and he knew.

"Uncle Peter . . ." she whispered. "He's dead."

# FORTY-THREE

"Objective accomplished, Teneby injured, return delayed." The message from Dunagh did not ring true for Hayes but did not raise real suspicion, either, until much later that day, when an alert communications officer reported an interesting flag.

In addition to receiving daily reports from various posts throughout the world, the British intelligence services subscribed to several wire services and CNN. This of course provided an overwhelming amount of information, far more than any office could process: an increase in the price of butter on the Russian black market, a trained dancing bear escaped from a carnival in Greece, Bosnian Muslim leaders' plea for an end to the arms embargo, vacationing MP receiving a speeding ticket in Majorca. All the bits and snips of news, from the seemingly trivial to the obviously important, poured in twenty-four hours a day.

In order to make any sense of them, these bits were fed automatically into a computer that was programmed to flag certain words and phrases. The flagged item was then passed to human intelligence officers, who quickly decided if the information was actually of any importance. Hundreds of topics were on a standing "flag" list, but there were dozens of others that were added for a short time, usually during a particular investigation or operation. Before Teneby and Dunagh were sent off on their mission, certain key words—"Mayaguana; Bahamas; shipwreck"—had been added to the computer files as a matter of course.

Chicago's Mayday call and the subsequent alert had been reported on several of the wire services. Since so few details were known, however, it was still a minor story, reported only in a couple of South Florida newspapers, but the computer, programmed to flag "Mayaguana," noted the item.

159

"The salvage boat was sunk?" Spencer asked incredulously. He had rushed over as soon as he got the news. "Sunk? On the bottom? And your man never *mentioned* it?"

"No." Hayes handed him the little message slip with the three scanty lines. *Objective accomplished . . .*

"Have you talked to . . . whoever it is in charge over there?"

"The Royal Bahamian Defense Force is coordinating the search. Since it was a US boat, their Coast Guard is expected to assist." Hayes took a deep breath. "It appears there were seven people on board at the time of the sinking, the American archaeologist, and his daughter among them."

"Oh, my God."

Spencer knew that it wouldn't take long before the story spread. It was guaranteed intrigue. If they were very lucky, it might be a couple of days before the British news services got interested.

"You shouldn't be damaged," Hayes said grimly. "I just thought you should know what to expect over the next couple of days."

"And what should I expect?" Spencer was furious. It was utter stupidity, typical overreaction. Explosives, covert actions, why hadn't they just waited until the damn body got to the lab, if it ever got that far, and deal with it then?

"Can't tell when our papers will pick it up, or how soon after they start finding out all the rest. We've had a bit of luck already; some cruise ship is having a minor mutiny in San Juan, and it's diverting both resources and media attention.

"But there is a search under way for survivors?"

"Yes, of course, but they haven't sent anyone to the site to examine the wreckage. Seems no one has the exact location, just the general area."

"Is that really possible?"

"Not indefinitely. No. Especially if any survivors are found."

"And do we expect them to be found?" Spencer asked sarcastically.

Hayes looked at him narrowly, the implication of the remark clear.

"We are still operating on the premise that the sinking was accidental."

"Oh please, Mr. Hayes, don't play with me. You send your

agents, out there to ... to blow up the coffin, and you say this could have been an accident?''

''The action was not intended to cause anyone harm, nor would I have authorized it had there been the slightest chance of such. I suppose you don't believe it, but that is the truth. We can do our duty to the queen without drowning twelve-year-old girls.''

''Why—why would you ever have set out to blow the thing in the first place!''

''My men were unable to call for confirmation, and made a decision based on the apparent situation at the time.''

''Of course.'' Stupidity or subterfuge, authorized or not, the thing had happened, and there was no averting disaster now.

''I've told Dunagh to stay put in Mayaguana, and dispatched a senior agent to investigate. He will arrive there later today, and report back as soon as he knows anything.'' Hayes stood, removing his glasses and placing them on the desk with an air of weary resignation.

''I believe that's all then.'' Hayes rose and crossed the room to escort Spencer to the door, a gesture somehow servile for him, and one he did not do well. ''I will let you know as soon as we hear anything more. Meanwhile, you'll just have to handle your end as best you can. I trust you have your own system over there, but if our damage-control people might be of any help, please don't hesitate to ask.''

''Certainly.'' Spencer turned quickly and walked out of the office. Once on the street, the whole world seemed slightly altered, as if the watery January sun was sapping the middle out of everything, leaving only shells and facades. There was no stopping it now. Whatever the outcome of the immediate crisis, the facts alone would outrage England.

At the very least, they would be a laughingstock, a case of shooting at a fly with an elephant gun. At the worst, the severity of the covert action might cause everyone to think the fear had been valid all along, that the body in the coffin, if that of the true Prince Edward, would constitute a real claim to the throne. There was no good result. The cure, as was so often the case, had been far worse than the disease.

# FORTY-FOUR

" 'Twas the last virgin sunrise, dawn of the fateful day, the sixteenth of April, 1746. From then on, the sun's rays have never crossed the fields of Culloden but that they warm the blood that lies ever in her ground." Lachlan Muir's dark eyes burned. The firelight carved hollows in his craggy face and cast his tall, thin shadow on the stone wall. The men sat silently around the plank table, glasses of whiskey and water in front of each one. The story was known to all, but the telling was honor to the memory, and so recited at the start of every gathering.

"When the brave Scots rose that morning, they were weary, starved, and cold to the bone. They faced the English army, out-numbered, and they knew . . ." Muir's voice dropped. "Yes, lads, they knew that many would die that day. They hadn't the numbers, nor the guns. 'Twas courage had carried them this far, in a triumphal march across Scotland with the bonny prince gathering the clans as he went, but courage alone could not stand against cannon."

The five listened raptly. Kyle McKay just waited. He was less inclined to ritual than Muir, but realized the power of such ceremony with the lads. They were all in their early twenties, four of them from Glasgow, one from Aberdeen, ill-educated, unemployed, angry, and alienated working-class youths. Billy had come up through borstals, Hugh had lost his job at the steel works when it shut down, barely two months after he started. Sammy had worked his father's fishing boat in Ullapool until the catch fell off and the diesel went up and the bank came calling.

There were dozens more like them in the group, but these five had been chosen for this mission for their unique mix of loyalty and having nothing else to lose. They would not question the leaders, as would many of the older Jacobites.

"Cumberland attacked," Muir went on. "For an hour, artillery blasted the Jacobite army, shattering the ranks and killing hundreds where they stood. Then the bonny prince gave the order to charge. The brave Highlanders, like a pack of hungry wolves, attacked the British line." Muir spoke faster now, seizing the lads with the battle fervor. "With sword and heart alone, they broke through the ranks, but the numbers were too great. British troops surrounded them, and hundreds more fell to the bayonet. But the slaughter had only begun."

Even McKay felt himself moved, as he anticipated the story's horrifying turn. No one, no matter how loyal or devoted, could ever say that the Jacobite action at Culloden made sense militarily. It was folly, pure and simple. The Highland troops had been surprisingly effective against the British while waging guerilla actions over rugged mountains, but they were at a loss on the open field. Cumberland had nine thousand troops, fresh, well-fed well-trained, and extremely well-equipped.

The Jacobites had a ragtag band of five thousand, a loose assemblage of clans, many of whom were quarreling for position and leadership. They had tried an ambush by dark, but could not find the British encampment and wound up exhausting themselves, wandering around all night. They had no artillery, and little ammunition for the small arms they did bear. Provisions had been poor for weeks, and now, on the day of battle, most of the troops were weak from hunger.

"Our men fought bravely and well. But finally the day was lost." Muir was circling the table, crouched a little, with a fanatical urgency in his voice. "Yet never was there such a shock as what happened then."

McKay looked around the table at the young men's faces. They were men without a future who had been given a noble past, men without work who had been given a mission, men without families who had been welcomed into the Party like sons. Muir went on, describing the atrocities, one after another, each worse than the one before, until the air in the small room was damp from their sweat and heavy with their fervor.

Cumberland's British troops began to ride through the field,

slaying the wounded Scots where they lay. Men raised their hands
in surrender and were received instead with the cold steel of an
English bayonet through the gut. They ran to the woods, but Cumberland's men hunted them down and butchered them. Hacked the
bodies to pieces. Burned the nearby villages, killed women and
children. Those they spared were plundered, every sack of grain,
all the cattle, every sheep, all stolen and the villagers left to starve.

Culloden was a story too bloody, too harsh for even the oldest
of the MacClannon grandchildren, a slaughter of such cruelty that,
even in its day, it stunned the world.

In the offices of Edinburgh today, computers hum and faxes
cross the globe. In the pubs of Glasgow, young factory workers
are more likely to slam-dance than strum a plaintive ballad. In the
tourist hotels around Loch Ness, innkeepers fluff up comforters,
polish the brass and dust the antiques, then retreat to their own
quarters, where they pop a tape into the four-head Hi-Fi Stereo
VCR with digital auto tracking and on-screen display and cook
up a bowl of microwave popcorn.

Scotland is a thoroughly modern country, with thoroughly modern people, but mention Culloden, and in the most gentle and
amiable face you will see a bit of the ancient fire of the Highlander
come alive.

For thirty-six years after the slaughter, kilts and bagpipes were
forbidden. Clan leaders were hunted down and killed. Jacobites
were exiled to the Colonies. The battle of Culloden in 1746 was
widely believed to be the end of the Jacobite resistance, but as
Hayes had observed, there is no memory like a Celtic memory.

"And from that bloody ground, our fathers and our clansmen
cry out to us still!" Muir pounded the table with his fist and the
whiskey rippled in the glasses. "They cry for justice! They cry
out for revenge." Muir grabbed his whiskey glass in one hand
and his water glass in the other. The young men likewise took
up theirs.

It was an ancient Jacobite ritual, though practiced even today
by the occasional Scot, in sentimental or tyrannical mood. The
glass of water was held in front of the heart and the whiskey
raised around it, drinking to "the King across the water." The
men all drank, then slammed the glasses down on the table. The

fire had burned down, and McKay was looking for a signal that he could now switch on the lights and get down to practical business.

Though red hair had always been associated with a fiery temperament, it was "Red" McKay who was the steady one in this group. It was his planning that had brought them thus far, his idea, ten years ago, to get their people infiltrated into British government and security agencies. McKay was a long-range planner. Once there were Jacobites in the government, in the media, even in the palace, they could begin the final task.

Lachlin Muir and Kyle McKay, Neil Swinny, Steven Dunagh, and about a dozen others who formed this core group had borne the flame handed from their fathers, and their fathers before that, for two hundred and fifty years. Theirs was a secret brotherhood, pledged for hundreds of years to one day liberate Scotland from British rule.

The Jacobites had long ago abandoned the mission of returning the Stuart line to the throne, and focused instead on simply abolishing the monarchy entirely. The goal was secession, and control of oil revenues, it would not matter then who was king. But now, through a marvelous twist of fate, by finding truth in an old fable, they had a chance that none had ever even imagined. Now they had a chance to do both.

The meeting went quickly from ceremony to substance. There were plans to work out, tasks to be assigned, projects to review. They had had to pull this all together so quickly, McKay was amazed it was going so well.

"But we still need the money," Muir insisted. "Damn Swinny, so sure he could get it out of MacClannon. What are we going to do if we can't even fly the coffin home?"

"We'll get the money," McKay assured him.

# FORTY-FIVE

A pretty young desk clerk with a face from a 1920's valentine led Adrian Spencer down the long back corridors to Mark Whitstone's office. The office, like the man's apartment, was tiny and orderly, with old furniture worn into the exact shape of him. The little room was adjacent to the preservation lab on one side and the storage vaults on the other. It was quiet except for the hum of machinery that kept the temperature and humidity at constant levels.

"I'm not sure that he's here today, sir," the girl said in a soft voice. "He's been ill a lot lately."

"He just phoned my office, I assumed this is where he would be."

Whitstone looked up as Spencer entered the room, and almost immediately his face paled and his frail old shoulders began to tremble. "Oh, Mr. Spencer—how . . . how good of you to come!" Spencer was surprised at the reaction. The secretary paused at the door. "Shall I bring some tea?" she asked pleasantly. Whitstone didn't answer, so Spencer just shook his head and she slipped away, closing the door behind her.

"I'm sorry to hear you haven't been feeling well, Mr. Whitstone. The winter has been rather brutal."

"It has. Yes. But I'm fine," Whitstone replied nervously. "I just had to talk to you. I'm afraid this has all got out of hand." Spencer felt a new flush of panic. Whitstone couldn't know any of what was going on. What was he talking about?

"My good sir," he said placidly. "You look like you've seen a ghost. What could be so terrible as all this."

"It will come out. Everything now. I tried to stop it, but I

166

couldn't. Too ..." He gasped a little, as if fighting back tears. "Too many know now."

"Know what, Mr. Whitstone?"

"All of it. The Prince ... the medallion ... all of it ... the queen ..."

"Please, sir. Try to calm yourself." Whitstone sat back down and Spencer pulled a folding chair over to the desk. "Now just tell me what has been worrying you."

"The ladies, those ... those *ladies* with their *clubs*. They *know*!" he said accusingly. "I told you it shouldn't go out of the room. Shouldn't go beyond us. It was too delicate ..."

"Mr. Whitstone," Spencer said cautiously, "I did relay your information on to the investigative branch, it is standard practice to—"

"Oh, my God ... investigative ..." Whitstone's eyes grew wide. "Oooooh. *That's* it then! They have been testing me. You mean..." his voice dropped to a whisper and he glanced around nervously. "The MI5? The Secret Service?" He was agitated and rambling now, and Spencer wasn't sure what to do. There was no way Whitstone could know about all that had gone on, so what had got him so upset?

"Mr. Whitstone, are you all right?"

The man's face had gone from white to gray, and his eyes seemed to lose focus.

"Oh, my God. I ... when I told you, you told them ... and then they must have ... The MI5? It's them, then. It had to be them ..."

"Calm down, sir." Spencer was unsure how to help the man.

"You shouldn't have told them ..."

"I had to, sir. It was a matter of—"

"No no no no no no. You told them about the letter!"

"What letter?" Spencer was completely confused now. "What letter are you talking about?" Whitstone drew a deep, ragged breath and gave a ghastly nervous smile.

"The letter. That Margaret found ..." One hand rattled spastically across the desk. "The letter ... she had the letter when ..." His body went rigid, his startled old face froze for a second in pain. "I know ... I know it ... wasn't an accident ..." The old man slumped over the desk.

Spencer jumped up, opened the door, and shouted for help, then grabbed up the telephone and told the desk clerk to call an ambulance. What letter? he wondered as he lay the man down. Whitstone had a pulse, but it was weak and very fast. He heard a screech at the door and turned to see the young woman, her hand to her mouth. Two others ran in from their offices, and Spencer took the woman's arm and led her out into the hall.

"Is he all right?" she asked plaintively. "Will he be all right?"

"I don't know. But I need to ask you something. Do you know who Margaret might be? Someone who works here in the archives perhaps?"

"Margaret . . . no."

"Think. An associate, a colleague."

"I don't know."

"She might have had some kind of accident?"

"An accident? Oh, Margaret Haversford?"

"Haversford!" Of course. The ancient-jewelry girl from the Victoria and Albert. She had discovered something more about the charm. Spencer's dread was mounting. What had the old man been trying to tell him? Why was he so terrified of the MI5?

"Yes, the girl who was mugged?"

"Mugged?"

"Last week, at Charing Cross station. He was all upset about it. She'd been to see him just that day, I think. What is this all about?"

"Where can I find her? Do you have her office number?"

"But she's dead."

"Dead?"

"Well, yes. It was all on the news." Spencer never paid attention to the prurient stories on the local news. "Her purse caught or something," the woman went on. "She fell on the tracks. A terrible accident."

# FORTY-SIX

By the end of the second day, Chicago had slipped into a steady but numbing intensity, all her energies focused on the search. She slept only in fits, when exhaustion overwhelmed her, dozing off at the helm, or at the chart table, then waking suddenly in a panic, afraid that she might have sailed right by them in her sleep. They could all be unconscious by now, injured, or at least suffering from hunger and thirst. They had been drifting for three days now, one day ahead of her. She had seen the spilled provisions on the ocean floor. She did not know how many souls belonged to the bones she had gathered, but perhaps it was only one. That meant there could be six of them at the most, a heavy load.

She stared at the chart, her eyes stinging. Over and over, she had plotted the possible course of their drift, studying the weather reports from the past few days, wind direction and speed, surface conditions, currents. It was the roughest of estimates, for wind recorded in the weather station in Nassau had little to do with conditions down here. A variation of a knot or two would have little effect on a drifting yacht, but it would make a huge difference to a tiny raft.

Four yachts and three fishing boats had come through the area since the Mayday was issued, all keeping a lookout, but nothing had been sighted. Dive-boat operators in the Turks and Caicos were on alert, but no reports had come. All she could rely on now was her own instinct, and a lot of luck.

Chicago stared at the chart and tried to make sense of it. There were numbers written on the notepad, the latest coordinates from the GPS. Now she had to translate these numbers into little X's on the chart, but she could not figure out how to do this. It was simple. It was the simplest thing. She had been doing this since she had to stand on a stool to reach the chart table. Numbers here, X's there, that was

169

her course. Her mind was blank. After three days with no sleep and way too much caffeine, her body felt jittery and her mind, like a great rusty tractor, could only rumble slowly toward it's dogged goal. Find Alex.

She thought of Mary Beatrice, poor woman, married off at fifteen to an old man she had never met. Did she ever feel this way about a man? Did she ever go about at night, touching the places he touched, as if some essence of him lingered there? Did she sleep with his shirt over her pillow to have the smell of him?

Somewhere out here, he was still alive. People had survived for weeks, months, in life rafts. He was strong, and he would be alive. She caught herself. No time for thoughts. She stood up quickly, panicked to have spent too many minutes below deck, but felt lightheaded and the cabin swarmed in her vision. Had she eaten anything today? It was hard to remember. She grabbed the tin of crackers and climbed up to the deck.

The breeze was freshening and the water was getting rougher. After two days of fair weather, a front was moving in. Poor Alex would be seasick, she worried. He had largely adjusted, being aboard the *Tassia Far* this long, but in a little raft, he would be bobbing all over. She could not bear to think of the real peril of the waves, the fact that they could swamp a tiny raft and drag it to the bottom, so she worried about his seasickness instead.

She took a bite of cracker, checked the compass, double-checked the time, and grabbed the binoculars. She had been steering a careful zigzag course across a mile-wide area that she had decided offered the best drift pattern for the life raft. The autopilot whirred as it adjusted the steering. She took another bite of cracker and grabbed the binoculars.

The sun had just set, and the light was fading, the most desperate time of day. It was now that the fear clutched at her. *How dare you try to be happy?* it hissed. *You really thought it would last, didn't you?* She pushed the voices away, but in her exhausted state they scratched louder tonight. Too much loss already, her mother Tassia, so beautiful in the coffin, surrounded by hibiscus and the scraps of velvet that the five-year-old Chicago had tucked around her face. The image floated in the clouds over the water, swirls of white cloth, swirls of white sand, the happy memories, then all gone. Stephan, her husband, not even bones to bury there, the body gone to the bottom of the sea.

And now Martha. It was probably Martha, she had decided, from the shreds of nightgown. Martha had been kind. She had married Ross the day before he left for war, a young sailor in the Merchant Marines. Chicago remembered Shep and her father talking their war stories one night. She had gone into the kitchen to find Martha washing dishes and crying. Twice boats had been torpedoed out from under him. Would he be three times lucky? Which of them was still alive?

She put down the binoculars and took a few deep breaths. Her watch began to beep. She had it set for every fifteen minutes, in case she fell asleep. At night, she changed it to every hour, realizing she had to at least nap, but this hadn't been necessary, she would doze off once, then wake before the alarm and was too terrified to fall asleep the rest of the night.

She still felt lightheaded, and her mouth was too dry to chew the cracker. She would have to eat something, she realized, had to stay strong for the search. She would cook some rice. Rice was easy. Easy to cook, easy to swallow. The small task gave her a boost of energy. Here was one small, focused job. Fill the pot, measure the rice. Add salt. At this stage of exhaustion, objects became slightly surreal, sounds and smells magnified. How pretty the pot was. So shiny, even the bottom. Alex must have cleaned it. She usually forgot the bottoms. How lovely the salt looked, streaming into the water.

When she went back up on deck, she felt immensely, ridiculously, lighter. In the overwhelming powerlessness, she had found one small stupid task she could complete. The wind was picking up, that was good, she would sail tonight, after all this motoring around. The moon was three-quarters full, maybe Alex would see the sail.

Chicago picked up the binoculars again and began another slow sweep. She had gone almost full circle when something caught her eye. Birds in the distance, seagulls, a flock of them circling and diving on something. Desperately, she stared. It was probably just a school of fish, but she was far enough from land that the scene was a bit unusual. She watched closely. There it was—something! Something . . . a little boat!

Her hands were shaking as she reached for the sighting compass that she wore around her neck and took a bearing on the object. She ran back to the helm, flipped off the autopilot, spun the wheel to change course, and pushed up the throttle. Her hopes soared, then quickly dropped again.

It was not the life raft at all, but the *Goose*'s skiff. She saw no one aboard. But they could be lying down, she thought. They could be sleeping, or sick . . . . The *Tassia Far* closed in on the drifting boat. Chicago, standing by the helm, strained to see any sign of life other than the screeching birds. Suddenly a smoke alarm went off below deck with a violent buzz. The rice—damn it! She swung down and found the galley thick with smoke, the rice a charred lump in the bottom of the now-ruined pan. Chicago grabbed the pot and, burning her hand on it, dropped it to the floor. Snatching a towel to retrieve the damaged pot, she took it up the companionway, and flung it into the water. She raced back to the starboard bow and there was the little boat, bumping gently against her hull.

She stared. A body was sprawled in the bottom of the boat. It was a man's body, in bloody clothes, his arms charred red by the sun. The gulls, frightened away by her presence, wheeled angrily overhead. It was so unreal, so oddly horrible. Even as she watched, one of the gulls landed on the gunnel and hopped toward the body. The world began to spin and Chicago fell back, leaning against the cabin. Was this to be the pattern now? Finding one horrible corpse after another?

Angry now, she screamed at the gulls, waving her arms to scare them away. They scattered, but would not abandon their victim so easily. They hung like specters in the sky. Who was this man?

She tried to remember Jack and Peter McGuire. She had only seen them for a few minutes when the plane landed to pick up Alex on Crooked Island. Jack was older, early fifties, she remembered. Could it be Peter then? She remembered the man shaking her hand, his hair whipping around his face, thick curly hair, gray at the temples. This man had straight brown hair. Was he the enemy then? A killer? Chicago felt weak, bludgeoned by death. Whoever he was, he had to be involved—but how? They drifted together for many long minutes. The gulls became bolder, swooping down even when she waved at them, eager for the taste of flesh. Finally she decided that, friend or enemy, she could not leave the body as it was, to be eaten by the gulls.

Steeling herself for the grisly task, she found a length of rope and a tarp. *Just get it over with,* she told herself. She picked up the boat-

hook, snagged the dragging line, and tied the skiff to the *Tassia Far.*
*Who were you?* she wondered as she climbed down. *Was it you that
killed Shep and Marty, and maybe the man I love?* The little boat
bobbed under her weight. She realized with a new shock, that
wrapped around the man's stomach in a crude bandage, was Stan's
T-shirt. He had been alive when he wound up in the skiff. She squatted at the man's feet and touched his ankle. The skin was warm.
Fresh blood trickled from the wounds where the gulls had pecked
him. The man groaned.

Chicago jumped back. He was alive! Jesus Christ, she was about
to drown him! Quickly, she scrambled back up on the *Tassia Far*
and ran to fetch a rescue harness. He was a big man, and she had to
hoist him a good six feet to her deck, so she rigged him into the
harness, tied it to the mainsail sheet, and climbed back aboard to
winch him up.

She steered him, while dangling from the line, close to the cockpit
so she wouldn't have to drag him too far, then she let him down on
the deck. It seemed impossible that he would be alive. Three days in
an open boat, wounded, with no water. His lips were blistered, his
breathing so shallow, his chest barely moved. Quickly, Chicago untied the bandage, brought up a pan of water and washed away the
dried blood. She found two wounds, one on his front, one on his
back. They had closed up, and though red, did not look badly infected. The man opened his eyes briefly, but did not seem to see.
Touching him revolted her. But she would keep him alive, she would
make him live to regret what he had done. She raised his head and
held a cup of water to his mouth. His lips moved slightly, but he
could not drink. He was about as near to dead as one could be. She
had to act fast.

She went below to the bow cabin, pulled up the mattresses and
lifted the hatch. Here, they stored all the rarely used gear and equipment. Even in these days of rapid communication and helicopter rescue, emergencies could arise on a boat that needed immediate
treatment. The first aid book gave clear and simple instructions for
treating major disasters at sea, including administering drugs, in-
serting a catheter, and setting up an IV. Chicago grabbed the two
plastic IV bags and the sealed needle kit, then opened the manual
with shaky hands to find out how to do this.

# FORTY-SEVEN

Annalee lay listlessly, curled in a little ball, her head resting on the pontoon. They had given her most of the water, usually by lying about their own portions, or pretending to sip when they were not, but even that was a scant cup a day, and she was suffering. This afternoon, she had begun to lapse into delirium. She thought they were on a car trip to the lake, where the McGuires rented a summer cottage, and begged someone to roll down the windows, complaining of the heat, asking if she could go in the water right away. Once she awoke in a daze, and seeing the water outside the raft, thought it was the lake and tried to jump in. Alex had caught her just in time.

He was working hard to keep his own lucidity, fighting the comfortable swirl of unconsciousness. He knew how intoxicating it could be, how easy it was to slip just a little, allow the mirages of the mind to lure one into surrender, and inevitably death. He had seen it happen. He had to stay alert. Had to watch all the time for rescue. He had flown searches before, and knew how difficult it was. They had one flare left, and one smoke bomb. The raft had come equipped with an air horn as well, but the water pressure from the plunge to sixty feet had deployed its charge.

". . . So there she was. Poor Lady Jane, beheaded in the end. She was only sixteen." Jack had gone back through another hundred years of the monarchy, relating more tales of royal intrigue. His voice was barely audible, strained by the long story, but he was not ready for quiet yet. The stars made him feel even more isolated, the pale moonlight shining down on his sleeping daughter, more desperate. He needed the connection of conversation. "We forget how much religion had to do with it all . . ." Jack went on, Alex straining to follow the train of thought. "Well, not

174

religion as much as power. The pope was a rival political force as much as a religious one. The Reformation sprang as much from a fear . . ."

The Reformation. The term came vaguely back to Alex, bringing with it the surprising memories of high school history class, the chalk and varnish smells of the classroom, the sounds of locker doors and pencil sharpeners. Jack's voice faded to a low background hum. Mrs. Tollerson, junior year history class. The Reformation. Carla Squires, one seat up and over, a perfect angle on the back of her leg, the round swell of her breast, an angle more enticing for its obliqueness. Cromwell. King Charles. Test on Monday. The incomparable feeling of freedom to walk through those heavy wooden doors on a Friday afternoon in late spring, when the vast prairie had finally begun to thaw and the rich odor of black dirt made him crazed.

The North Dakota plains, that vast exotic emptiness, a platter of land, wearing gravity like armor. King Charles, King James, the Reformation . . .

". . . and then as soon as Spain got involved . . ." Alex was startled for a second to see blue water all around, not the green prairie.

Jack smiled. "I'm so sorry. I've been bludgeoning you with history, haven't I? I do get caught up in it. We spent the whole winter stacked up with books, Peter and Mizzy and I." His voice broke at the mention of his brother. Neither of them wanted to dwell on his fate. They had no choice. They could not keep him in the boat. Alex was glad the man was muscular, and did not float long. Between the three of them, they had been able to construct a few scraps of Bible verse, and the Lord's Prayer for a service. Annalee had not cried, though since then, she awoke screaming from every sleep.

Jack looked at Alex questioningly. "You know, I don't know what you studied. Here we've been in a life raft together for three days and I know almost nothing about you. What's your field?"

"My field?"

"Some military training, I'd guess; you knew what that bomb was all about."

"Didn't do us much good, did it?" Alex said ruefully.

"You saved our lives. You mentioned you were in Vietnam?"

"Barely. Things were pretty much over with when I got there. I was seventeen, almost eighteen. It was 1973 and I wanted to get out of North Dakota."

"You enlisted?"

"In the Navy. I really wanted to see the ocean." Alex gave an ironic laugh; he'd seen enough for a lifetime now. "But I wound up flying. I already had a pilot's license. My uncles had a crop-dusting business, and a flying circus on the side, so I learned to fly pretty young. Mostly I wound up flying small planes—taxiing people around . . ." He hesitated, never sure how to explain his life.

"I'm sorry. I don't mean to pry. Please, I'm just a scared old professor trying to make conversation." They were silent a few minutes. The last of the daylight faded out, swallowed by the inky sky. Stars appeared. Jack felt ashamed at his need right now for the talk to continue. He craved sound as much as water. He couldn't bear to have this black night go silent.

"Did you play football? You look like you would."

"I played in high school." Alex was happier with this subject, and, realizing the man's need for connection, pursued it. "Did any of your sons play?"

"Warren played, high school and college, and John looked like a star for two years, then broke his leg. Trevor, my middle boy, wrestled."

"I wrestled, played hockey." God, wouldn't that feel nice right now, Alex thought, to walk into an ice arena! "I play a little soccer, race bicycles now and then, did a few triathalons . . ." He stopped abruptly. There was a sound.

"What?" Jack sat up.

"Shhhh. Listen." There it was again, a faint low sound, like a foghorn, still distant, but very real.

# FORTY-EIGHT

Word was in from the new agents in Mayaguana, and it was not good. Dunagh and Teneby had both vanished entirely, leaving nothing behind but an old copy of *National Geographic* magazine. Traces of blood in the hotel room. One seat on a flight to Provenciales. Dunagh had not called again since his initial contact. Hayes felt himself slipping into a crazy despair. This couldn't be happening to him. Three years to retirement, a careful career, now all would be ruined. And on top of it, to be betrayed by his own men.

Damn it, where was Spencer? He should have been back by now. *Probably going to leave me out to die alone,* he thought bitterly. Head of palace security indeed. Did he have any idea how silly his routine little motorcades and crowd surveillance would have been over the years without the MI5 behind the scenes, rooting out the real threats? He had to take chances. It was his job. He had planned this well. The men had been vetted. He couldn't have known.

"Damn," Hayes muttered to himself. How messy could this get? The intercom buzzed, the secretary announcing the Home Secretary and the Lord Chancellor. How much should he tell them? If things went drastically wrong from here on, and he hadn't informed them completely, they would be angry. He would need their support, and they would feel betrayed. On the other hand, if he could still straighten it out without them, his career might be saved.

It wasn't fair. He had served well. One mistake ought not to condemn him. What was left for an old man if not the honor and respect of his peers? How was he to spend the next ten years if ostracized from the right clubs, shunned by members of his own class? Move to America? Buy one of those goddawful "mobile homes" and drive around Disneyland?

"Send them in," he said calmly. George Burton, the Home Secretary, and Randolph Shiftly, the Lord Chancellor, entered with serious expressions, never expecting to be summoned to a meeting with the Director General of the MI5 for light conversation.

"Gentlemen, thank you for coming over so soon." Hayes waved them to the adjoining small conference room. "Adrian Spencer is expected as well, but has unfortunately been delayed. In the meantime I'll bring you up to speed. I'm afraid we have a bit of a situation on our hands."

Lord Shiftly just frowned. He had gone through a few too many "situations" with the Secret Service in his tenure. For the next fifteen minutes, Hayes sketched out the story from the time Whitstone first contacted Spencer, to the dispatch of the agents, to the recent news of the sinking of the *Golden Goose*.

"So as you might imagine," Hayes summed it up, "further investigation of the accident will probably uncover our interest in the wreck of the *Christiania*, and raise suspicion."

"Suspicion for which there is some basis?"

Hayes looked at Burton steadily, neither confirming nor denying. They all knew the game they were playing. How much should I know? What could hurt me in the end?

"Mr. Hayes, you have just explained to us the repercussions that this King James business might have on England." Burton was testing the waters. "One might suppose that a cautious response to this situation might have been to try and prevent the coffin from being raised in the first place?"

Shiftly leaned back in his chair and rested his chin in hand, too fully aware of the implication here.

"One might further assume," Burton went on, "that a man of your position and expertise, seeking to serve his country, and with the means of an organization such as the MI5 at his disposal, might consider a way to fulfill that wish." Hayes felt a slight twinge of hope, like a window had cracked and a beam of light was shining into his dungeon. He gave the Home Secretary an encouraging nod.

"Oh, Jesus." Shiftly folded his arms across his ample stomach. "What did you do, Crawly—try to blow the thing up?"

"If we were considering the use of explosives," Hayes went on carefully, "the salvage vessel would not have been our target."

"The sinking is still officially an accident," Burton agreed with a strained tone. "Should, however, things come up appearing a little less accidental, one would like to have an explanation at hand."

If Hayes were the hugging sort, he would have jumped over the desk and hugged the Home Secretary right now. What style he had, how well he played.

"Of course." Hayes cleared his throat and ran one hand carefully across the side of his thin hair, collecting his thoughts before he continued. "We suspect that our agents, who were sent merely to observe the operation, discovered—or suspected—there was a treasure involved, and motivated by their own greed, betrayed their country and their cause."

"How refreshingly venial," Shiftly sneered. Obviously he wasn't buying this, but neither was he pressing for more.

"So naturally, we have taken immediate action to locate these rogue agents?" Burton pressed.

"We have enlisted all local island law-enforcement officers to help locate Dunagh and Teneby. I've appraised the British ambassador in Washington, and he will contact the State Department in the morning."

To his great relief, there was relatively little scolding. Both men were civil, though angry. England did not need this sort of nonsense right now. An international event, rogue agents; indeed. Nothing to be done now but try to set it right. It would be sticky at best. There should be an immediate diplomatic intervention. Offer of financial restitution, certainly. Perhaps there were some English planes that could be sent to join the search.

For the next hour, the men plotted the damage control for an accident none of them would admit happened. Hayes waited for half an hour after the two men left, but still did not hear from Spencer. With a mixture of worry and annoyance, he finally got his coat and left.

The night was cold but clear, and after the long, tense day, Hayes decided to walk a while and clear his mind. The meeting had gone well, and he offered himself a cautious congratulations. Treasure, indeed. Well, it was as good an excuse as anything.

\*    \*    \*

Hayes had not gone two blocks when he heard the purposeful step of someone behind him. He turned, and saw, to his relief, that it was only Spencer. His curly white eyebrows and mustaches shone in the moonlight, like three little moths fluttering toward him.

"Spencer, where the hell were you? Leave me to the wolves now—is that your strategy?" Spencer did not reply, nor offer his excuse, and this put Hayes on guard. "I told you you wouldn't be involved," he said with some contempt. "But a little help with the inquiries now would be sporting. Don't you think?"

"I was talking to Mr. Whitstone," Spencer said, glancing around, suddenly a bit nervous about confronting the man this way.

"Ah, and how is the dear old troublemaker?" Hayes began walking again, and Spencer fell into step beside him.

"He's in hospital as a matter of fact. Had a stroke this afternoon."

"A stroke?" Hayes stopped, clearly understanding something more in the man's words. "What is it?"

"I'd like to know what happened to Margaret Haversford."

"Who?"

"The young lady curator at the V and A, so convinced the old medallion was meant for the Queen's love child."

"Oh, yes. She had an accident in the underground?"

"So it seems." Hayes stopped and pulled the collar of his coat up against the cold.

"Mr. Spencer, I cannot dance round about anymore tonight. Are you trying to tell me something?"

"When Mr. Whitstone learned that your office had become involved in this case, he got extremely upset." Spencer paused. It was a dark night on a lonely street. Perhaps he should have waited until tomorrow. Hayes, an innocuous-looking man now, with the thinning hair and spotty hands, but there were stories . . . *oh, don't be stupid!* Spencer summoned his nerve.

"Mr. Whitstone believes that Margaret Haversford's death was not an accident."

# FORTY-NINE

The last blast of the air horn faded out into the distant night. They had to be somewhere close. They *had* to be. The skiff most logically would have been lost the same time as the *Golden Goose* had sunk, and would have drifted in a similar pattern with the life raft. As darkness fell, the wind grew stronger, the water choppier. The weather was changing. If they weren't found soon, their chances dropped enormously. The hours were endless. There was little to do but wait, and change the course every twenty minutes from zig to zag. She had been motor sailing most of the time, with only the jib up since the winds had been so light.

The radio was on, tuned to Channel 16, but she hadn't heard from any boats since early that morning, and the reports regarding the Bahamas' rescue efforts had been similarly fruitless. The exhaustion was deep. Her body felt strange, hollow, scoured inside, like she was turning to dust. Any time now, she would see them. She would feel the slight bump of the life raft against her hull, and there they would be. Alex would climb up and they would sail away from this shit, leave the damn coffin and go back to their own lives.

While searching the first two nights, she had blasted the air horn every half hour; tonight, she increased the frequency of the blasts, hoping that the charge would hold out. Even if they couldn't answer back, at least they might hear her, know she was near, feel some hope.

The man stirred and shifted, his arm flopping off the narrow cockpit bench where he lay. He was an ordinary-looking man, as best she could tell with his face so swollen and red. The scar under his chin gave him a sinister edge, but otherwise, he could have been anyone. It had taken several tries to get the IV into a

181

vein, but once hooked up, the fluid had an immediate effect. His heartbeat was stronger, and the breathing secure. She had scrubbed out the wounds, and doused them with antiseptic, backing it up, as the book instructed, with antibiotics.

Who was this man? Where had he come from and why? Were the stab wounds Alex's handiwork? Had they fought? Alex was a martial arts expert. She had seen him fight. This man looked strong, but Alex would have won. Whoever he was, she didn't trust him, and though she thought him still too weak and injured to even live, she had shackled his feet together with the chain and padlock she used on the dinghy when docked.

He lapsed in and out of consciousness, but was now starting to sip from the cup she held to his lips. She had cooked up a simple oral rehydration solution, with sugar and salt. Although the seas continued empty, Chicago was newly hopeful.

The radio crackled and she jumped alert, but the message was far away, the static heavy. Nothing. Nothing to do but sail and think and hope. They would be hungry, she thought. She should have something ready. Something easy. Not rice, though, not rice. Chicago went below and opened the cabinet. Noodles—that would be okay. Oatmeal. That was good. She took the box of oatmeal off the shelf and put in on the counter where it would be ready. What else now? There was nothing else. Nothing she could do. Nothing. The face on the box of oatmeal stared at her, such a placid face, a peaceful, smiling face, a satisfied, kind face, a remote face from a gentle world. A world she would never know. Suddenly her knees could not hold her, and she sank to the galley floor, wedged between the cabinets in the narrow space. For the first time, Chicago sobbed uncontrollably.

# FIFTY

"What was that?" Jack and Alex both heard it.

"It sounded like an air horn," Alex said, trying to suppress his excitement.

"Well, shoot the flare!" Jack reached for the last flare, but Alex caught his hand.

"Not yet. It's still far away. We're low in the water, she might miss us."

"You think it's Chicago?" The thought that it could also be the enemy went silently acknowledged by both men. Annalee, roused by the sudden activity, opened her eyes.

"Wonderbread?" she asked, staring at Alex. Jack put his arm around her and pulled her onto his lap. "No, honey," he said softly. "Wonderbread isn't here. He's at school. That's what we call my son John," he explained to Alex.

"There's dolphins out here," Annalee mumbled, still half asleep. "One is blue." Her lips were swollen. "The blue one has flowers in his mouth." She drifted back to sleep. Alex and Jack sat silently, straining to hear in the darkness. When they did hear, fifteen minutes later, the sound seemed farther away.

It was an excruciating hour before they decided the sound was getting closer, but neither man was sure in his judgment at this point. Alex stuck two fingers in his mouth and tried to whistle, but his mouth was so dry the sound was feeble. He wet it with seawater, flinching at the sting of salt, and tried with little better results. The shrill sound pierced the night. There was no response. Finally, after another half hour, after two more blasts of the air horn that sounded as if they were now getting closer, they decided to shoot the flare. One flare, their only hope. Alex stood to get it as high as possible, while Jack steadied his legs. The life raft was

183

rolling and pitching like crazy by now. The flare made a loud whooshing noise, bright flame shot toward the sky and scarlet sparks fell hissing into the sea.

Chicago was just coming out of the companionway when she saw the faint glow on the horizon. At first she didn't dare to believe it. It was just a far-off ship, or heat lightning reflecting off the low clouds. But still, it could be. She took a bearing on the light. From this height, Chicago knew she could see about four and a half miles to the horizon. She had hope now, direction, and with it, renewed vigor. Her best chance was to speed toward the sight of the flare. The cool aluminum wheel felt powerful under her hands, as she spun it to pick up the new course. They were close.

# FIFTY-ONE

Lachlin Muir and Robert McKay waited in the car, parked near the hedgerow at the top of the hill, watching the MacClannon estate.

"What about a couple of the grandkids?" Muir suggested, as a jumble of little boys went leaping over the stone wall that ringed the backyard. "Be easier to nab."

"Christ, that's all we need are a couple of bawling kiddies to take care of. Use your head, man."

"Well, the old man's bound to move if he thinks we'll harm the wee ones."

"First of all, it's bad for the cause. Wouldn't go over a'tall to be seen as kidnappers. No, the daughter's far better. Look—there she is, coming out now."

They watched Birdy come out the back door with three of the family dogs yelping at her heels. She picked up a walking stick and set off down the path toward the old croft buildings. That was no good, too many laborers hanging about.

"What about the wife? She drives herself to town most afternoons."

"We might have to keep her three or four days, lad. Don't know when Dunagh's going to have the coffin up, and even if MacClannon coughs up the money this afternoon, we still have to arrange the cargo plane from Miami. I don't want the old biddie to have a heart attack and die on us. Just be patient. See, she's heading over toward the road now."

They waited until Birdy and the dogs had walked some way up the road, then Muir started up the car and drove after her. As they neared, he slowed, and McKay leaned out the window. In rough jackets and caps, riding in an old battered car with tools in the backseat, they looked every bit like itinerant laborers.

" 'Scuse me, lass." McKay leaned out the window as the car slowed. "Would you know where's the croft round here what's being made a museum?"

Birdy laughed. "Not a museum exactly, but I think it's the one you mean. Back over the rise here."

"Oh, but it's not being fixed then?" He looked crushed, and Birdy felt a stab of sympathy for the man. There was so little work around these days.

"It is. It's going to be a working croft, like the old times. For the schoolchildren to visit."

"Oh, well, that's a fine thing. Would you know if the foreman's about?"

McKay was trying to think fast. He had intended to jump out and grab her, but the dogs might pose a problem.

"He should be." Birdy glanced at her watch. "But I think they've a full crew." Shit, he thought. He was about to grab her through the window when Birdy, guiless and never suspecting anything sinister, offered the opening herself.

"But I know there's some Americans bought an old manor house down the way, fixing that up I've heard, and might be wanting some carpenters." McKay beamed.

"Oh, the wife would be happy if I come home today with a job, I'll tell you truly. Here, I've a survey map in the back, could you show me the place?"

From there it was a matter of seconds. The car stopped by the side of the road, McKay climbed out to rummage in the backseat, Birdy was pushed inside, McKay leaping in after her, wrestling her down as Muir sped off.

# FIFTY-TWO

The two men strolled alone across the meticulously groomed lawn of Balmoral Castle. Because of his position as a leader of industry and a major philanthropist, MacClannon had met the prince before on several occasions. There were a few ceremonial dinners and official functions, a charity ball or two over the years, which neither man had particularly enjoyed and from which both fled as soon as politely possible, and, of course, the annual Royal Highland gathering at Braemar in Deeside. But the acquaintance had never gone beyond this.

The prince seemed smaller, older, far less royal without ceremonial garb or tuxedo. He even seemed a little cockeyed, his stride disjointed, one shoulder dipping slightly before the other as he walked. The royal posture, so perfect on horseback, so elegant in formal pose, was relaxed out here. He walked like a man physically unbound after long restraint, who had to consciously remember the muscles needed for each step.

He wore plain twill trousers and a faded hunting jacket gone baggy in the elbows. Of course the sweater beneath the coat was expensive cashmere, and the cap was from Savile Row, but otherwise, he looked like any common country gentleman. His boots were well-worn and the seam near the top of one had already been mended, while the other was beginning to unravel. MacClannon found this a comforting detail. A man loyal to a good pair of boots could not be so bad.

\*     \*     \*

"I suppose you know why I've asked you out here?" the prince asked simply.

"Wouldn't be for measuring, would it?" MacClannon asked with his usual irony. "I'd guess my crown size about seven and a half, and I would think the ermine cloak, or cape, or whatever you call it, ought to be a one-size-fits-all. I've a few inches on you, but it drags a bit anyway, doesn't it?"

The prince smiled. "You really haven't much reverence for the Crown, do you?"

"My sentiments have never been disguised, sir."

"And your loyalties?"

"Rest assured, Your Majesty, I've no intentions of raising an army against your mum."

"But you would see us put out?"

"It's the monarchy I'd put out, sir, not your family. And by vote, sir. By law."

"You will never have these votes." MacClannon thought he almost heard a note of sadness in the prince's voice.

"Never is a long time in the history of this island," he said. The prince gave a nod of concession to that point.

"If this business is true, however, you would not need the votes," Charles went on. "You simply claim the throne, then as king of England, issue a decree. Dissolve the monarchy with a stroke of the pen."

"That simple, eh?" Both men walked on silently. Devotion to royalty aside, MacClannon still felt a bit intimidated to be here, and constrained to be talking so personally.

"Tell me something, MacClannon." The prince stopped and rested both hands on his walking stick. He looked out over the moors as if searching for something. "Put your average Englishman on the shore of a lake with a boat tipped over. He sees my two sons drowning, along with his own two children. He can only save two. Where is his loyalty then? Who does he choose to save?"

"His own, of course. Though I've met a few children who might give a moment's pause before the plunge."

The prince seemed to strain for the humor in the remark.

"Yet many men, including your own father I believe, have given their lives, and their sons' lives for the Crown."

"For England, sir, not the Crown."

"Yes, of course." MacClannon was growing more puzzled. "The SNP is trying to change the Constitution. We're not anarchists."

"Ah, but would that you were," the prince said strangely. "Would that you were . . ." It was a clear cold day and distant mountains carved a rugged outline against the sky. "Shall we turn around then?" The prince swept his hand back toward the castle. "I don't want to keep you, but you're welcome to tea. The boys are still here, you ought to meet them at least, before you depose them."

Now it was MacClannon who was unsure about the humor.

"Perhaps in a decade or so, when they're looking for employment, you can find them something in one of your companies."

"I put no stock in these stories," MacClannon repeated. "I have no interest, even if there were some ridiculous chance I could, of taking your throne."

"Why not?" The prince stopped and faced him squarely. "Why the bloody hell not? It's a perfectly good throne. Hard on the lower back after a while, but you could get one of those orthopedic cushions . . ." He gave a tight little chuckle and a quick thin smile, took his cap off, and smoothed back the thinning hair. He glanced around the castle grounds, and his gaze seemed momentarily panicked. MacClannon had another odd chill.

"They're clever boys. I'll be sure they learn a useful trade."

"What would you have me do, Your Highness?"

"Do? Why, your duty, my good sir. Only your duty."

MacClannon thought hard all the way home. The day had been too strange, starting too early with the meeting at the standing stones. Now this odd chat with the prince of Wales. What next? He could never have imagined the terrible announcement that awaited him at home.

# FIFTY-THREE

"She's going away!" Annalee cried in terror as they saw the lights of the *Tassia Far* turn.

"No. She's doing a search pattern," Alex explained in a controlled voice. "She couldn't tell how far away we were when she saw the flare, so she's sweeping a larger area." Alex guessed they had drifted a mile since she had first spied them. He did some rapid calculations. She would travel back three or four miles, make another quarter mile turn and repeat the pattern. Meanwhile, they would continue drifting in a more or less straight line at three or four knots. The *Tassia Far* could motor at about 8 knots, but the waves would slow her down. In his exhausted state, the calculations were confusing.

"We might just have to wait a little," he said, the words almost swallowed as a sudden huge wave hit the little raft.

"We'll keep shouting anytime she gets close, but we might just have to wait for daylight." It was like some cruel, blind courtship dance across the waves.

For hours it continued, the low bleat of the air horn, and sometimes, when the wind didn't snatch it away, faint shouts in reply. Clouds had blown in and covered the moon, the sea was getting sloppier, with four- to six-foot waves. The tension was thick in both boats. Chicago swept the water with a spotlight but saw nothing but foam and troughs. If the water got much rougher, a hundred yards would be as good as a hundred miles. In the life raft, Alex, Jack, and Annalee watched as the light came closer and closer, then turned abruptly away again.

"What are you doing now?" Jack asked the puzzlement as Alex tied a lifejacket to the end of a line.

"With waves this high, it's hard to see us even if she's close."

189

He tied the orange life jackets on the line each about three feet apart.

"It looks like a kite tail," Annalee remarked.

"Exactly. The more we have bobbing out there, the more there is to see." Alex threw the tail out in the water and they watched with satisfaction. One of the life jackets was always viable atop a wave.

# FIFTY-FOUR

Lachlin Muir opened the door carefully, fully expecting the wolf to spring at his throat, but Birdy sat quietly on the bed, simply radiating her fury with a smoldering black glare. His nose throbbed, and his eye was beginning to show a deep purple. The hour-long drive to this remote farm had given his testicles time to recover, but his little finger, which she had yanked out of joint, still ached.

"So the banshee's settled down, has she?" he said, smiling. "Or is it just conserving your energy you are?"

"Piss off," she snapped.

"That's no kind of language for a princess to be using now, is it?" He had brought a telephone, which he now plugged into the outlet. He was about to sit down, thought better of it, and spun the chair around and straddled it instead. No use giving her an open target should she choose to pounce.

"You're a scrappy one all right. Did ye take one a' them self-defense courses or somethin'?"

"I have brothers."

"Ah yes." He laughed. "I've a few of those myself, and the scars to prove it."

"What do you want with me?"

"Now look here, lassy, there's no reason for this to be such a trial. I've explained it all. We really hate hav'n to do this, but we don't see no other way. We need your father's help. Scotland needs his help.''

"Kidnapping is a fine way to start your heroic mission.''

"Yer right, lass. And if we had more time, any other way, you wouldn't be here now. But we have to move. ''Where's your friend today—still licking his wounds?''

She had given McKay a bit of a bashing as well.

"He's gone to the islands,'' Muir told her. ''To bring your grandfather's body home.''

"The coffin?'' she scoffed.

"Aye lass the coffin. I'm leaving shortly, and I won't see you again until the exchange. There are four lads guarding the place. They won't hurt you. They won't even see you. There's a woman to see to your needs. We've tried to make it comfortable for you.'' There were several paperback books, and some magazines. Clean T-shirts and underwear were folded neatly on another chair, and there were tiny wrapped bars of Crabtree and Evelyn soap by the sink.

"Again, I do apologize.'' He got up. ''Now I'd like you to phone your father. Tell him you're all right. We won't give him time enough to have the call traced, so talk fast. We need the money wired today. Tell him to wait by the phone for another call with instructions.'' Birdy took the receiver. Muir pulled a pair of pliers out of his pocket. He picked up her other hand.

"If you try to tell him anything else; if I think you are giving him a message in some sort of family code, I will crush your knuckle. We will try very hard not kill you. But things can get ugly.''

# *FIFTY-FIVE*

"It wasn't us." Hayes calmly slid the report across the desk to Spencer. "I don't know whether to be saddened or flattered by your assumption." Spencer opened the file and saw a good inch of police reports, coroner's reports, and evidence summaries on Margaret Haversford's death.

"I realize we have a certain reputation," Hayes went on. "But novels and movies aside, the fact is, sir, my office simply does not do this sort of thing. And if we did," he added with a grim smile, "we would have done it better. Pushing a girl in front of a train is not, shall we say, discreet."

Spencer still felt suspicious as he scanned the pages.

"But blowing up the coffin was?" Spencer replied coolly.

"There were reasons." His tone was chilling and full of implications. *You do not know everything, Mr. Spencer.*

"But what about the letter? Mr. Whitstone said she was carrying an original letter, borrowed from a family friend. The police report doesn't list it among items in the bag they recovered." Hayes sat forward and folded his hands like a patient schoolteacher dealing with an exceptionally dull student.

"I phoned the chief inspector first thing this morning and related what you had told me. They went over to the hospital to have a chat with your Mr. Whitstone. I'm afraid the old fellow is in a bad way. All hooked up to machines. They're not expecting him to pull through."

"So he couldn't talk to them?"

"No." Hayes reached into the top drawer and pulled out a fax which he handed to Spencer. "But they did take his fingerprints."

Spencer read the fax twice, then asked incredulously, "They're certain?"

"All over her bag. They've a man at the archives looking for the letter, and they're searching his apartment now. There may be other physical evidence, hairs on his coat or something, but the prints on Margaret's bag were clear. I'm sure he didn't mean it," he said with some compassion now. "I suppose he really thought just to steal the letter. But Margaret put up a struggle. It really was an accident, Mr. Spencer. A tragic accident."

# FIFTY-SIX

Annalee spun across the slick rubber, grabbing at her father, as another wave crashed over them. It was practically routine by now, lying low, clutching each other as the waves hit, then frantically bailing out the water until the next deluge. The sea was getting wilder by the minute. Five-foot waves that to a real boat would cause only minor discomfort, threatened to capsize the little raft. Alex had given up on the kite-tail idea, retrieving the life jackets for their proper use, and using the length of rope to tether, each of them to the raft in case they were dumped altogether. The strong wind had done in the already damaged canopy, so there was pretty much nothing left. They were in constant danger of swamping.

Annalee sat up again, hair dripping around her thin face. She looked like some pathetic little Walt Disney animal, the motherless bunny, or lame colt, frail and lost. She wiped the water from her eyes and began to bail again with impossible vigor. Annalee was still young enough to hurl herself at hope. Chicago was about to swoop down on them at any minute!

"We'll have watermelon," she croaked as she bailed. "Macaroni and cheese; Mom's kind, not the box. Can Chicago make that?'' Alex decided not to puncture this small hope with the truth of Chicago's cooking and assured her that real macaroni and cheese would definitely be on the table that night.

"And a huge glass of orange juice ..." she went on as she scooped the last of the wave from the boat. "... and a beer for you and Dad ..." Jack nodded automatically at his daughter's menu as he kept watch for the *Tassia Far.* Twice now, they had seen her, twice now she hadn't seen them. The first faint blue of daylight was edging over the horizon, but the sky was thick with clouds and the wind was getting stronger.

Annalee sat up on her knees, and her dark eyes burned with a fevered excitement. "And ice cream. And ..." A huge wave was roaring down on them, its crest like a hatchet.

"Watch out!" Alex grabbed her arm and pulled her down as the wave hit. Jack ducked, but it caught Alex full in the face, knocking him backward against the pontoon. He choked, the salt-water burning his throat. His lungs felt seared, and he gasped for air. Annalee landed in his lap and he grabbed her, then Jack slid into them. The raft tipped perilously, plunging Alex head-and-shoulders backward under the water. He was really choking now. He felt Annalee's knees against his ribs. The raft was about to capsize.

It felt like a hot stake had been driven down his throat. Then suddenly Jack pulled the girl back and the wobbly raft was level once more. Alex sat up, choking. The world swarmed before him, the dizzying orange of the raft, the inky sea, the faint turquoise of sunrise in the sky. Sharp blows on his back, shocking the breath into him.

More air now; his hands were tingling, his vision clearing. Alex knelt hunched over, six inches of water swirling around his hands and knees. Miraculously, the bailing can had survived the near capsize. The can was so small, and there was so much water. They would never make it. A few more waves ... how long could they last. The coughing subsided, Alex sat back on his heels. Now he wondered for a second if he really *had* died and was seeing a vision. ... for out of the dawn, barely visible in the scalding light of the rising sun, was the white bow of the *Tassia Far* bearing down on them.

# FIFTY-SEVEN

It began to rain, a warm steady rain that flattened out the waves and sweetened their skins. They waited silently as the *Tassia Far* approached, a chimera in the mist. Time slowed and sounds were magnified, the sound of the water lapping at the raft, the gentle drumming of the rain.

Chicago looked so small. Standing alone at the helm, she looked as small and scraggly as Annabel Lee, Alex thought. She had not bothered to put on her slicker, and her clothes were drenched. She guided the boat alongside. Alex could not read her expression. He tried to control his own, for now, only now that the ordeal was over and rescue at hand, was a sickening fear seizing him. He tried to stand, but found his knees too weak to hold him. Chicago was shouting something, Jack responding, Alex couldn't hear it. Everything was shutting down.

It had always been like this for Alex. Calm in the crisis, no matter how long, no matter how difficult, then once it was over, sometimes day later, it would hit him like a truck. It was a weakness he despised but could not control, a renegade physical response in a body otherwise so disciplined.

". . . the line! Grab it, Alex! Alex?'' Jack was holding the ladder, struggling to keep the pitching life raft near the *Tassia Far.* Dumbly, Alex picked up the line and pulled in the raft. If a giant shark lurched up at them now, if the bad guys showed up with guns blazing, Alex knew he could leap back into action. But this simple task, to climb aboard the boat, was stupidly beyond him.

Jack steadied the ladder and guided Annalee up. Chicago grabbed the girl's life jacket and hoisted her onto the deck.

"Go ahead," Alex told Jack. His voice sounded far away; there was a steady roar in his ears. He slid over to steady the ladder.

Jack climbed awkwardly, one rung at a time, and stumbled as if his feet had forgotten solid ground entirely.

"Well, what are you waiting for—a brass band?" Chicago leaned over the railing. "Tie that off and get your ass up here!" She fought back tears. She knew what was going on. Alex tried to pull himself up. Shit. The waves were bucking the raft and his legs wouldn't hold. He clung to the ladder. The rungs were slippery, hard to grasp.

Then Alex felt her hand on his, her fingers curling around his wrist. Her palm was calloused, her grip strong. "Come on, Alex." Her voice was quiet and steady. Alex felt strength flowing into his legs. He climbed up on the deck, into her arms. He could feel her heart beating. She was trembling. Alex pulled back and looked into her face, a haggard, exhausted but beautiful face, her pale eyes shiny with tears.

"You're here," she said in a quavering voice. "You're back."

"Yes." He stroked her wet hair, felt a shudder go through her.

"You're hurt?" She touched the side of his neck where Dunagh's knife had cut him.

"It's just a scratch. We're fine. Are you okay?"

Chicago nodded. "The others . . . ?"

Alex just shook his head and saw the pain in her eyes. She took his hand. "Come on. I have to radio . . ."

"No." Alex stopped her. "Not yet." She felt a new alarm. "Why? Alex—what is it?" Suddenly Annalee screamed. Chicago turned and saw what had alarmed them. The stranger was sitting up.

"I found him last night," Chicago explained. "Floating in the skiff. What is it, Alex? Who is he?"

"I don't know."

# *FIFTY-EIGHT*

*"Two Englishmen are being sought for questioning about an American salvage vessel that sank under mysterious circumstances in the Bahamas last week ... Mysterious sinking, two Englishmen involved ... American treasure hunters lost at sea ..."*

The stories so far were vague, and noninflammatory, except for the tabloids which declared simply: "PIRATES."

Hayes, together with the ministers, had decided to go up front with the mention of the two men in the press reports, even though no independent sources had found them out yet. That was only a matter of time. The diplomatic channels had been busy. The Americans were being cooperative. The wife of the missing archaeologist had been contacted, and was being questioned.

How much did she know? Hayes wondered. And what would she tell? She would certainly know about the coffin. She had to be kept quiet, at least for the time being. Convince her that her husband and daughter, if alive, could still be in danger. Details, there were so many details. It was frustrating to have to rely on someone else's finesse for this important aspect.

*"... the Englishmen were sent to observe the salvage of the* Christiania, *since the wreck being investigated was a British ship and could contain historically significant artifacts. 'Treasure hunters traditionally wreak havoc on history,' said Dr. Malcom Breyer, marine archaeologist. 'It is vital for government agencies to maintain watch and control to see that precious artifacts are not destroyed in the name of fortune hunting.'"*

*Ah, God, bless you, Dr. Breyer,* Hayes thought as he folded the paper. There was also a sidebar piece on recently recovered undersea treasures, featuring photos of jeweled crosses and pyramids of gold bars, the implication clearly being, *here is what tempted these agents to treachery; it was greed pure and simple, we had nothing to do with it.*

The story was starting to get extensive coverage in the United States. That couldn't be helped.

*"Seven, possibly eight people are reportedly still missing, including a twelve-year-old girl. England has offered support in the search efforts already under way."* That was from an American television news report.

The trick now was not to suppress the news but steer it, manipulate it into the reality they were creating. It was like a game of chess. Anticipate, guard, protect the Queen. Finding Teneby and Dunagh would be a major step. God, he did not want to end his career on such a stupidly botched operation!

There was a short rap on the door and George Shorter came in. He was deputy press liaison, part of the damage control machinery.

"Bad news?" Hayes guessed morosely after a glance at the man's face.

"I'm not sure. The life raft was reported found this morning—empty."

"No survivors?"

"It appears not."

"Who found it?"

"The woman who discovered the *Goose* had been sunk."

Hayes glanced over the fax, but it told him nothing more. "What do we know about this woman—that she was on the *Golden Goose*, originally, then left?"

"She and a man, boyfriend we understand, were hired as divers, but they stayed on her sailboat. It's registered to a Chicago Nordejoong in Miami—not much else on her right now. They seem to have been hired on for the salvage."

"But she wasn't around during the explosion?"

"Apparently they left for a more secure location when the storm hit. We don't know yet why he returned ahead of her."

"Well, find out. What have you heard from our men down there?"

"It looks like Dunagh at least went to Providencales. It's an island in the Turks and Caicos, south of the Bahamas. Also known as Provo. A bartender said he was asking about flights there. Also said Dunagh told him Teneby wasn't well. We checked the flights out of Mayaguana, and we're certain *one* of them left.''

"So our lads have gone on to Provo?''

"Yes, sir.''

"Good. I want every harbor, road, and airport under surveillance, but tell our chaps not to get too bossy. Natives can get so touchy. Still no activity at the wreck site?''

"RBDF has been monitoring it, mostly with fly overs. It's quite a way off shore. So far no boats.''

"So whatever Dunagh was after, he either got it that night or hasn't come back for it yet. What does that tell you?''

The other man shrugged. "It was either small enough to be brought up in a sack or large enough that it needs some equipment.''

"Right. Let me know as soon as our men arrive in Provo. Our highest priority is to find Dunagh and Teneby.''

# FIFTY-NINE

"Talk to us,'' Alex said simply. "Start at the beginning, and don't waste our time.'' Teneby was still weak, but no longer delirious. It was early afternoon, and they were all in the cockpit of the *Tassia Far*, sailing back to civilization. The rain had stopped, but the sky was still cloudy and the water choppy. There was a good steady wind that should get them to Provo by evening. There was an airport there, with more regular flights than Mayaguana and a full marina. After the long search, the *Tassia Far* was low on fuel and water.

There would also be a hospital in Provo, or at least a clinic. While Alex and Annalee were bouncing back, Jack McGuire was suffering heart palpitations, nausea, and dizziness. Though fit for a man of fifty-three, the dehydration had been more of a strain, and he was not responding well. He had drunk several quarts of fluid by now, but had produced no urine and that didn't seem like a good sign. His legs and hands were swollen.

Annabel Lee, though weakest to start with, had made the most rapid recovery. A few pints of Chicago's sugar and salt solution, some orange juice and peanut-butter-and-jelly sandwiches, and she was practically glowing with vigor. She sat in the cockpit, her hair finally clean and untangled, her skinny body lost in Chicago's clothes. She held Lassie on her lap. She had seized on the snake for comfort as if it was a teddy bear. Teneby was clearly uncomfortable with a boa constrictor so close. Annalee did nothing to ease that fear, letting it slither over to within two feet of him before pulling it back.

"I really don't have much to tell." Teneby spoke slowly, his lips still swollen from the sunburn. "But sinking your boat was never meant to be a part of this—"

"That's not the beginning," Alex interrupted coldly. "Who sent you?"

"No one." Alex leaned over, deliberately grabbed the man by the shirt and slowly pulled him closer.

"Is there something about my face that makes me look particularly stupid today?"

"Alex ..." Jack was surprised by this harsh side of the man, and glanced at his daughter. As if reading his thoughts, Annalee refused to even look at him, ducking that glance of parental banishment.

"You are not a treasure hunter or a pirate," Alex offered. "You are a British agent."

"That's absurd." Teneby jerked away, and shifted back against the cushions. His feet were still tied. "I'm sorry for all you've been through, but I think you had too much time to ... to invent fantasy out there."

"I didn't invent a HICER bomb," Alex challenged. Teneby could not mask his surprise. "The bomb that destroyed the *Golden Goose* was unusual." Alex explained about the HICER shell to the others.

"Like putting a firecracker under a tin can?" Jack offered.

"Exactly. And a HICER bomb is beautifully untraceable. The concentrated force usually destroys the bomb mechanism, and the shield itself is ultimately pulverized."

"You obviously know your stuff," Teneby countered. "So you know that anything can be bought on the black market."

"Not this. Now since you happened to get lucky and live through it so far." Alex relaxed his tone a little. "Why don't you do yourself a favor and help us sort this out. Tell us about the coffin."

"I don't know anything about any coffin." Teneby eyed the snake as it rippled over the helm, a good three feet of its body extending in midair, little tongue delicately flicking in his direction. Alex held out his arm, giving the snake support to continue closer.

"Honey," he said casually to Chicago, "do we have any rats left in the freezer? I think Lassie is hungry."

"She should be, she hasn't eaten for three weeks."

"What do you think would happen if we tied a couple of rats around our friend's neck here?" Teneby shrank back as the snake's tongue explored the collar of his shirt. Though his rational mind knew the snake was not poisonous, his more basic response was fear. He had never even seen a snake this close. He did not even visit the reptile house at the zoo. He felt the weight of its body as it began to creep slowly over his shoulder.

"Around his neck?" Chicago tickled Lassie's tail, encouraging her to move faster. "I don't know. But she doesn't usually squeeze for more than a couple of minutes."

"I think it would depend on where you hung the rats," Annalee chimed in. "Like if you hung them right here," She stroked her neck on either side of her trachea. "That might be a good place. There's a lot of stuff to squash in there. Arteries, I think." Chicago was surprised, Alex was not. He had just spent three days in a life raft with the kid. Jack McGuire just sighed.

"Okay—okay. We knew about the coffin." Alex gently lifted the boa constrictor off the man's neck and draped it over his own shoulder. "We were trying to avoid an incident," Teneby said carefully. "We were just supposed to keep an eye on your salvage operation. If the coffin was found, we would get rid of it. The coffin, not the boat," he clarified quickly. "Dunagh, my partner, went down to rig the charge. I waited in the boat to pick him up. I don't know what happened. Why he did this. I saw the commotion, saw you getting in the water and the other chap swimming after the skiff. I figured you had seen him, and I went in to pick up my man."

"You shot Shep and Marty," Annalee said accusingly.

"No. I tried to shoot low, to scare them off. I still didn't even know about the bomb. I picked up Dunagh. Next thing I knew, there was a knife in my back. I turned around and he stabbed me again, then pushed me overboard. Then the thing blew. I woke up in the water, with wreckage all over. Dunagh was gone. We had weapons in the boat, I suppose he shot your people." Teneby paused to drink some water, moving slowly with the pain of his wounds.

"I floated a long time on a seat cushion or something, then I saw the skiff and managed to swim to it. Your man was dead inside. I got myself in. The outboard was shot up, too, so I could only drift. That's the whole of it."

"Had you ever worked with this Dunagh before?" Alex pressed.

"In the Falklands a bit. I didn't know him well. But he had clearance." He remembered Griffith, his assigned partner, conveniently injured at the last minute. It hadn't seemed suspicious then.

"Why would it be so awful for England if this coffin is found?" Jack pressed. "I just don't understand."

"There was an infant who survived the wreck of the *Christiania*," Teneby said.

"Edward's son?"

"Yes. The pirates returned him to Jamaica. He grew up there, prospered, and his descendants eventually returned to Scotland. One of them is now a leader in the Scottish National Party."

"Which means what?" Alex pressed.

"That he could lay claim to the British throne."

"What do they know back in London right now?" Alex switched tracks a little. Teneby hadn't had much time to consider this aspect.

"Dunagh must have phoned the home office and told them something," Teneby speculated. "The chief would have been suspicious."

"Enough to send another agent?"

"I don't know."

"Who stands to benefit by Dunagh's blowing up the boat?" Teneby gave a morose sigh.

"We clearly lose."

"We being the British government?" The man would not reply.

"How do you lose?" Alex pressed.

"Overreaction. It lends credibility."

"Credibility?" Jack leaned forward excitedly. "You believe it! You know exactly who it is in that coffin then!"

# SIXTY

"There! Look there! I think we have it!" Dunagh leaped across the boat and leaned over the side. Far below was a vague dark shape on the sandy bottom.

"Let's check it out!" Dunagh ordered. Kyle McKay grabbed his mask, lowered the boarding ladder, and climbed down for a clearer look. "Spot on!" he cried excitedly.

"All right then—take her up a bit," he ordered the helmsman. "Drop the anchor well clear. Ready the gear, lads. Let's get His Royal Highness up and on his way."

They had searched for a day and a half. Without the exact coordinates, which Shepard had guarded closely, Dunagh knew it would be difficult to locate the site. There were a dozen of these small reefs and cays out here, and he knew only an approximate distance and a compass direction from Andrew's bay in Maya-guana. For this trip, they had come from the opposite direction entirely. Today's overcast sky and choppy water had made it extra difficult.

"Leave off the wet suit for now," Dunagh instructed McKay brusquely. The tension was wearing on him, and he was still hurting from his wounds. "Thomas, you, too." Thomas was a local divemaster who had come with the boat. Dunagh was glad to have him. Finding Jacobite scuba divers had not exactly been an easy task. McKay had only done his basic training, and that some years ago.

Thomas had been recommended as the best salvage man on the island. Best in the business of salvage meant not only finding and retrieving what you set out to, but staying quiet about it after the fact. In this case, the price had been five hundred US dollars. Funding was getting tight. Dunagh hoped Lachlan Muir was busy shaking up some money back home. A cargo plane had been reserved from Miami, ready to fly at a moment's notice and receipt of thirty thousand dollars.

"We have no idea what sort of shape this box is in," he explained. "So everything has to go easy. You do nothing without a signal from me, and everything exactly the way we went over it."

How many years he had spent waiting, working for the cause, and how much he had risked now. His very life. Dunagh knew he would be caught and tried, if he lived to stand trial. At the very best, he could expect fifteen or twenty years in prison. He would be respected. He would be a folk hero in Scotland. His poor father, God rest his soul, would finally be proud of him. But he would still be in jail for a long, long time.

"The coffin," Dunagh resumed his instructions in a controlled voice, "must reach Scotland intact. That's all we're working for."

They got in the water and descended quickly, each man busy with his assigned equipment. The coffin lay undisturbed, still half buried in the sand. Thomas and Dunagh, working on either side, dug out the sand from around the bottom, then worked heavy straps down under the base. McKay tensed, and watching carefully for instructions, handed over the lift bags, which Dunagh secured to the straps.

These looked like miniature hot air balloons. They were open at the bottom for inflation, and had release valves on top, to vent off the air as it expanded during ascent. It was a delicate business, and too much air, or uneven distribution of lift, could send the object rocketing to the surface, or tip it halfway up where it could plummet again to the bottom.

Dunagh and Thomas took out their regulators, held them under the bags, and pressed the purge valves, letting out small bursts of air. One-second blasts, each time testing, looking for any motion. This first step was intended merely to raise the coffin off the bottom a fraction of an inch, just enough so that they could wiggle a heavy tarp under it. After the coffin was wrapped in the tarp, nylon cinch straps were slipped around and pulled tight. For good measure, and to give them more handholds. Dunagh and Thomas also tied a net around the box.

The whole operation took almost fifty minutes. Once wrapped, it was ready to be moved. Dunagh pointed McKay to his place. He would steady one end, swimming up with it as it rose. Thomas and Dunagh faced each other across the coffin, each controlling two lift bags. With one more short blast of air in each bag, the coffin had enough lift. Slowly, the men began to swim up. As they rose, Dunagh and Thomas vented off the air, keeping a steady pace. It was all so smooth, so incredibly smooth. Fifty feet, forty feet, thirty, the timbers of the wrecked *Christiania* faded behind them, as its most important passenger was carried skyward.

*"Drop me to the bottom of the sea,"* the young prince had pledged his bride so long ago. *"And I'll come back to you some-how."* Now, after three hundred years, the last of the Jacobites were helping James Francis Edward keep his promise.

# *SIXTY-ONE*

"You know you can't get away with it, Swinny," MacClannon said bitterly to the man who had been his friend and partner, and who was presently holding his daughter hostage. "It's all over the media by now. Do they know that? Your boys out there? Do they really expect just to land, unload your damned king, and walk off down the path?"

"We're expecting things at the airport to be very civil," Swinny explained with only a hint of threat.

"And when the hell are they going to get here? Neil, you don't even know what's going on down there!"

"The plane is on standby now. Dunagh will call as soon as they're ready to leave." Swinny was nervous. Two days now Dunagh and McKay had been searching for the coffin. Every minute's delay was giving the English more time. "We know you want Birdy back safe; and we know you have friends at Scotland Yard. I'm counting on you to keep them off our backs."

MacClannon looked at him closely. "I've arranged my end. You'll be allowed to land. But once my daughter is released, I have no control. You know that."

"Of course. We'll stand to our deeds, Cory. If we're caught," he added with a questioning tone that hung heavy in the air.

"I told you, Neil, I'll have none of it!"

"You don't have to betray us, though, to have none of it."

"Then don't tell me anything to betray," he snapped. "I don't care where you go or what you do after Birdy is back. We part at the airport and I don't care to ever see your lying face again." Swinny looked down and MacClannon immediately caught his hesitation.

"We never said anything about the airport, Cory," Swinny said reluctantly. Cory felt his rage about to burst out of control. He turned and grabbed hold of the mantle with both hands, squeezing hard so his fingers would not leap up and grab one of the swords that hung there.

"As soon as the coffin arrived, you said."

"Arrived at the laboratory, Cory. Not the airport. You know how badly the English want to stop this thing! We can't take the risk."

"Risk! There will be a hundred television cameras at the airport!" MacClannon seethed. Cause or no cause, this was betrayal as sure as the Campbell's had been.

"You can have my head if you like, old friend," Swinny said sadly. "Once the thing is done. But we've come too far to risk it all now. We'll take Birdy with the coffin and drive them both to where the testing will be done. Once there, we'll let her go. I swear it, Cory. She won't be harmed."

# SIXTY-TWO

She could see them—just ahead. The little boat spinning toward the horizon, caught in a current, lost in the foamy troughs. Faster! She had to sail faster. The sails began to flap, but when she picked up the sheet, she could not move it—it weighed a hundred pounds. The ship was as big as a building. She leaned her whole weight against the helm, but could barely turn it. The wind snapped the sails and the mast creaked, while overhead, thousands of gulls circled, crying viciously.

Why could she not change course? Desperately, she ran to the stern and looked down, fifty feet or more, to the muddy green water. The rudder was jammed. She climbed down the outside of the boat. The timbers rotted under her touch. Her fingers gouged into the wood. Something was caught in the rudder. She kicked at it. It was a woman's body, her long pink nightgown swirling through the water. Quelling her revulsion, Chicago reached down to free it. Suddenly, one bony white hand lurched up out of the waves and grabbed her ankle. Chicago kicked and screamed.

Annalee jumped back, startled.

"What is it? What's wrong?" Chicago jumped to her feet, crashing her shin against the helm as she staggered awake. Her heart was pounding. The sun had come out. Afternoon. "What's the matter?" she asked, panicked.

"Nothing. I'm sorry. You were having a bad dream." Chicago sank back down on the cushion and brushed the sweaty hair off her face, checked her watch. It was two-twenty. She must have slept nearly an hour. A dream—yes, it had to be a dream.

"Where's Alex?"

"He's still sleeping." Chicago jumped up. Of course, Alex had gone below for a nap, she was on watch and must have dozed off. "It's all right" Annalee said. "The autopilot was on, and I've been watching. We got one satellite fix, and I wrote down the numbers. Shep showed me how it worked on the *Goose*, sort of."

"Thanks. That's great."

"You looked really tired."

"I guess I was." She tried to quiet the pounding in her chest. "Everyone's okay?" Annalee nodded.

"I saw a boat."

"Where?"

"Still far. That's why I woke you." Annalee handed the binoculars to Chicago and pointed. "Do you think it's the enemies?"

"What? . . . No." She looked at her watch. "We should be getting close to the Caico Islands. It would be a dive boat or ferry." It was too far to make out much beyond the shape of the distant boat. Chicago put the binoculars back down, checked the compass, and looked at the sails. Everything looked good.

"How you doing?" Chicago asked. "You feeling all right?"

"Yeah. What was your dream?"

"Just weird stuff. Where's Lassie?"

"I put her below, in the closet in your cabin. Alex said to, since the man is in the bow where she usually stays. Can I try steering a while?"

"Sure." Chicago leaned across the cockpit and switched off the autopilot. "Sit up on the bench there so you can look down on the compass." Annalee took the helm, and the *Tassia Far* swayed a little under her novice hand. "Don't watch it all the time," Chicago suggested. "Think more about the feel of the boat, and the sails. If you're on course, they'll stay pretty full."

Chicago adjusted the sails a little. The wind was steady, and they were on a good course. The two sat silently a long time, and Chicago liked the girl for this.

"I had some weird dreams in the life raft," she said after a while.

"I'll bet you did." Chicago waited, but didn't press for elaboration.

"Is my dad going to be all right?"

"He'll be fine. We'll be in Provo soon." Jack had been growing steadily worse, and they were worried about his kidneys. A helicopter rescue was still an option, but one they were reluctant to take. That might risk alerting the unknown villains to their location.

"My uncle died in the life raft," she said with a blasé tone that wasn't convincing. "We had to throw his body overboard."

"Alex told me. I'm really sorry." What a feeble sentiment. "But your dad isn't going to die."

"Lots of people died in history." She stared out over the water. "Are you and Alex in love?" she asked as if this were the next logical step from people dying in history. Chicago hesitated.

"I think . . . well, yeah."

"Did you think you would die if you never saw him again, while you were searching?"

Chicago nodded, still unable to face that very fear.

"But you wouldn't really," Annalee went on sadly. "No one dies for love. Except in songs. Or really old people sometimes. Like Shep and Marty. If only one of them had got killed, maybe the other would die, too. In six months usually." Chicago pictured Alex sleeping in their cabin right now. A week ago, she had been trying to reconcile herself to a life without him, now she could barely suppress the urge to go check on him to see if he was breathing. Annalee gave her an embarrassed glance. "I pretended sometimes; in the life raft; that he was . . . well, sort of like my boyfriend. In case we did die or something."

"No one special back home?"

"Boys mature slower," she said matter-of-factly.

Chicago smiled. "Well, was he a good boyfriend? In your imagination, that is?" Annalee laughed and nodded. "I guess."

As if on cue, Alex appeared in the companionway. His hair was ragged and his face creased from the sheets. He moved stiffly. He looked a lot like a guy who had spent three days adrift. "I'm a new man." He grinned.

"That's too bad, we were just deciding we kind of liked the old one," Chicago replied. He climbed up, squinted at the light, and stretched. "I'm all rested up." He touched her gently on the back as he sat beside her. "Why don't you get a nap?"

"I just did. Annalee's been running the ship." She handed him the binoculars. "There's a boat in the distance. I can't tell what it is yet." Alex looked at the boat, then got up and looked at the compass. He frowned.

"What is it?"

"Probably nothing. How far to the horizon? Four miles?"

"Standing on deck, it's about four and a half. Why?"

"I looked at the chart on my way up," Alex explained a little too calmly. "From where we are right now, three or four miles out in that direction puts them pretty damn near the site of the *Christiania*."

# SIXTY-THREE

It was ten P.M. in London, the bitter end of a long, troubling day. Spencer, Hayes, Home Secretary Burton, and Lord Chancellor Shiftly were once again planning their strategy.

So far, they were holding their own in the media circus. The real story, from the switched infants to the Jacobite cause, was complicated enough, and the immediate events—sunken ship, archaeologist, and young daughter lost at sea—were dramatic enough that the tabloids hadn't had to scratch below the surface.

Adrian Spencer turned a pencil over and over on the conference table, running his fingers down the length from point to eraser, eraser to point. If they had only listened to him in the first place. Ignored the whole thing. Filed it away, as it should have been, stamped "No Further Attention," none of this would be happening now.

"Anything further on your agents?" the Lord Chancellor asked.

Hayes hesitated, his voice betraying the strain. "We have confirmed that Steven Dunagh, one of the agents in question, has been a member of a secret Jacobite organization."

"Jacobites?" Shiftly asked incredulously. "Did I hear that right?"

"The files should have been found weeks ago. The whole thing was inexcusably sloppy."

"What the hell are you doing with files on Jacobites? Shouldn't they be extinct or something?" Shiftly rustled with disgust.

Burton, tired of the man's bluster, tired of the whole mess, felt his own patience wearing thin. "Surely there can't be any Jacobites around today, Mr. Hayes. Whatever would be the point?"

"They're old men mostly. History buffs, like to go on 'what if-ing' their Sunday afternoons away. But there are a few active in the various antimonarchy sects, as well as the SNP," Hayes reported gravely. "They claim to have originated as a loose band after the Glencoe massacre, then consolidated over Culloden."

"Are you joking, sir? Culloden was seventeen . . . something."

"Seventeen forty-six."

"Two hundred and fifty years is a long time to hold a grudge," Shiftly snorted.

"And you keep files on them?" Burton pressed.

"How the bloody hell do you think they've kept themselves in business all these years?" Shiftly interrupted crossly. "For every man hour spent on the KGB or the IRA, there's ten spent on the communist bird-watching clubs and Knights of the bloody Holy Grail or whatever. How many genuine subversives do you think there are in England anyway?"

"Well, what do these Jacobites have to do with all this?" Burton continued in a more civil tone.

"As I've said, we have come to believe that one of the agents we sent to Mayaguana, Steven Dunagh, may be involved with this . . . group . . ."

"So one of your lads was a mole. Is that how it is, Hayes? You've been infiltrated again. Christ! Why not just hire the bloody Girl Guides to run this place."

George Burton gave him a withering glance and drew himself back to his aristocratic poise.

"But what, sir," he asked civily, "would be the point of these Jacobites sinking the American's boat?"

"To cause us embarrassment and lend credibility to their claim perhaps," Hayes explained "And also, I'm afraid, to secure the coffin so they can have the body identified." Hayes was having a hard time with this. He had barely digested the news himself. A secret Jacobite organization, who would have thought? Some department simply dropping the ball. A proper vetting should have hit on Dunagh's Scottish roots, as well as his associations with this subversive group. Goddamn Jacobites indeed!

Steven Dunagh's personal file showed only that he came from an unremarkable middle-class background, raised by an aunt and uncle in Manchester ever since his parents died when he was six. The family was originally from Scotland, but it hadn't seemed important. Still didn't.

"We are not talking about the parlor anarchists here," Hayes responded coolly. "These Jacobites are a highly secretive antimonarchist, Scottish Nationalist sect. They seem to operate at a sophisticated level."

"So he's a mole, eh, Crawly? Is that what you're telling us? He's a mole, and you people screwed up? Christ ..." The Home Secretary leaned back and folded his arms in disgust.

"Could you enlighten us a little bit more about this organization, Mr. Hayes?" Burton was a master of the upper crust tone of disdainful condescension. "Do they have an agenda?"

"Their goal is Scottish nationalism. Secession and complete independence. They seem to be very well organized, and geared to long-range plans. They placed Dunagh with us six years ago, or recruited him once he was already in."

"And they're antimonarchists? So why are they going on about declaring this ... MacClannon fellow the rightful king of England?"

"One doesn't always expect consistency from these groups." This caused a rumble of agreement around the table.

# SIXTY-FOUR

"It's him." Teneby handed Alex back the binoculars. Sailing west into the lowering sun made it hard to see Dunagh's face, but Teneby could tell it was Steven Dunagh by the compact, muscular shape, and the way he moved.

"You're sure?"

"Yes."

"And that must be the coffin." Alex studied the boat a few long seconds.

"Oh, God, does it look all right?" Jack asked. "Can you tell?"

"It looks pretty well wrapped up." Alex handed the binoculars to Jack. He turned to Chicago. "How soon do we get there?"

"Getting into the harbor is tricky. We'll reach the entrance in about an hour, but then there's a virtual maze of coral to get through. If the channel markers are all in place, I'd guess a half hour or forty-five minutes to wind our way through. With the sun low, it's trickier. If we have to get a pilot boat to lead us, add at least another twenty minutes. Then we need the tide to get through the last channel into the marina. I figure we have until about eight tonight. If we miss the tide, we have to anchor outside until morning."

"But that's not far, is it?"

"No, a couple hundred yards. We can go in with the dinghy."

"But they'll have all the same obstacles, won't they?" Jack asked. "To slow them down as well?" He was too sick to stand up, and was lying in the cockpit.

"That's a local dive boat," Chicago explained. "They know the path through the coral, and they draw a lot less than the *Tassia Far*. Plus they go faster than we do." They had dropped the sail and were now motoring at about seven knots. "They'll be docked within an hour."

213

"Damn."

"What are we going to do?" Annalee asked with a mixture of fear and excitement. The recent traumas had blunted her enthusiasm for adventure.

"I don't know yet." Alex got up and walked out to the bow, watching in frustration as Dunagh's boat sped toward the harbor. Chicago followed him, worried and angered by the look in his eyes. She sat on the narrow pulpit rail, and propped a foot on the anchor. They sat silently for several minutes, practiced by now in the art of each other.

"Alex, this is not our fight," she finally said simply. He continued to watch the boat, moving steadily toward the harbor entrance.

"They're killers."

"They'll be caught and punished. It doesn't have to be by us."

"They have the coffin."

She grabbed his arm. "What the hell do you care! It's not important! Listen to me, Alex ..." She loosened her grip, slid her hand down his arm. He took her hand and held it lightly. "Isn't it you who's always going on about how you have to pick your battles?"

"Me?" He smiled. "Did I say that?" She was not in the mood for humor. Her stomach was knotting. "I like Jack, too, and I'd be sorry to see all his research lost, but that coffin is not going to change a damn thing. So what if it shakes up the damn Royal Family a little—so what? Might do them all some good. God-damnit, Alex; we're alive. We're safe. King James the whatever is dead. All we have to do now is get Jack to a doctor, turn Teneby over to the cops, and sail off into the sunset." Alex brushed her hair back off her shoulders and kissed her forehead.

"You don't feel like righting a few wrongs here?"

"Who would we be helping? We don't even know! Who do we believe—this Teneby guy? What if he's lying, and Dunagh is really doing the right thing? Have you thought about that?"

"Yes."

"This is not like last time. There is no nerve gas in that coffin. You're not saving the world, you're not even ... I don't know, rescuing anyone! It's just some old bones. Bones that aren't going to change anything."

"Hmmmm. That life raft was no pleasure cruise."

"Revenge? Is that what you're after? Makes a damn lousy motive and often gets you killed ... Who was it said that!" Alex remembered the very moment he had told her that, sitting on the dock, in Miami the first time he knew how painfully he loved her.

"I'm not sure I can argue if you're going to keep quoting me."

"Alex, look. I know you ... you're wanting to leave. I ..."

"Wait a minute. I don't know where you get this ..."

"It's true. We both know it. You weren't jumping to take this job for the six hundred bucks. You need the adventure. You want to go back to being ... whatever—this ... fixer of things. Well okay. That's who you are. And you're good at it, and ... maybe the world needs you." Her eyes were filling up, and she had to make herself talk fast. She had thought about so much over these long desperate days. "So go. Go and fight the good fight. But, Alex ..." She squeezed his hand, "this just isn't it." God, how he had changed her! A year ago, she would have just cursed him out, probably pitched him overboard, and gone on with her life.

They were both a little surprised. Alex pulled her close and felt the quiet tears soak his shirt, spreading in a tiny warm patch against his skin.

"Well ... maybe you're right." Chicago pulled away and searched his face.

"What did you say?"

"I said, I think you're right. It's not our battle."

"You mean it?"

"Well ... yes. Mostly." He looked into her eyes, such an unworldly shade of blue. "Babe, I ... I love you. You're right. About me getting restless. I need to do ... something. But I promise you—I want to ... I don't know what it is but I want to *honor* ... your love. Is that right? I want, if I do get killed, that it's worth it."

"Oh, thanks." She laughed through her tears. "You're promising me a noble death, is that it?"

"Well, I hadn't thought of it in exactly those terms."

"We might have to discuss the parameters of noble ..."

"Okay." He kissed her deeply. "Come on below and I'll show you something noble." He swung her around and they kissed again. How amazing that he was here again! His good flesh hers to feel and hold. Chicago thought of his toothbrush, the bristles mashed down, and chuckled.

"What?" Alex peered at her. "What's so funny?"

"Nothing."

"What?" He grabbed her.

"Nothing!" She was back to her tough old self.

"Well you're laughing . . ." he stopped abruptly, staring toward the island. Alarmed, Chicago turned.

"The boat's turned around. They're heading this way."

# SIXTY-FIVE

The meeting broke up shortly after eleven, with little resolved except for more damage-control measures. Inflammatory stories on antimonarchist groups would be planted in the media, an exposé perhaps, a Sunday feature: *Shocking new revelations from secret government files. Separatist groups plot to assassinate the queen . . .* A prominent forensic anthropologist would be encouraged to release statements casting doubt on the reliability of DNA testing on bones so old, bones tainted by seawater.

Most importantly, as Spencer had pointed out, the DNA testing would do no good unless the body of King James the second were exhumed for comparison.

"He's buried in France," Hayes informed them. "We'll have our solicitors ready an injunction."

"Bloody frogs," Shiftly murmured. "They'll be all *oui oui messieurs* up front, while behind our backs they'll be out sharpening the shovels."

"Still, with a prompt go at the courts, we can tie up any questions of exhumation for a long time," Burton agreed. "Anything else, sir?" he asked, looking impatiently at his watch.

"We'll investigate MacClannon thoroughly. There has to be

some scandal can take him down a peg or two, sully that perfect family image. There's talk one of his sons is a homosexual."

"Oh, Christ, Hayes." Shiftly slammed an exasperated palm on the table. "First of all, that's a laughable complaint these days, unless its the old man himself caught with a boy or something. God, you probably need two boys now."

Spencer felt a new flush of worry. "Mr. Hayes, I'm not sure that would be the prudent course to pursue, either. The press's treatment of the Royal Family has already been fairly unkind this year."

"What he means is," Shiftly interrupted. "you start talking queer and Prince Edward will be eaten alive."

Rumors about the queen's youngest son had been circulating for years, helped not a bit by his foray into musical theater.

"Forget the slander," Burton suggested. "We've never been terribly good at manipulating public sentiment. What about your agents? What do you intend to do with them?"

"They will be brought in," Hayes said simply. "And their cooperation secured."

# SIXTY-SIX

Alex dodged around the mast, vaulted over the cockpit, swung through the companionway, and yanked Teneby away from the radio. The man swung reflexively, but Alex easily deflected the blow, twisted his arm, and wrestled him down by the time Chicago showed up with the fish club.

"What did you tell him?" Alex shouted in the man's face.

"Nothing I . . ." Alex slammed him into the table brace.

"Don't lie to me."

". . . the police" Teneby gasped as he raised his hands in defense. "I radioed the police." Annalee sat at the top of the companionway, watching, Jack right behind her, trying to keep her back. Alex dragged the man up on the couch.

"I couldn't let him get away." Teneby's face was white with pain. The sudden exertion had drained him.

"You're lying. It was too quick."

"Something else then. Someone already waiting."

"Other agents?"

"I suppose. Yes." Teneby held his side. "I'm sure they've sent people by now. They must have traced him from Mayaguana. It's been three days."

"Annalee, go get me some rope. A mooring line, by the rail in the stern," Alex directed. He glanced at Chicago, and nodded toward the aft cabin. "We might have trouble." Chicago edged around Teneby and went to the locker. Like most sailors, she carried firearms. Like most experienced sailors, she carried a couple of cheap old guns to be dutifully turned over to customs while in port, and then the real guns, which never left the boat.

She bypassed the closet with the old weapons, and opened this secure and less obvious cubbyhole built beneath one of the berths. There was a well-oiled double-barreled shotgun and a Smith & Wesson .38-caliber hammerless revolver. "A good girl's gun," her father had explained when he picked that one out for her. There was also Alex's bag, which she removed unopened. Unlike most sailors, who didn't have ex-CIA agents for boyfriends, there was a small collection of serious weapons that she left to Alex's care. He had taught her to use them, but she hated even knowing they were aboard, and had never even touched that bag since it was stowed there.

Alex tied Teneby's hands and feet and locked him in the bow cabin.

"Annalee, you and your dad stay in the aft cabin. Don't come out for anything—understand?"

"What are you going to do?"

"Nothing, I hope. We'll just be sailing along minding our own business."

"I've done some hunting," Jack offered. "I can shoot." He was swaying, and his skin had taken on a gray pallor. Alex was sure the recoil from one shot would knock him out.

"Thanks, Jack—but just take care of Annalee." He double-checked the shotgun and slipped it up on deck. Chicago pulled on a windbreaker and tucked the pistol into the pocket.

"Go on and take the helm," he instructed. "Just act normal, but keep your shotgun close. I'll be standing here on the ladder out of sight." Chicago climbed up on deck.

"Alex, there's a launch just come out of the harbor. I think it's chasing them!" He peeked over the transom. A small boat, perhaps a police speedboat, with two or three men in it, was definitely pursuing the dive boat. Whether that was a good or a bad thing remained to be seen.

As he leaned against the companionway ladder, Alex tried to think through all the possible contingencies here. Dunagh may or may not know who they were. If so, what would he want with them? He may or may not know Teneby was aboard; would he want to save the man or kill him? He heard the dive boat approaching and saw Chicago lift a hand in a friendly wave.

"Shit!" Next thing he knew she had dropped to the deck between the cockpit seats and was reaching up for the shotgun. Alex reacted instantly. He stood up, braced his elbows on the doghouse, and trained his sights on the approaching boat.

They were ten, fifteen feet away, two men on the deck, ready to jump aboard, heavily armed.

"Sorry, mates!" a man's voice called out. "Don't resist and we won't shoot! We just need to have a little chat!"

"Hard to starboard!" Alex hissed. Chicago rolled over and gave the wheel a hard spin to the right, then scuttled back to reach the throttle and shove it full up. The *Tassia Far* arced away, but the dive boat was only momentarily delayed by the evasion. One of the men jumped to the helm, and with a rev of the engine, it easily closed the distance once more.

"I'm not up on my maritime law," Chicago asked. "What's the rules for shooting here?"

"Pull the trigger," Alex said in a cool voice. "That's the only rule we need." As the dive boat swung alongside, he stood up cautiously, making sure the Uzzi was obvious.

"Get out of here," he demanded.

"We need assistance."

"The Coast Guard is on the way. Back off."

"You don't really want to shoot," Dunagh shouted.

"You're right. I'd rather blow you out of the water. Now back off."

"Sorry, Yank, we can't do that," McKay explained in an slightly more civil tone. "I'm afraid there are a lot of chaps back there trying to keep us from landing."

"So don't land."

"There's no need to have this get ugly," McKay continued, "but we do have our business here." He glanced nervously toward the approaching patrol boat. "Drop your guns—I promise you no one will get hurt."

"Drop yours and I'll believe that . . ."

Dunagh shot a nervous glance toward the speeding police launch, his shoulders tensed, his knees braced. Alex read the signs and dropped just as the man opened fire. Chicago screamed and covered her head. A bullet hit the helm, ricocheted off and embedded in the fiberglass inches above her left knee. Alex returned fire, spraying a heavy volley across their deck. The men dove for cover. The bow of their boat scraped the side of the *Tassia Far* with a sickening crunch. Chicago scrambled for the helm. Alex grabbed her jacket and pulled her back.

"Stay down!"

"They'll ram us!"

"Get down here." He pulled back into the companionway and squeezed out around her, crouching by the helm. He handed her the shotgun.

"We don't want anyone getting hurt!" McKay shouted. "We're just asking for some company to the airport. Keep the police off our backs."

"Company? A hostage, you mean."

"Damn it, man—let's get on with it!" They heard Dunagh, then both men talking, arguing by the tone, but too low to be heard clearly.

Chicago, terrified for her boat, started to climb up. Alex grabbed her shoulder and he yanked her back down.

"Goddamn, Alex—"

"Cut it out! Stay down!"

"What the hell are we supposed to do!"

"Wait for help . . ." Another brief, teasing round of fire erupted from the dive boat. "Get on the radio . . ." He said to Chicago.

The radio was already crackling with commands from the police boat, voices squeezed with panic and confusion. Another hail of bullets raked across the deck. The police boat, too small and exposed for this kind of gunplay, sped away and stayed its distance.

"Hold your fire! Enough!" Dunagh shouted furiously. "I've got a grenade. Come out now or your pretty boat goes down." Alex ducked below and looked up through a hatch.

"He isn't joking," he said tensely. He opened his bag, found a small, thin knife and tucked it into one of his sneakers.

"What are you doing?" He pushed past her, but she grabbed him. "You can't go!"

"I don't think they want to kill us. They're backed in a corner."

"So that's dangerous!"

"Not if they're given a way out."

"Stop!" she cried desperately.

"What?"

"Ten seconds!" Dunagh shouted. "I want to see everyone up here in ten seconds or I toss this grenade."

"I got to go."

"No!" Chicago clutched his shirt, her hands shaking. "I'll go. They won't kill me sooner than they won't kill you." Alex smiled.

"How's that again? They won't kill who when?" He kissed her. "I'll be fine. Anyway, it's my turn."

"What . . . what do you mean your turn!"

"Shark rescue—" He tapped her chest, trying for a little levity. "Your point. Overboard . . ." He pointed to himself. "Mine. Life raft . . ." He shrugged and bounded up the ladder. "You're one ahead of me. You know I hate to lose a contest here. Now give me your shirt."

"My shirt? What . . ."

"It's white. We're surrendering."

"We are not."

"Shut up. We can't fight hand grenades." Chicago was trembling with rage, frustration, and fear. He couldn't leave again. She couldn't stand it.

"Well, we're not surrendering with my damn shirt!" She reached into the galley. "Use a goddamn dishtowel!"

Alex grinned, snatched the towel and gave her a fierce hug.

"I'll be fine. I'll be back in no time. I love you." he lifted the white towel up through the hatch and shouted to Dunagh.

"Come up easy now," Dunagh commanded. Alex braced his hands and pulled himself slowly up through the hatch. "Don't move." McKay jumped onto the deck with a pistol in one hand and a line in the other.

"How about a fender there, pal?" Alex suggested as the two decks cracked together.

"We won't be that long," McKay said with a touch of apology. "Why don't you tell the others to come up, and we can be on our way."

"You don't need them. I'm your hostage."

"We don't want you."

"Hey, what? Is it my breath or something? Come on . . . I'll change my shirt."

"Shut up!"

"Really, I can be a very nice guy once you get to know me."

"I said, shut up! Get over there." Dunagh shoved him with the pistol.

"Drop your gun," he shouted at Chicago. "And get up here. Everyone on deck. You . . ." He nodded toward the water behind Alex. "In the water." Chicago watched McKay walk to the rear of her boat. He yanked up the hatch and pointed the pistol inside.

"Leave the girl," Chicago pleaded steadily as she surrendered. "She's only a kid. I'll go with you."

McKay looked to Dunagh for an answer, although he was quickly losing faith in the man's control, it was still his operation.

"Take them both," Dunagh said hoarsely. "What are you waiting for!" He jabbed at Alex with the pistol. "I said, get in the water!"

"Where are you taking them?"

"Goddamn you, man, you're not listening, are you?"

"They'll be safe," McKay interrupted. "Our fight's not with you. But there's too many want us dead and the body there destroyed. The lassies here will protect the king." He steered the trembling Annalee toward the dive boat. Chicago ran to her side and put an arm around her.

"When will you release them?"

"Soon. Now get in the water. It's either that or I shoot you. I'm sure that police boat will come fetch you out once we're gone."

"It's okay, Alex. We'll be all right." Chicago smiled and climbed over to the dive boat as McKay followed with the gun at her side. Dunagh, still angry and growing increasingly more nervous, swung a heavy forearm and pushed Alex overboard.

# SIXTY-SEVEN

Cory MacClannon sat slumped over the scarred old table, rolling the glass between his fingers, staring into the amber liquid as if the answer was melted in there, just waiting to assemble in some form he could read. All the lights were on in the kitchen. The table, counters, serving trolley, and chairs were stacked with plates and platters, cups and spoons, every drawer and cabinet emptied. The radio was on low, turned to a classical station, but the orchestra was overcome by the constant scruchhhh scruchhhhh sound of Maggie MacClannon scrubbing cupboards.

This was the only way she knew to handle worry. She had done this all her life, having learned it from her mother, who had learned from her mother, a long heritage of scrub therapy. Fortunately for Maggie, their lives had been so smooth and bountiful for the past few years, that enough grime had built up in the corners of the old house to keep her busy all night.

"Swinny won't hurt Birdy, Mum. You know he couldn't do that. He's known her since she was born."

"He's already hurt her," Maggie said bitterly as she slammed a can down on the counter. She bit her lip and began to put things back in the cabinet, arranging everything with a sharp precision that had never reigned in this kitchen before, and would not be long-lived.

Cory was alarmed to see his wife holding tightly to the counter, her tiny body clenched. He downed his whiskey but resisted the urge to pour another. He wanted to stay clear-headed. He got up and pulled his coat off the peg by the door.

"Where you going this time of night?" Maggie asked.

"To talk to Swinny," he replied steadily. "I've made a decision."

# SIXTY-EIGHT

"I'm with the FBI." Alex flashed the bogus ID, one of many he had collected or manufactured over the years. He had not needed to wait for the police launch, but had pulled himself back aboard the *Tassia Far* by getting a handhold on an open porthole.

"There are two hostages on that boat. I need you to radio all your people and keep them away. No one is to approach or threaten them. Can you do that?"

"What's the FBI got to do with this?" the officer asked suspiciously.

"We've been asked by the State Department and the British government to help out." Alex wasn't sure how much the man knew, and had to be careful not to overplay his hand. "That was good work, intercepting them at the harbor entrance—but I need your help now. I need to get to the airport—some other way besides through the harbor. Is there a beach near a road?"

"Round back dere," the man said doubtfully. "By the resort."

"Can you take me there? Just drop me off. I've got to get to the airport as soon as possible."

"They're going to the airport?" He had the radio transmitter in hand.

"Wait—don't call anyone ..." Think fast! What would make them afraid to interfere? Certainly British agents wouldn't have told them all the details, wouldn't have mentioned old bones and switched kings. "The box ..." Alex hesitated. "That big crate they have on the boat contains some old nuclear weapons ..." He watched with relief as fear seized the man's face. "From a sunken ... ah, submarine. They're not stable. They're leaking radioactive material, and if anything happens to the box, even a crack or something, the whole island could be contaminated."

"Sheet!" a younger officer murmured in fear, and turned to watch the dive boat as it disappeared around the corner into the harbor entrance. "Das bad stuff."

"I have to get to the airport."

"What you gonna do alone?"

"Nothing to cause trouble. I just want to make sure everything stays calm."

"Deres no flight out today, you know. Tomorrow, the soonest."

"That's good, but they might be planning something else. Hijack a small plane or something, fly to Miami—I don't know. But I do know they want to get that crate off the island as soon as possible."

The officer thought over the plan for a few long seconds. So little ever happened out here, beyond the occasional tourist robbery. This could be his big chance. But nuclear bombs—that was bad business.

"Okay. I take you round the beach, you can get a taxi there to the airport."

"And you'll tell everyone to hold back?"

The man nodded.

"Two more things," Alex went on hurriedly. "There's a man below in the aft cabin who needs to get to hospital right away ..." He suddenly remembered Teneby, still bound and gagged in the bow cabin. Alex felt the urge to leave him to suffer for a few days as they all had on the life raft. His eventual decision against that was based not on compassion, but on the hope that with a prisoner in his control, the officer would have some satisfaction and pride, and stay the hell out of his way.

"There's also a man tied up in the front cabin. You can turn him over to the British." He pulled a small roll of bills out of his pocket, a hundred dollars from the emergency cash supply. "Now I need you to find me a pilot to take this boat in, anchor her safely, and keep an eye on it until I get back. Would you take care of that?'' He handed the man the cash. ''If I'm delayed for any reason, I'll add twenty bucks a day.''

The officer took the money and nodded. It was by no means a bribe, but it was understood that the officer himself would be looking after the *Tassia Far.*

''Give me two minutes to get some things together.'' He returned shortly with a knapsack, always packed and ready, with passport, useful ID's, guns, credit cards, and cash. The officer came on deck as Alex jumped into the launch. ''Key's in the ignition,'' he said. ''And don't worry about the snake, she's friendly!''

# *SIXTY-NINE*

''This is my decision. If we're going to do this thing, I want to do it right.'' MacClannon, too agitated to sit, leaned on the back of his chair. It was after midnight, but he had called Swinny as soon as the idea had taken shape and insisted he come over right away. ''Your lads are too coarse, too reactionary, they lend us a bad association. Terrorists. They're calling us terrorists now. If we're going to go this route, by God let's do it right.''

''What are you thinking, Cor?''

''No more skulking around. No dragging the king through the back doors like he's some poor relation who had the ill manners to die at your dinner party. If you claim I'm the king, then by George, let's treat me like one. When that plane arrives in Edinburgh, I want the royal treatment. A red carpet and an honor guard. Pipers and a proper hearse, and lads in white gloves for pallbearers. The Scottish flag draped over the coffin for all the world to see.''

Swinny was listening with interest, glad to have Cory coming around, but, as always, a little afraid of the man's rampaging enthusiasm. It was this ''by God let's do it attitude'' that had

made the man so successful in business, but always with himself
close in the background to tend to the details.

"Ceremony, Neil! Isn't that what the monarchy is for? Pomp
and circumstance. How will it look to the world if we start off
our reign with hostages and hired guns and vans careening off to
secret laboratories? No—this is our chance for all of Scotland to
come together, to feel the pride that will carry us up and away
from England forever." His eyes blazed with zeal, and in this old
stone room, Swinny could easily imagine themselves five hundred
years ago, clan chieftains planning for war.

"Every news program in England will be there to film it. Hell,
there could be Americans, too! Pageantry! That's the way to go.
We demand our legitimacy right from the start! Give them no
chance to discount us by our crimes."

"Pipers, an honor guard, a red carpet, hmmmm . . ."

"We all walk up to the plane, myself and Maggie. And the family.
I'll wear my tartan." Cory paced it off as he spoke, with the desk
serving as the aircraft and the press stationed by the potted palms.
"The pipers walk in playing; they divide in two and flank the entrance so. Then the honor guard. Or maybe the red carpet first. When
do they usually do the carpet—I can't recall ever noticing."

"After," Swinny said definitively. "Only the nobility walks
on it."

"Right." So the color guard, then the carpet, then you, carrying
a staff . . ."

"What staff?"

"We'll find one. Or a scroll. That would be good."

"Or a great seal!" Swinny laughed and poured them both another whiskey. "I could borrow something from the village post
office—that great heavy thumper thing . . ."

"Good, good." Cory laughed. His face shone with animation,
and Neil was beginning to feel relieved.

"Okay, so the pipers—there and there. The honor guard, over
here. The red carpet. You with the seal. Then Maggie and I and
the children. No, wait. I think that's a little cluttered for a proces-
sional, don't you? They go up ahead. We have a little box roped
off for them right by the door to the plane, so they're all in the
picture—good?"

"That's good. The new Royal Family. Have the little girls in their Christmas frocks."

"Yes, yes, then Maggie and I walk down to the door. I go up the stairs . . ."

"With the pallbearers . . ."

"Yes . . . wait . . ." He paced furiously, deep in the logistics of all this. "No. Not yet. First I go up alone. To pay my respects. Here's the shot." He stood by the desk, hands folded solemnly. "The coffin right here, just visible through the door. Then the lads come up to carry it down. I follow. There we are. We will have set the image." He flopped in the chair, exhausted by the show.

"Then we go on to the lab as planned?" Cory nodded.

"No one will dare interfere at this point."

"What about Dunagh and McKay? Can we get them off the plane first? We've a hiding place ready for them."

"First?" He had forgotten they would be there at all. What would be best? "No. No. There will be cameras going from the minute it lands, and they did kill quite a few people. We don't need that image right at first. No, they stay on board."

# SEVENTY

"You know we could be a movie of the week," Annalee said in a subdued voice as the truck drove slowly away from the dock. Her hands and Chicago's were tied to the coffin, forcing them to hunch over a little, bumping their knees.

"What's that?"

"A movie of the week? You know, on TV. Real-life stories that happen to people. Like babies who got switched in the hospital and now the parents want the real kid back, or surrogate mothers who want to keep the babies, or kids get molested at preschool, or this woman has repressed lives, or no, I mean, repressed *memories,* or fifty different personalities. Stuff like that. I'm not allowed to watch them,'' Annalee confessed. "But I see the commercials.''

"I've never watched much TV,'' Chicago said apologetically.

"Do you think they'll let us go now? Once the coffin is on the plane?'' She spoke as if Dunagh weren't actually sitting two feet away.

"I don't know,'' Chicago answered honestly. Dunagh ignored them. His wrist, too, was tied to the coffin, and in his belt were a couple more grenades. If threatened by the police, he had explained; he would pull the pin and hold the spoon down with his thumb. If he was shot, and lost his grip, the grenade would explode, killing them all.

Alex jogged through the scrub, his feet sliding in the sand, sharp-leaved plants whacking at his shins. Solid ground was a foreign planet, and his legs were stiff and sore. He skirted the edge of the resort, though there was really no need. He looked a little rougher-edged than the typical tourist, with his faded clothes and worn sneakers, but not enough so to call attention to himself. When he reached the gardens he slowed to a fast walk, winding through the flowering hibiscus and hanging plants.

Two well-oiled women strolled languidly toward the pool, tropical drinks in hand. One took a chunk of pineapple off the rim of her glass and bit into it with a sensual pleasure. The other was lamenting over lettuce. Her salad was only iceberg. Why couldn't anyone get good lettuce on the island? At least romaine. Was that so much to ask?

Alex felt like he had stepped through a hidden door into some kind of weird parallel universe. It had been a month at least since they had been on any sort of populated island, and he felt like he was still on life raft time. He hurried to the hotel entrance where two taxis waited in the shade, the drivers playing dominos on a piece of plywood laid out on the trunk.

"Taxi to the airport, please.'' The man from the first cab stood up slowly. Looked at his watch.

"No more planes today.''

"I like airports.'' The driver shrugged, said something to his friend in rapid patios, and got in.

\*   \*   \*

Alex paid the driver and walked into the cool interior of the terminal. Polished empty hallways stretched to empty ticket counters. The airport was almost deserted. He looked out the observation window to the tarmac, and scanned the rows of small planes parked near a hangar, then glanced around again, looking for someone who might have information on the plane's owners.

He saw two white men, with postures so stiff, skin so milky, and jaws so clenched, they could only be British agents. Help or hindrance? How badly was the coffin wanted? Bad enough to sacrifice a couple of hostages? They were accompanied by one of the two young officers from the launch. Alex ducked into an alcove by an Avis rental car desk, almost upsetting a framed poster of paradise. Palm trees, white sand, turquoise water, the perfect couple strolling along, he in gauzy white pants, she dangling a sunhat.

He peeked around and saw the men joined by two others, Americans he decided by their shoes and walks. The State Department would have been contacted by now. Who would they send— operatives or attachés? It didn't matter at this point, whoever it was would only interfere. The best thing to do right now was for everyone just to ease off.

Alex was pretty sure that while these men were fanatics, they were not brutal, and with the possible exception of Dunagh, would be hesitant to actually kill. Dunagh was edgy and tense, and probably stood the most to lose. If he landed in Miami, he would be safer than if he returned to Britain. There would be nice calm negotiators to greet them. England and the US would not want an incident over this. That must be the plan. That would be a good plan.

He heard the men hurry down the hall, radios crackling.

"Suspect turning into airport now . . ." he heard one say. Alex paused a second more.

"Can you take them?"

"He's got the hostages . . ."

"Take Dunagh."

"I don't have a clear shot . . ."

"Damnit, man. You know our orders. It has to end here. No one's getting on that plane."

Shit! They couldn't really mean to sacrifice hostages could they?

For a stupid king? Quickly, Alex darted out and sprinted off in the opposite direction. He jumped over a rope, and headed outside. The sun had just set and a cooling breeze swept in from the ocean but the tarmac was still baking with the heat of the day.

"Hey! Hey, you!" A cry from behind. The Brits had seen him. Alex hunched along the wall, sprinted around the corner, and ducked through the rubber flaps of a baggage portal, back inside the airport. He heard the two men running closer, heard the unmistakable click of automatic weapons. Alex crouched, waiting, the sharp smell of his own sweat filling the tiny baggage space. *Damn! Would I shoot me if I were them?* he thought quickly. *Come on, come on.*

The footsteps stopped. They would be pressed against the wall, edging up; soon enough, a hand with a gun would . . . Alex sprang as soon as he saw the hand, grabbing, twisting the gun away, diving into a somersault with the force of his body flipping the agent with him. A shot rang out. Flecks of concrete flew up around him. With a quick blow, Alex knocked the man out, sprang to his feet, and threw himself into a sort of handless cartwheel toward the other agent.

The man was confused by the move. He had never seen anyone fighting this way. It was like a gymnast gone crazy. He parried with karate, but couldn't land a blow. Alex kicked him solidly, then scissored his legs out from under him. The man crashed to the pavement, the breath knocked out of him, saw only a flash of a hand rushing toward his head, then slipped into blackness.

Alex jumped up, panting from the exertion, then ducked back against the wall. Did Dunagh and McKay see any of this? The truck had stopped, he noticed, about a hundred yards away, by the row of planes. Which one? And how could he get on it? There were no pilots in sight yet, they must be inside somewhere. Quickly Alex grabbed the agent's pistol, ducked back through the baggage door, and looked for a passage that would lead to a hangar or cargo area. It was a small airport. Soon he heard voices and came out into a hangar just in time to see two men, a pilot and co-pilot, walking toward the door.

"Stop right there!" Alex ordered. The two froze, startled to see the pistol trained on them.

"You, too!" Alex commanded a mechanic who he saw out of

the corner of his eye, edging toward another door. "On the floor now!" The three dropped quickly. "I'm really sorry, guys. I don't have time to explain. You, over here bring that rope." The mechanic cautiously crept over and handed Alex a length of rope. "Tie him up," Alex pointed at the co-pilot. "You give me your clothes quick."

The pilot frowned and didn't move. "Who the hell are you?"

"Stay calm and listen close. This isn't a hijacking, you won't be hurt." The pilot looked distinctly unimpressed, and only slightly worried. He was a big guy. He looked like he'd been around, and sometimes lived to tell about it. The mechanic had tied up the co-pilot, and now waited for further instructions. "Slip knot. Around your wrist." The mechanic complied.

"Clothes! Now!" Alex really hoped he wasn't going to have to fight again. He was not yet twelve hours out of the life raft, and had eaten little. The adrenaline was running out, and his vision swarmed for a few frightening seconds. The pilot pulled off his shirt. Alex sat the mechanic down in a chair and finished tying him down.

The minutes seemed like hours, but finally, Alex had the pilot also tied up, and was changing into his clothes.

"Which is your plane?"

"The Fokker," he replied sullenly. Alex felt his stomach lurch again as the significance of that became clear. The Fokker was a twin-engine long-range craft, easily capable of crossing the Atlantic. "Where are you taking the coffin?"

"What coffin?"

"Your cargo. It's a long story. Where?"

They heard shouts from outside. Alex peeked out and saw McKay, obviously looking for their pilot.

"Be right there," he shouted. "Where you hired for?"

"Scotland."

"Shit. Where's your flight bag? You have a shaver?"

"Hey, buddy, do I look like your fucking valet?" Alex just rummaged through the bag and found the electric shaver. Dunagh had fought with a shaggy-haired man in a raggy T-shirt with a five-day growth of beard. With the pilot's crisp white shirt and jacket on, his hair wet and combed back neatly, and a fresh shave, he could probably get away with this. They hadn't had that good

a look at him, and it was in tense circumstances. Alex had seen
trained agents unable to identify an attacker moments after a fray.

"All right. You'll wiggle out of that in a few minutes. Tell the
police no one is to interfere with that plane. There are hostages
on board. Call the U.S. State Department. Tell them . . . shit. I
don't know . . ." Who could vouch for him over there these days?
"Tell them, call over to Langley, my name is Alex Sanders. Someone should remember me there."

The pilot's expression narrowed a little. He knew Langley was
CIA headquarters.

Alex walked toward the plane, urging every muscle in his body
to stay calm and hoping Chicago or Annalee would not recognize
and reveal him. McKay, Dunagh, and Thomas were loading the
coffin on the plane, straining against ropes to pull it right from
the truck. Alex, affecting a thick southern accent, apologized for
the wait, climbed right into the cockpit.

He resisted the urge to turn and look as they loaded the coffin.
He checked the instruments, familiarizing himself with their layout. It had been years since he had flown a Fokker, but he was
happy with the choice. It was a good sturdy plane, the mainstay
of cargo transport in Africa, where it could handle short rough
runways and harsh conditions.

"Anyone chasing? Any police? Can you see?"

"There's no one, Dunagh, relax," McKay said soothingly. "It's
all clear—we've done it, man! Relax."

Everything had to stay very calm. Alex heard McKay directing
Chicago and Annalee to seats, and was glad to hear nothing from
Chicago in the way of protest. She was usually a little too hot-
headed and vocal to do well in a situation like this one. If they
had schools for hostages, she would be lucky to earn a D−. He
wished there was some way he could let her know he was there,
ease her worry.

"Y'all ready there, fellas?" he called back. "We need to git
on out'a' here 'fore these clouds close us in."

# SEVENTY-ONE

"C'mon, lads, we've mighty work to do tonight." Neil Swinny ducked through the low doorway of the cottage and roused the lads who were sleeping on the kitchen floor. "Wake up. Up now." Another door opened and Lachlin Muir came in from the bedroom pulling on his trousers as he went.

"What's happened?"

Birdy, who had already awakened when the car drove up, leaned her ear to the wall to hear what was going on. She pressed the light on her watch and saw that it was just after midnight.

"Dunagh's on the way," she heard the muffled voice declare with excitement. "He phoned from the dock in Provo, and they were on their way to the airport. Should be on the way right now, and landing in ten to twelve hours." The lads scrambled into clothes, still sorting out the news from their recent dreams.

"I've the van waiting, we need to leave soon."

"Clewe!" Muir called back to his wife. "Get Birdy ready to go. Have you called the others?"

"Everyone. It's all in motion now." Swinny had quickly passed on the news to the other Jacobites, each of whom already knew his or her specific job. Some would be calling the media, some arranging the ceremony, others would be busy at computers, sending out press releases, putting their own spin on the event. This was the chance for which they had been waiting for three hundred years, and the stakes were high.

In London, Crawford Hayes sat alone in his office. It was out of his hands now. Scotland Yard would handle things at the airport. No more for him to do now but prepare for the inquiries. Teneby was in custody, swearing he had no part of it, no idea.

That might help a little. Dunagh as rogue agent. No way to have known. Jacobites, indeed. Who would ever have thought to check out such a thing? He might yet come out all right.

At Buckingham Palace, Charles had just arrived, summoned by the queen. He had been briefed on the way over, and felt a curious, detached sensation, almost pleasure.

"Charles. Welcome home. Has the country done you some good?"

"Was I in such need of being done some good?"

"Of course not." The queen put on her glasses with a defensive gesture. "I only meant you look well. Why must you always twist things?" She looked particularly old tonight, her face drawn with worry, her infamous royal posture almost yielding to a slump. He was surprised to see the stack of tabloids on her desk. Usually she simply ignored them, unless, as had happened with the infamous toe-sucking snaps, they had infiltrated every media niche throughout the world.

The most clever of this latest batch was a doctored photo of a village fair baking contest, with Maggie MacClannon's face pasted in for the winner. She was holding up a luscious prize-winning cake, while the queen sulked in the background, staring gloomily at her entry, a store-bought sweet bun.

"Sorry." Charles gave a brief tinny smile, clasped his hands behind him, and strolled past her to the fireplace. The two Corgis were stretched out on the rug. Both looked up as he approached, then rested their heads down again, not expecting to be petted.

"We need to discuss this Scottish business." His mother got right to the subject.

"Ah, yes."

"Mr. Spencer says you've been following it?"

"Yes."

"Well, it does seem to have gone rather awry. I've been assured of an inquiry, but in the meantime, we must prepare a response."

"I would think this is one of those 'don't dignify with a comment' affairs."

"It would be if it hadn't already gone so far. I am told they will be flying into Edinburgh tomorrow." She fluttered one hand briefly as if flicking off something sticky in the atmosphere. "It will be a circus." There was nothing, Charles thought, like that tone of royal contempt. "The Americans have been most gracious, though, and the prime minister is going to make a statement condemning the actions."

"And which actions are those?"

"Which actions? Why, the terrorist acts, of course."

"Ahhhh, right. I thought perhaps he would be condemning the coup."

"What coup?"

"Why, the one that drove poor old James off in the first place."

"Charles, I do recognize, if not appreciate, your penchant for sarcasm, but this is not the time. England does not need an upheaval, nor does the Royal Family."

"You don't think so?"

"No, I do not."

"Ahhhh."

"Oh, Charles, please. This is difficult enough. We are trying to avoid an international incident. If the Scottish sympathizers are not placated, they can cause a great deal of trouble. Now please don't be obstinate, just promise you will be here tomorrow for a statement."

"I am always at your service." Charles reached into his jacket pocket and pulled out a piece of paper. "In fact, I have already written my statement on the way over."

The queen sat down and began to read. She looked up after the first paragraph, her face severe, then hurriedly read through the rest.

"I've told you we are not in the mood for sarcasm."

"Nor am I, Mother."

"What is the meaning of this then?"

"It is my statement of support." She crumpled the paper and threw it into the fireplace.

"For Cory MacClannon."

"I've met the man, you know. He's a fine chap."

The queen stood, returned to her desk, and sat down. "Very well. I will tell Lord Fairlane that you will not be making a statement tomorrow."

"But I fully intend to."

"You can't be serious. There is no legitimacy to this claim. It is absurd."

"A good barrister could make quite a show in court."

"This isn't going to any court."

"Why not? As you say, we have nothing to fear."

"It's a waste of time. England has more pressing concerns."

"You're afraid, aren't you?" Charles walked to the desk and spread the tabloids gently with his long aristocratic fingers. "They don't really like us so much any more, do they?"

"I am confident in the support of our people."

"They don't like us," he repeated in a quiet tone, as if pleasantly awed by the idea. "The monarchy may have outlived its usefulness regardless, but we've exhausted our entertainment value long ago."

"I will preserve this family."

"Will you? What would you do, Mother, to protect the throne?" Charles noticed for the first time that she was wearing slippers; pale-blue terry-cloth slippers. It seemed somehow indecent, this way, and he felt a pang of shame.

"I never expected treachery from my own son." This accusation stiffened his resolve, and Charles turned away.

"Oh, come now, Mother. In the fine tradition of royal treachery this is pretty mild, don't you think?"

# SEVENTY-TWO

High thin clouds covered most of Scotland on the morning of the king's return. Wisps of vapor skated across the cold black lochs that carved the rugged countryside, lakes, long and narrow, deep as time and still as morning. On a day like this, with the quiet gloom and the chill mist, the most modern Scot is tugged by the ghosts of the land and stirred to a disquiet passion.

~In Inishail, the clouds striped the horizon and settled as frost on the windows. Aeowulf's new puppies, staggering out of their warm straw nest for the first time, found the world a harsh and dismal place and bundled home to suckle. In the old manor house, the MacClannon family, those members who had been able to sleep, had been up since dawn, and were now assembled in the great hall. The granddaughters, pleased and showy, twirled in their best dresses, hair ribbons swirling out in colorful tracers. The little boys, just as proud but embarrassed to admit it, fidgeted and played with Gameboy. Kevin and Ian, who actually understood the idea of their grandfather being crowned king, were planning what they would do as princes. It mostly involved skipping school, having their own private video arcade, and declaring war.

"I'd send soldiers to kill all the bad people," Kevin announced while sweeping the room with an imaginary machine gun. The younger children knew only that they would be going to Edinburgh, and must be on their best behavior. They all knew that they were helping Aunt Birdy somehow, though the details of her kidnapping had been withheld from them. Still, with the unique perception of children, they knew this was not a party affair. It felt very much like Uncle Andrew's funeral last summer, in fact.

There had been much hair-brushing and shoe-brushing, and a minor crisis when Michael's kilt was discovered to have slipped off the hanger in the closet during the year or so since last worn, and was wrinkled beyond reason. Twelve yards of heavy pleated wool seemed a trauma to iron, but Anna the housekeeper attacked it with a practiced hand. All three of the sons, and Grace's husband, wore their kilts. The MacClannon women wore the clan sashes, with Maggie in more formal dress, displaying the riband and chivalric decorations bestowed on her husband. When Cory MacClannon himself entered the room, there was a sudden and awed hush.

While the younger men wore the simple dress of kilt, sporran, and tweed jacket, Cory was resplendent in full ceremonial attire. Beneath the short velvet doublet, with its silver buttons, he wore lace jabot and sleeves, and his kilt was fastened with his grandfather's cairngorm. His sporran was also a family heirloom, a beautiful pouch of silver and badger fur, which usually lay wrapped in tissue paper in the cedar chest and was taken out reverentially only on special occasions for a good grandchild to examine.

Tucked in his right stocking was the beautiful ivory-handled knife, the *sgian dubh.* A big sturdy man to begin with, in the kilt he looked taller, stronger, a warlord from the halls of the mountain king.

"Saints, look at the lot of you," Grace said appreciatively as she regarded the MacClannon men. "It will be a mob of women and no Jacobites we'll have to contend with now."

"Thank you all," Cory said gravely. "This means a lot to me. You've brought something for Birdy?" Grace held up a dress in a dry-cleaner's bag. Swinny and Muir had agreed that Birdy would be allowed to join the family at the door of the plane for the photographs, in return for no mention of her kidnapping. With Cory's endorsement now, and all the press attention, the Jacobites no longer feared an ambush from the English.

"You are a grand lot. Very regal. A final touch . . ." He crossed to the mantel and carefully took down one of the ancient swords that hung there, slipping it into the scabbard that hung from his waist. "The cars are ready?" Michael nodded and motioned for the children to get their coats.

"Neil and some of his lads are here, too. They're waiting outside."

"Well, then, let's not keep our subjects waiting." He held out his arm and Maggie took it. They looked every inch the royal couple as they walked toward the door.

# SEVENTY-THREE

They were two hundred miles over the Atlantic, with the first stars beginning to appear before Dunagh recognized that the pilot of the chartered plane was the same man he had fought with hours before. There were a few tense minutes, and a lot of shouting, but obviously, since there was no one else to fly the plane, there was precious little could be done about it.

"Just don't be thinking about any tricky stuff on the other end,"
Dunagh warned him. "We'll be home then, and I'll have nothing
to lose."

Since then the flight had been uneventful, if long and uncomfortable. The plane could fly on autopilot much of the time, but
Alex was too tense to nap. Dunagh would not let him leave the
cockpit, or even talk to Chicago. Annalee slept on and off, always
awakening with nightmares. Flying east, the time change was disorienting, the sun was rising only six hours after it had set in the
Caribbean. It was shortly after noon when they began the final
approach to Edinburgh.

"We have clearance to land," Alex reported. Dunagh was
crouched over his shoulder, monitoring the radio conversation.
"They're holding off other flights, and promise no interference,
but he says your men have organized some sort of ceremony."

"Ceremony?" Dunagh began to protest, but McKay restrained
him. "Ease off, man, let's hear some more." The tension and lack
of sleep had pushed him to the edge of psychosis. "Can you ask
him for a little more explanation, please?" Alex radioed the response and they waited for a reply.

"I have a message from Swinny," the air traffic controller reported in a crackly voice. "MacClannon cooperating fully. Small
ceremony at plane. Large media turnout. Please remain in plane
and wait for further instructions."

"No—no—forget it . . ."

"Wait . . ."

"They'll storm the plane!"

"Shush, man—let me think. Give me that." McKay reached for the
microphone. "Hello . . . uh, hello. This is . . ." he hadn't thought about
code names or what even to call themselves. ". . . Tell them we
will stay on the plane as requested, but make sure they know we
have hostages on board."

"Did you say hostages?" the distant voice constricted, and mut-
ters could be heard in the background.

"Yes. Sorry. Two. Well, three counting the pilot, I suppose,
so make sure we are not attacked. Please. In any way. Do you
understand?"

"Affirmative. Hostages on board." McKay handed back the

microphone and went to the back of the plane while Alex finished receiving instructions to land.

"We'll be on the ground shortly," he explained as he pulled his suitcase out and snapped it open. "You're not dressed for the weather in Scotland, that's for sure." He handed Chicago a long-sleeved shirt and light sweater for herself and Annalee. "I didn't bring much in the way of warm clothes myself," he explained apologetically. "But this will keep the chill off."

"Do you have a brush or a comb?" Annalee asked. McKay found one, and the girl started working on her tangled strands.

"Do you know how to braid?"

"Sure." Chicago took the comb and Annalee settled in front of her. "You want a French braid?"

"Can you do one?"

"Of course. I used to have long hair." She combed the wispy side strands back and began to weave them into a French braid.

"My poor mom must really be going nuts. If I show up in some newspaper picture all scruffy, she'll really die."

"I'm pretty sure she wouldn't notice at this point." Annalee's hair was warm and heavy. Annalee was bringing out all sort of maternal instincts she hadn't felt in a long time. She and Stephan had talked about having children, "little boat babies," but then he was killed, and she had gone on with a solitary life. It seemed too huge a risk, to create someone you would love so much. She looked at the coffin and thought of Mary Beatrice, all those desperate days wondering if her child was still alive across the sea. There was a break in the clouds, and sunlight suddenly poured in the window, falling like a golden sword across the coffin.

"I wish we got to see inside. I wish Uncle Peter got to see." Annalee's voice trembled.

They felt the pressure change as the plane dropped through the clouds, and they saw the Edinburgh airport below.

"Final approach everyone. Fasten seat belts," Alex shouted back. He was exhausted and tense.

"Time, Cory. They've just landed." Swinny opened the door of the lounge and MacClannon saw the small retinue he had assembled for an honor guard. They looked so young! One barely in whiskers. They were the angry young men these fanatics had preyed upon for their stupid cause. Poor lads wanting for glory and bursting with zeal, frustrated and looking for a villain to blame. They stood solemnly, though with the bristle of excitement the young cannot disguise.

As angry as he was, MacClannon could not help feel sorry for them. He had had to work hard as a lad, but there had always been something to work hard at. There were jobs, no matter how ugly or dangerous; today there was nothing, nothing but the grand talk and stirring ceremony of Muir and his gang. He hoped this would not turn out too badly for them.

The press had mobbed the family when they arrived at the airport, but now the cameras were held back by ropes and a line of police. Cory searched the faces, looking for those he might know. He had tapped all his connections for this day. It was vital that the police not go overboard. Fortunately, this was Scotland, and there weren't many guns around. Muir and the lads were not armed, nor was Swinny.

He led them to a glass door, where the pipe band was already assembled on the tarmac. MacClannon's heart was heavy, and his hands, much to his embarrassment, were damp and trembling. He felt Maggie squeeze his arm, and looked down to her reassuring smile. God, he hoped he was doing the right thing.

The plane taxied to a stop and the pipe band, as planned, began to march. The mournful strains made the atmosphere even more peculiar. A hearse drove up, and two lads pushed a boarding stair over to the door of the plane.

When the band had finished, Swinny spoke into a radio and Cory clutched his wife's hand. At a slight stir, they all turned to see Birdy being led into the little room. She wore the dress her sister had brought, and smiled tightly as she was ushered to her family. There was not time for relieved hugs. The door of the plane opened. The English watchers all went rigid, and the marksmen on the roof trained their sights.

"Here you go, Cor." Swinny almost gasped, his throat tight with nerves. "Do us proud now." He opened the door, and the MacClannons walked out to their strange new destiny.

There was to be no speech. MacClannon had pointed out that with all the chaos of the planning, they had forgotten the fact that they still did not even know that the king was actually in this coffin! The whole saga had grown so Byzantine that they had overlooked the very real chance of being held up in the near future as complete and utter idiots, with no body to rest their claims upon.

They walked out on the tarmac, the sons and daughters and grandchildren first, then the royal couple themselves, Cory Fitzroy MacClannon, looking as fierce and noble as any Highland chief, his tiny wife statuesque with defiance. The children stood, as arranged, by the side of the stair. One of the honor guards stepped forward to take Maggie's arm. The door swung open, and Cory MacClannon walked up the steps alone, his heart pounding.

He entered the plane. Dunagh and McKay stood stiffly to one side of the coffin. It was an awkward moment. No one knew quite what ceremony to stand on. "Gentlemen," MacClannon said with a slight bow. "You do me honor."

Dunagh nodded stiffly. "Sir. We are glad to have been of service." He had a pistol tucked in his waistband. McKay was not armed, but a weapon lay within reach by the open door.

MacClannon quickly surveyed the scene. The pilot still in the cockpit, was he a hostage as well? And over there, toward the back of the plane, a woman and . . . *my God*, he thought as he saw Annalee, *she's just a child!* He glanced toward the cockpit, and caught Alex's eye, and gave a slight nod. "I am sorry for the trouble to you, and to you ladies."

He turned his back to Dunagh and McKay and looked at the coffin. The ropes and netting had been removed. Buried as it had been, the surface was still smooth. Cory felt, with some surprise, a flood of emotion. He had never considered the reality of this moment. All along, it had occupied an abstract and certainly bizarre place in his thoughts, but now here it was, real and solid as this gray day. He stroked it lightly, as one would the bedcovers of a sick child. *Whoever you are, you poor soul, it will soon be over.* MacClannon looked up at Chicago and Annalee. He made a small gesture with his hand and mouthed the words "Stay down." Then he slowly reached for the handle of the sword.

With a startling cry, and a motion much faster and smoother than he had any right to expect from his old body, MacClannon drew the sword, spun around, and slashed at Dunagh. It was a wide, low swing, for he was not committed to a slaying. The blade sliced across the man's stomach, and Dunagh fell back, more from shock than injury. Alex reacted immediately, vaulting out of the cockpit and grabbing his arm as he reached for the pistol. Mac-Clannon leapt to the door and kicked at the gun. It spun toward the open door but caught halfway out. McKay lunged for it, but MacClannon waved the sword at him, forcing him back.

On the tarmac below he saw Michael and John wrestling with the Jacobite guard. They had known about the plan, and had tried to race aboard, but the young men were on them, holding them back. Birdy and Grace grabbed up the children and were racing to safety.

"Start the engine!" MacClannon shouted as he reached for the door, but Alex was struggling with Dunagh. Dunagh, infuriated by MacClannon's wound, fought like a maniac. It was hard to move in the cramped space, and Dunagh went in low and hard, catching Alex at the knees and knocking him down. He was brawling like he had so long ago in the streets of Glasgow, get in, stay in, and hammer hard. It was a pit-bull attack, and Alex caught several powerful punches before he shoved the man off, spun him around, and hurled him against the coffin. Dunagh's head cracked against the iron and he fell unconscious.

Alex staggered back and McKay jumped on him, knocking them both to the floor. MacClannon, frightened by the blood he had already drawn, couldn't slash at him again, and instead whacked him hard across the back with the flat of the blade. McKay gasped, and Alex rolled him off. MacClannon caught him by the hair, pulled out the small knife, and held the tip to the man's throat.

"Alex!" Chicago cried. "Stay!" she ordered Annalee as she ran out to help.

"Shut that door ..." MacClannon panted. Chicago saw the mayhem on the tarmac, kilts flying, police sirens wailing. No way to tell what help or harm would come from that scene. She kicked the gun the rest of the way out and pulled the door into place.

"You all right, lad?" MacClannon looked at Alex.

"Yeah." His head was swimming as he struggled to get up. Chicago climbed over McKay and crouched by his side.

"I'm fine," he winced. There was a sudden loud banging on the plane, voices shouting.

"Come on, man!" MacClannon cried at Alex. He reached in

his sporran and pulled out a small flask. "Pour some of this down his throat, lassie. We need to get out of here."

"Out where?" Chicago snapped. "What the hell . . ."

"Please . . . I've a plan." MacClannon wiped the sweat from his forehead, and Alex saw the keen look in his eyes.

"Have you fuel enough for another wee flight?" Another wee flight was not what Alex had in mind right now.

"How far?"

"A hundred and fifty kilometers or so."

Alex pulled himself up, leaning on Chicago. "Yeah. I think we can manage that." She started to protest, but stopped. What the hell? They had come this far. She just shook her head and steered him back toward the cockpit. MacClannon felt a light touch on his shoulder, and saw Annalee standing beside him with a couple of cords.

"I can help you tie him up," she offered. "I know how."

There was louder pounding, and a police car drove cautiously up alongside the front of the plane. MacClannon grinned, took the rope from Annalee, tucked the knife back in his stocking, and brushed off his kilt. The radio was snapping with traffic, the tower trying to find out what had happened inside the plane. In the airport terminal, the MacClannon family waited nervously to learn, too, what was happening inside the plane.

"What say you, sir?" MacClannon shouted. "Will she go that far?"

"We can make it," Alex announced as he started the engine, "if we lighten our load." Dunagh and McKay were unceremoniously ejected at the end of the runway. The MacClannons cheered with relief, and the plane once again took to the sky.

# SEVENTY-FOUR

"Well, that's it then," Spencer said dismally as they watched the events unfold live on the television. "I'm terribly sorry, Your Majesty."

"Sorry? Whatever for?" Prince Charles smiled.

"This whole awful business. It never should have gone this far. I cannot help but take some responsibility."

"Nonsense, Mr. Spencer." The shades were drawn in the study, casting the men in blue shadows from the screen. Charles clicked off the sound but continued to stare as the news announcer, looking comically confused at the turn of events, mouthed words and pointed toward the sky.

"I suppose it's time I went down," he said with resignation. "You've had a look at my statement. What do you think?" Spencer had been surprised when the prince asked him to look over the paper. There were certainly enough royal advisors and speechwriters for that sort of thing.

"I think it's very good, Your Majesty. The expression of sympathy for the Americans killed is quite touching."

"And the rest?"

"Very good as well. The queen will be pleased."

"Respectful amusement, with ah . . . a hint of royal disdain, is what Lord Fairlane suggested. Have I got that?"

"I believe so, Your Majesty." Spencer was puzzled. He knew the brooding, sarcastic side of the prince, but this was different. Spencer waited, but the prince still sat. On the television, Maggie MacClannon was seen, the family surrounded closely by police, trying to shoo away the cameras.

"How is your Mr. Whitstone doing?" Charles asked suddenly.

"Poorly, I'm afraid."

246

"What a shame." Charles finally got up and switched on a light. "He gave us all such a good ride. If things hadn't gone wrong with that boat sinking . . ." he pulled his jacket on and checked his tie in the mirror. "There's to be an inquest, you know. Several MP's are calling for Hayes's resignation."

"So I've been told."

"What do you recommend, Mr. Spencer?"

"Begging your pardon, sir. That's not my place to say."

"You will be questioned."

"Yes, sir."

"You think it was wrong of Hayes to order the coffin destroyed?" Spencer hesitated. "You would not have done it?" Charles pressed.

"No, sir."

"Well, then. I suppose I talked to the right chap." He smiled and folded the statement back up, watching with sly pleasure as an incredulous look slowly spread across Spencer's face.

"Your Majesty . . ." His voice was trembling. "I believe we should be going down to the press conference."

"Oh damn it, Mr. Spencer—don't stand there like . . . like a butler trying to ignore the indiscretions of your master! You understand what I've just told you. I told Mr. Hayes to have the coffin destroyed. Is that clear to you?"

"Please, Your Majesty . . ." Spencer was struggling now. Was he more disturbed by the prince's drastic action, his meddling in national security affairs, or the fact that he had bypassed Spencer's trust and went to Hayes instead?

"It wouldn't have gone anywhere otherwise," Charles declared. A red flush of emotion had bloomed on his face. "It was too old, too obscure, too remote. A baby switched, eighteenth century Jacobite politics. I wanted something more dramatic, more immediate. If this archaeologist had recovered the body, gone about his tests and proofs, it would be dragged out over months or years. Quite likely turn up nothing at all in the end. But I knew that if people thought someone had tried to destroy the evidence . . ." He turned back to the mirror and began to comb his hair. "Never in a million years did we suppose this Dunagh fellow would twist it all up this way."

Spencer could stand the darkened room no longer, and walked

slowly to the window, trying to sort all this out in his mind. He opened the shade. It was indecently sunny.

"But why, Your Majesty?" he finally asked. "You knew it would hurt the monarchy."

"The monarchy has hurt itself, Mr. Spencer." There was a look of deep sorrow on the prince's face. "And I'm so tired of it all." The brief glimpse was gone, and once again, Charles wore the mask of a placid royalty. "I suppose . . . I suppose I was playing commoner. But it was stupid. And it was inexcusable." He tucked the paper into his pocket. "And ultimately, it was futile. For we will go on. The queen will still be queen. I would like however, to beg your pardon, and now to ask a favor." Spencer waited silently. "At the inquest. In regard to Mr. Hayes's decisions in this matter; if you could find a way to be . . . gentle."

"Of course, Your Majesty." How well they all played.

"Very good then." He opened the door, paused as if to say something else, then started to leave.

"Your Majesty." Charles, too, paused. "Your ah . . . your security will be intensified in light of the expected Scottish unrest . . ."

"Unrest?" Charles smiled.

"We're not sure what will be going on now that MacClannon has the coffin."

"Oh, I wouldn't worry about it, Spencer." Charles gave a wry mile. "I don't really think MacClannon intends to keep the old bloke around very long."

# SEVENTY-FIVE

"Is it really deeper than the ocean?"

"That it is, lassie. Miles deep. And the bottom is all pits and caverns and the like, so you can't just send down one of those fancy remote probes or submarines to feel around for it. Once

there . . . he's there. The Loch never gives up her dead. I feel bad
for you, girl . . ." MacClannon went on sincerely, seeing Annalee's sadness, "I truly do, and for your poor father. But you do
understand, don't you?"

She nodded reluctantly.

"I would like to try and make it up to you a little. There's still
a lot of the wreck there to bring up, isn't there? What your father
likes to do, eh? His archaeology? And that takes a lot of money,
I'm certain. Could I offer to pay for this, do you think? Would
that make it a little easier?"

Annalee had fallen asleep on the kitchen table many a time
listening to her father and Uncle Peter going over and over the
budget for the excavation, trying to find ways to squeeze loose a
few dollars here and there. Of course it would make him happy.
It could mean years of diving, research, but not with Uncle Peter.
Not with Shep and Marty. Annalee felt strange. Like everything
had broken. She tried to fight back tears.

"Yes. He'll be happy." MacClannon took her hand. He had
heard most of the story by now and was horrified at the traumas
these people, and this child, had been forced to go through. Wasn't
the world ever going to get any better? Would they always be
scrapping and fighting for power and pride. His allegiance to his
country, his work for Scottish independence, seemed mean and
petty now.

"It's just not a good idea. Twisting up the past this way, unset-
tling the dead."

"I know." She wiped her eyes on the sleeve of the oversize
flannel shirt, and felt as wretched as her fading nickname, Les Miz.

"Would you really be king, though? If it really was Edward
in there?"

"I don't believe in kings."

"Well, then . . ." She glanced at Chicago, looking for support.
"Would it hurt to look inside? Can we, please?"

"Look in the coffin?"

"We might not even find out anything, but I have to look!
Please! For Uncle Peter."

"But how will you know?" She explained about the medallion,
and about the two pieces of a charm that should fit with the cross
around the prince's neck. MacClannon looked at the heavy coffin.

As much as he wanted the whole thing to be over, he had to admit he was curious.

"Can we get it open, do you think?" Alex put the plane on autopilot and found a crowbar, a hammer, and some sturdy screwdrivers.

"We can try."

As the plane flew over the bleak, rugged land, the four of them worked on the coffin. They struggled, and sweated. Finally, as the dark slash of Loch Ness became visible in the distance, Alex wedged the crowbar deeper in the crack, stood, and together with MacClannon, they threw all their weight into it. With a screech and crack, the lid moved. Annalee yelped and tumbled backward. A smell filled the little plane, a salty, musty, slightly spooky odor, like the ocean at night under a pier. MacClannon stiffened. No one spoke. The tension was thick. Finally, with all four of them lifting, they moved the lid aside.

Although the coffin had been well sealed, over three hundred years, water still had seeped in and only some of it had leaked out again during these two days in the atmosphere. Almost six inches still remained, a clear, dark pool in the bottom of the coffin.

"I'll get a flashlight," Alex whispered. They were all whispering now, unable to break the sepulchral spell. The flashlight cast an eerie light, both reflecting off the surface and rippling below, the first light in centuries to breach the peace of the grave. The bones were amazingly white and clean but the jostling of travel had shaken them into disarray. There was a thighbone, some ribs and tiny wrist and finger bones, like crushed marble, and finally, the skull. It was clean and smooth, and the empty eye sockets haunting.

"I've got to get back to the controls. We have to land soon," Alex said as he left them.

Slowly, Chicago moved the flashlight over the bones, searching for the medallion. Annalee placed one trembling hand on Mac-Clannon's arm. Her dark eyes were enormous, but her voice was steady.

"The medallion will have sunk to the bottom," she whispered. "May I feel for it, please?" MacClannon, though surprised, and frankly a bit revolted by her boldness, knowing nothing about her unique ease with such things, nodded. Annalee rolled up her shirt sleeve, and gently dipped her hand into the water. Her small white fingers looked ghostly in the light. She moved the bones as if they were made of glass, one by one, delicately, trying not to stir up any sediment.

The plane rumbled on, and Alex called out that they were approaching the loch. "I don't have fuel enough to mess around here," he shouted. She caught her breath and worked faster, beads of sweat shining on her lip, her fingers now submerged in the sand and muck of the bottom.

"We have to stop, Mizzy," Chicago said gently. The girl nodded, and put her other hand in, palms down, feeling across the bottom, the bones clacking softly against her wrists. Suddenly her bottom lip began to tremble and she blinked rapidly. Her face went white, and she pulled back sharply. In her hand, untarnished, still attached to a scrap of silver chain, was the cross.

# SEVENTY-SIX

Despite the cold gray winter day, there were still a few intrepid tourists at Loch Ness that afternoon. An earth science class from a nearby high school was out on a field trip. A few police officers, alerted by the Edinburgh authorities as they tracked the plane to its destination, stood around trying to figure out what exactly it was they were expected to do. A busload of Japanese tourists, eager to carry home pictures of the famed monster that prowled the deep, had twenty or more video cameras trained on the lake when their attention was diverted by the low-flying plane.

Surprised and interested, especially when the door was open and people were seen standing inside, they trained their twenty or more lenses on the plane. MacClannon, Chicago, and Annalee stood well back, braced against the wall of the plane and securely lashed to cargo ties. By a combined effort they had inched the coffin close to the door. Now, they just had to wait for the perfect moment. When they were well over the middle of the loch, with no boats below, Alex gave a steep, sharp turn, tipping the plane to a nearly impossible angle. They were pressed against the wall by the centrifugal force, and Annalee screamed with fright. Then the coffin, after a second of hesitation, rumbled out.

Alex felt the plane lighten immediately, then straightened out and circled lower. Cory MacClannon felt a flush of joy as he watched the splash. Here in the deep cold water, his however many greats-grandfather, James Francis Edward Stuart, ill-fated prince of the realm, would at long last rest in peace.

# SEVENTY-SEVEN

Chicago stood on the bow of the *Tassia Far*, looking down through the clear, shallow water. She lifted her right hand a little, and felt the boat respond immediately, gliding just a bit to starboard, away from a chunk of coral. Alex was at the helm as she guided them through the labyrinth of coral that led to the harbor entrance. It was almost a magical feeling, working together this way. Not talking, not even looking, just giving these small hand signals: forward, slow, port, starboard.

She would guide and he would steer, or she would steer and he would trim the sail, or she would rescue him and he would rescue her.

They didn't know where they were going now, except vaguely south. They would explore some more islands and spear a couple more fish, and maybe wear out a few more toothbrushes together. It didn't matter how long anymore. The sea was calm and the wind was steady. They sailed out past the breakwater, and when the sea turned from turquoise to azure, they raised the sails together and found a course.

*       *       *

"I think I see them," Annalee said wistfully as she stared out
the plane window during takeoff. "I think that's the *Tassia Far*
now, just leaving the harbor." She watched for a few seconds
until the island disappeared completely, then turned away from the
window. The sight of all that empty ocean gave her a sick feeling.

She pulled her feet up onto the seat and hugged her knees.
Annalee's hair was neatly tied in a ponytail. She wore a cotton
short set that her mother had bought for her in the hotel gift shop,
an awful thing with flowers on the pockets and lace around the
neckline, but Annalee hadn't uttered a word of protest.

April McGuire did not look like someone who had spent three
days on a tropical island. She still had her Wisconsin winter pallor.
She had flown out as soon as she heard, and stayed with her
husband in the hospital, while they waited for Annalee to return
from Scotland. Even now, she was having trouble convincing herself that her husband and daughter were really all right. She was
nervous and edgy. She touched them a lot.

Cory MacClannon had invited them to stay as long as they
wanted at Inishail, but Chicago was anxious to get back to her
boat, and Annalee was ready for the adventure to be over.

"It's weird to think I'll be back in school tomorrow," she said.
"It seems like a year. Not just ten days."

"You can take a few more days if you want, honey," April
assured her.

"What can we have for Uncle Peter?" Annalee asked. "Like
a tombstone, I mean." They had planned a memorial service for
Saturday. "Is there anything like that? When you don't have a
body to bury?"

April looked to her husband for help on that one.

"I don't know, Miz," Jack replied sadly. He was just now
beginning to acknowledge his brother's death. Before, he had felt
desperation, guilt, a raw, raging sort of pain; now it was slipping
into a huge abiding loneliness.

"Maybe we could put his name on something, Dad. Maybe
when we put the Christiania artifacts on exhibit in a museum, we
could dedicate it to him."

Jack nodded. April squeezed his hand. The plane climbed above
the clouds, and a hundred images crowded the young girl's mind.

*Sunlight under water . . . the timbers of the ship, like the ribs of
some great dinosaur . . . Mary Beatrice, kissing her baby goodbye
. . . Alex and Chicago. They were so cool. They were like in that
movie, where the woman had to walk across Russia in the snow
to get to her husband . . . they would really do that . . . if Mom
would let her join the hockey team, maybe Adam Kordinsky might
get to be her boyfriend. He had dark-brown eyes. Fire on the
water . . . chunks of the* Golden Goose *burning all around them
. . . water . . . dolphins . . . King James . . . William and Mary.
Queen angelfish . . . sharks . . . the coffin . . . the feel of the bones
against her arms. Bones . . .*

Annalee opened her eyes. Her mother was sleeping, her father
just staring at the ceiling. Thinking, too, Annalee knew. A million thoughts.

Quietly, she pulled up the purse her mother had bought for her.
It was straw, was embroidered with sea horses and had little shells
sewn on it. Annalee hadn't said a word about that, either. She
opened the purse. Jack turned his head and smiled at her. Annalee
reached in and pulled out a woolly bundle. It was a red knit cap,
wrapped protectively around a little antique porcelain box. Maggie
MacClannon had given it to Annalee when she saw her admiring
it. Each side was painted with a different miniature scene.

Now she carefully unwrapped the little china box and lifted the
lid off. Inside was another scrap of cloth. Annalee looked at her
father with that look that had worried him since she was two
years old and capable of conscious mischief, that sweet, innocent
expression that seemed like purest radience to one who did not
know her well.

She unwrapped the little bit of felt, and Jack saw two small
objects, each about an inch long, smooth and white. Bones. No,
she couldn't have. She wouldn't have.

"Here, Daddy," she whispered as she handed them to him.
"It's fingers, I think. Maybe toes."